NICOLAS FREELING

TSING-BOUM

VINTAGE BOOKS
A Division of Random House
New York

First Vintage Books Edition, June 1982
Copyright © 1969 by Nicolas Freeling
All rights reserved under International and Pan-
American Copyright Conventions. Published in
the United States by Random House, Inc., New
York, and simultaneously in Canada by Random
House of Canada Limited, Toronto. Originally
published by Hamish Hamilton, London, in 1969.
Library of Congress Cataloging in Publication Data
Freeling, Nicolas.
Tsing-boum.
I. Title.
PR6056.R4T75   1982   823'.914   81-52876
ISBN 0-394-75261-9   AACR2
Manufactured in the United States of America
Cover photograph: Ron Tunison

Tsing-Boum! Tsing-Boum!!
Soldiers are lovely boys
—*Wozzeck* (ALBAN BERG)

FOREWORD

In January 1968, sharing the news with earthquakes, fires, avalanches, and missing submarines, the Vietnamese People's Army had encircled and was besieging a fortified group of five thousand-odd American Marines. On Sunday the 28th, press reports were that the defence was being built up hurriedly to ten thousand men or more, that the fortress was being supplied by helicopter under great difficulty with considerable losses, and that a general assault was believed to be imminent. The report concluded with the words: "Dien Bien Phu is still a magic word in Vietnam."

General Giap was believed to be commanding in person. Back in 1953, press reports used to print the "General" between inverted commas.

American air superiority and firepower is, of course, so overwhelming that we are all quite confident in the American authorities who are quoted as saying, "A new Dien Bien Phu is utterly impossible." It is with no more than faint unease that we recall General Navarre's omniscience and omnipotence in January 1954.

Since all but the name is now as good as forgotten, a short aide-mémoire is of some use. Dien Bien Phu is a wide shallow valley, possessing an airstrip, appearing to possess opportunity for manoeuvre, and supposed fifteen years ago to be of great strategic value. It is in the high plateau land of North-West Vietnam, near the Laos border.

French troops occupied the valley. The Vietminh were allowed to invest all the surrounding hills. This had no importance, given the French power in artillery and aircraft. Indeed it was encouraged. The general idea was to attract large numbers of Vietminh troops to a point where they could be destroyed by superior firepower.

Some fourteen thousand French Union troops passed through the valley. Vietminh troops were estimated at roughly thirty thousand.

These French troops, unprepared and largely unprotected, were bombarded with artillery fire of extraordinary intensity. Few among them retained sufficient morale for counter-attack, and the defence of the camp, lasting from March 13th till May 8th 1954, was undertaken by roughly 2,500 élite troops, mostly paratroop units. Legend ran that these were mostly Germans of the Legion: in fact they were a very mixed lot, but largely Vietnamese with French officers, together with elements of Legion, Moroccan and Algerian units of the regular colonial army. The commanders of these bits and pieces came to be called the "paratroop mafia."

This group of relatively junior officers, headed by Lt. Colonel Langlais with Commandant Bigeard as his second-in-command, conducted their defence with the utmost resolution. They were overrun only when they had no more ammunition to fire.

The main source book, for anyone interested, remains *The Battle of Dien Bien Phu* by Jules Roy. The aptly named *Hell in a Very Small Place* by Bernard Fall contains the statistics much useful detail. Colonel Lanlais, Dr. Paul Grauwin and Captain Jean Pouget have written well on the subject. General Navarre, commander-in-chief in Saigon, General Cogny, theatre commander in Hanoi, and many other persons, have published long volumes of explanation and accusation.

Even the shortest account of the battle would be too long and out of place here. But the following remarks which I have collected show buoyant confidence on the French side changing to total abandon. These quotations, printed in chronological order, are taken from press reports and eye-witness accounts.

2nd January 1954: "The French Command is certain of inflicting a severe defeat upon the Vietminh at Dien Bien Phu." (General Cogny to the assembled Press.)

5th January 1954: "Dien Bien Phu is not a fortified camp. It is a base for offensive operations." (Colonel Castries, the camp commander, to Mr. Graham Greene.)

11th March 1954: "The hour has come to pass to the attack . . . Dominate your fear and your suffering." (Vietnam People's Army Order of the Day, signed: Vo nguyen Giap.)

14th March 1954: "We go to disaster, and it is my fault." (Colonel Piroth, the one-armed camp artillery commander, to Langlais. Next day Piroth committed suicide.)

8th May 1954: "No, no, *mon vieux,* no white flag. You are submerged: you do not surrender." (General Cogny, by radio-telephone from Hanoi, to Castries.)

CHAPTER ONE

Van der Valk was not best pleased: why did they have to go discovering crimes at dinnertime? That other people, too, had had their dinner interrupted—that someone, he had just heard, had got his life interrupted as well as his dinner . . . niggly old bastard, niggly old bastard, he repeated.

Aubergines too, done in the oven with a delicious cheesy chewy top layer. He still had his fork in his hand when he put the phone down; his wife had sniggered, so that he banged the fork down crossly and did not see anything funny in his own behaviour until he was outside the street door buttoning his raincoat. Raw grey day with a cold wind and constant heavy showers. Not really astonishing since it was late in the autumn, but since this was Holland, and since one was in a bad mood because of the aubergines, he said "Typical August" in a loud cross voice: nobody heard because nobody was there.

He had to wait a good minute on his doorstep, getting himself into a more professional state of mind. Somebody was dead—who had not had dinner. The medical examiner would be putting his fork down too with deep regret (bet you he wasn't eating aubergines, though). And what about the car-patrol police? He was commissaire in charge of the criminal brigade, and there could not be too many buffers between him and a violent death.

He looked at his watch—two minutes to one and what was holding up the car? Where there is no vision the people perish, thought Van der Valk sententiously, taking his hat off and wedging it more firmly against gusts. A sodden cardboard box with gay liquorice allsorts printed all over it skittered along the pavement and came to rest at his feet. A Peugeot station wagon with its little lighthouse winking on the roof did the same thing and he got in just as it began to rain again.

"Whereabouts?" The telephone message had said it already but it had not stayed in his mind: getting a silly old bastard as well as bad-tempered.

"Van Lennepweg." Of course. A dusty, wide, dreary boulevard on the outskirts of the town. New quarter, endless blocks of municipal flats, palaces of the people. A municipal murder.

No use asking the driver for any details; he was simply another man who had had to put down his knife and fork to answer the phone while his mouth was still full. The Peugeot turned into the Van Lennepweg; detestably dead: a ramshackle, cheap, unfinished look. Draughty bus-stops on pavements that were far too wide, an excuse to block them with carelessly parked cars, metal bicycle stands, tinny publicity hoardings. Hero lemonade, Caballero cigarettes, Wolf lawnmowers and Pressing—One Hour filed before his eye as the auto slowed.

"There it is." In front of Aspro stood an ambulance. A group of some fifty ghouls of all sexes and age groups were enjoying life, held in check by a uniformed policeman. Muttering and elbow-joggling broke out as Van der Valk arrived; he gave the front row a look of deep distaste. When younger he had often got irritated enough to hustle them off; quite useless—back they seeped like water next moment. The people, getting a real sensual pleasure. Not—do them justice—from the sufferings of others, not even from their sudden skill at hindering the professionals. Just from being there, near enough to catch a word—good as appearing on television. The people—he had known them stand there watching a man bleed to death, apparently incapable of movement or emotion. They perished so easily and there was so little he could do about it.

It made Arlette, his wife, so angry and wretched that he recalled her shaking one of the boys, about ten years old, shaking the child till his head was ready to come off, white with disgusted fury, hissing, "Let me catch you once again staring at people in trouble and I'll kill you, you hear me." The child had been watching a fire . . .

He banged straight through and they shuffled back a step. "Fourth floor," said the policeman. There was no lift; it was one of the low blocks and the fourth floor was the top. On the landings were more people standing in open doorways, with the television ranting unheeded behind them. Chewing still, some of them. Van der Valk's leg hurt, as it always did on stairs. He ploughed on through a smell of frying margarine and tinned peas. Dutch beehive—no smell of dust; all the housewives kept their bit of passage clean, and any backsliders would be dealt with by the Good Neighbours' Association.

On the fourth floor the doors were shut, dull little doors of plywood and pale grey paint. A policeman stood in the passage. "In here." The technical squad was already there, three or four of them with their bits of string and chalk and plastic bags, the cameraman flitting busily away. Ordinary municipal flat: tiny hallway with kitchen and lavatory, a fair-sized living-room on the Dutch pattern, half for sitting and half for eating. Passage to what would be either two or three bedrooms and a bathroom. There was plenty of light, for the big window ran the whole length, and in the kitchen a glass door led to a tiny balcony with a few clothes pinned to a washing line. The floor was woven fibre matting and everybody was looking at a scatter of bright metal shells. The sergeant straightened up as he came in.

"No footprints—wiped his feet very carefully before coming in. Cool you'd say. But he fired seven shots. Seven! What d'you think of that, chief?"

Van der Valk got the point. Even one gunshot is a rarity in Holland. Seven is exaggerating.

"Who's dead?"

"Housewife."

"Where's the husband?"

"Don't know, sir; haven't had time. She's there behind the armchair."

The young woman lay raggedly, blood coming out of her mouth. Pretty young woman but one couldn't tell; dead faces told one so little.

There was a strong smell of burning.

"What caught fire?"

"The potatoes boiled dry," said the sergeant, almost apologetically.

Van der Valk touched the huddled face.

"Happened about half an hour ago—why all the delay? Did nobody hear? Seven shots!"

"Television going—and it's a noisy building at lunchtime. People coming home, doors opening and shutting. There's a child—neighbours are looking after it. The neighbour that gave the alarm."

"Have those shells sent to Ballistics in Amsterdam. Seven shots—must be some kind of automatic weapon. Looks like sheer hysteria—and the fellow just walked out calmly, huh? Nobody saw anything either?"

"Not as far as we know now, sir," said the policeman stolidly. He'd had enough to do keeping the mob quiet!

The medical examiner came in, looked briefly, and said, "Good God!" He straightened the body out.

"Heaven help us. Literally shot to pieces. Died within seconds. You'd think she'd been machine-gunned."

"Perhaps she was."

"Professionally killed is all I can say."

"Some professional," muttered the sergeant.

"A professional . . ." said Van der Valk lumpishly. He pulled himself together.

"Camera finished?"

"Blanket job, chief. Top to toe—but it won't take long in a place like this."

"I want the keys, and all identity stuff—look in her bag. I'm going to see this neighbour." He looked across the room at his own sergeant. "Half an hour. Who has seen a stranger in the building?"

"Have you seen a man carrying a machine-gun?" muttered the technical sergeant.

"Have you seen the fingerprints on the lavatory flush?" returned the other, stung.

"Who gave the alarm?" asked Van der Valk.

"Concierge."

CHAPTER TWO

The plastic tiles of the passage were by now marked with so many muddy footprints as to have become very dirty. Two ambulance men passed him, wearing downtrodden looks at having to carry a dead body down four flights. He knocked at the door opposite, which was opened at once by a pale worried-looking man with a sensible artisan's face. Van der Valk showed his badge and put his finger across his lips.

"Child here?" he said softly. "She know yet?" The man nodded first and shook his head after. He beckoned Van der Valk in with a relieved look: somebody who would tell him what to do.

Around the table sat a woman and three children.

Two were fair-haired and one was dark, a girl of around ten. A plate of food was in front of her but she was not eating. The atmosphere stank of strain.

"Sorry to interrupt." He pulled up a chair and sat down. His driver appeared in the doorway.

"I phoned for a few extra hands."

Van der Valk nodded and turned to the man.

"If you've finished eating be kind and tell him what he wants to know—name, where you work, that stuff." He turned back and found the child's eyes looking squarely into his.

"So. You're having dinner with the neighbours today because your mamma is ill. We've taken her to the hospital. And now we have to look after you, don't we? I'm a policeman, here to look after everything. Have you just come home from school?"

"Is Mamma dead?" bluntly, in a small firm voice.

"The doctor is busy with her and I mustn't bother him yet awhile, because she's certainly badly hurt. Have you more brothers and sisters?" The woman opened her mouth and he held up a finger.

"One moment, Mevrouw."

"No. I came home from school and Mevrouw Paap told me Mamma wasn't home but I knew something had happened."

"We none of us know yet exactly what happened. We will work that out—that's my job. Now you eat some dinner at least because otherwise it's not polite, while I talk to Mevrouw, right?"

"Don't play with your food," she said sternly to her own children, "eat up and then show Ruth your toys; I'll give you your pudding when I'm ready."

He followed her to the bedroom, where she turned to him in consternation.

10

"It was ever so queer . . ." she began breathlessly.

"A second. It's easier if I ask and you answer. Do you know who found her?"

"I did. I heard such a crashing noise and I thought —I don't know—that somebody had fallen off a stepladder or something. Well . . . I hardly know her— knew her . . ." She broke off, confused.

"Yes. You saw her?"

"There was nobody in the passage but I couldn't get it out of my head—I fell off the stepladder once— or down the stairs carrying a tray of crockery . . . So I thought I'd ring at her door in case she'd hurt herself."

"Who opened the door?"

"But that's what is so queer, the door opened and there was nobody there, well one doesn't just plunge in so I called out 'Mevrouw Marks' and then again louder, and there was no answer and there was such a funny smell, a bit like fireworks, and I went on into the living-room, and I saw her lying there, and I got such a turn, and I was so frightened I ran back here and locked myself in, and then I was worried . . ."

"You saw nobody?"

"Not a soul."

"What time was it?"

"About quarter past twelve. Well, I thought, there's that child coming home from school, and mine too, and I can't let her see that, I have to catch her, and then luckily my husband came back. He works only in the next street. I told him there's something horrible happened and he ran and told the concierge to phone the police quick and they were here quite fast. They just walked in."

"You'd left the door there open then?"

"Yes, but I shut mine because of the children— she's seen nothing, thank God."

"You said you hardly knew Mevrouw Marks—you know her husband?"

"Well—I'll try and explain—you see she isn't Mevrouw Marks—or at least I don't know. He's called Zomerlust—he's a soldier. He's away mostly, but he's generally back at weekends. But I remember asking the child her name when she was—when they came here, and she said 'Ruth Marks,' so I said, you know, Good morning Mevrouw Marks, but she never made any remark, but she didn't talk to people. Like I say I hardly knew her, just to say good morning."

"Was she friendly with anyone else—that you know of?"

"I don't think she was friendly with anyone much. Very reserved. I mean she'd always smile and speak a word, not impolite, but you never got any further. Commissaire, what am I going to do with the child? I mean, I can look after her of course, but . . . her clothes and everything . . . I mean to say . . ."

Van der Valk had to do sums quickly in his head. This soldier would not be hard to find, but it appeared that the child was either from a previous marriage or illegitimate. Possible snags there. This woman had been shot with some kind of automatic weapon. A soldier's weapon?

One called the social assistant. Kind, brisk, experienced women. But institutions, however kind, would have one effect that was certain: the child would shut up and refuse to talk. She was ten. What might she know, and what might she be capable of telling? He made a sudden decision.

"I'll take her." He nearly smiled; relief showed on

the good soul's face like milk spilt across her clean kitchen floor.

"Don't think I don't know my Christian duty, Commissaire . . ."

"No no, I'll take her. Right now—sooner the better . . . Mevrouw, I'll be coming to see you again, maybe this evening. I must warn you against something. Urgently. Solemnly. Don't talk. Not to anyone, not your neighbours and especially not the Press. Say I've told you not to." He had no particular right to tell her anything of the sort, but the tactic was good. "The Commissaire told me"—it gave her importance, and an illusion that she knew splendid secrets.

Ruth was holding a doll, quite uninterested in it but with a sage obedience to what was expected of her. He had lost the habit of talking to small children. They like it better when you are brusque than when you are slimy-avuncular. Children like to know where they stand.

"You put your coat on, Ruth—yes, take your school things, you're coming with me."

"Are we going to see Mama?"

"Not straight away, because the doctor hasn't given us permission. We have to take charge of you. I know a place where they look after children whose mammas are in hospital but I'm going to take you to my own house. Mevrouw Paap has been very kind, but she's got a lot of work."

"What about my things, my clothes?"

"We'll pick them up later, don't worry. Come on, Ruth."

"How do you know my name?"

"Mevrouw Paap told me, otherwise I should have

13

asked you. Miss Marks? I'm Mr. van der Valk. How do you do, Mademoiselle? I am very happy to make your acquaintance." She gave a litle giggle. "We have a car with a light on top and if you like you can make it flash." She didn't know what he was talking about —he was used to boys.

"Office, chief?"

"No, my home. You've had no dinner," to the child sitting beside him, "but you know something—neither have I."

'And neither have I," said the driver, with feeling.

"I'm not hungry," said Ruth.

"No more am I, come to think of it, but perhaps we can have a glass of milk. Look, this is where I live. I won't be more than a minute, Joe. And this is my wife. Her name is Arlette. That's a French name."

"I know. My name's Ruth."

"Arlette, this girl's mamma has had an accident and her papa is away, so she's going to stay with us for a while."

"He's not my papa, he's my stepfather," calmly.

"Good," said Arlette. "I need somebody to help me very badly. Let's see—the car battery is flat and I've got to charge it, and I've got a horrible great heap of ironing, and the dinner was ruined so I've to make a nice supper—can you cook, Ruth?"

"Yes. Not much, though."

"But you can help me and I will be very happy."

"Yes, but Mamma will be worried."

"I'm going off to fix that now," said Van der Valk, getting milk out of the refrigerator like Archie Goodwin in a Nero Wolfe story. "I've got to look at my orchids now but I'll see your mamma isn't worried."

Arlette's eyes were flashing light signals like a D S overtaking everybody on the autoroute. He didn't know what it was but Arlette would certainly cope until he could tell her more.

"I refuse to be like Archie Goodwin." But he drank a second glass of milk before dashing out to the car.

CHAPTER THREE

In the office, wheels were turning at a great rate and everyone was in a bustle. Probably, he thought, for the same reasons as himself: smelt publicity. Couldn't blame the Press if they did play it up; who would have expected to find a woman assassinated by seven bullets (could it really be a machine-gun?) in a municipal housing block in provincial Holland? Nothing so glamorous had happened to him for years. There had been the girl in the white Mercedes, but she had only stabbed her lover with a mechanic's pocketknife— though she would certainly have gone for a machine-gun had there been one handy. He grinned; dear Lucienne, whom he had himself been in love with in a half-baked sort of way. Still married to her ex-boxer? The central heating was too hot as usual; he took his jacket off.

"Branle-bas de combat." The phrase pleased him. We will now advance upon Marks in skirmishing order. And behold, she is not Marks; she is Marx. A telephone call to the town hall, a flurry in their precious files, and he heard that Esther Marx was married to Joseph Egbert Zomerlust in France (in France), and that shortly afterwards a female child registered Ruth Sabine Marx had been born—in France—to said Esther. Aforesaid Marx was not classified as alien, being married to Dutch citizen. Registered as housewife with no further profession. Zomerlust was a sergeant, professional soldier, place of work Juliana Barracks within municipal boundary.

Van der Valk phoned the technical squad and got the sergeant, whose title was in fact Wachtmeester. Very proper and appropriate.

"Anything showing?"

"No. We're developing prints as fast as we can, going over everything with the low-power glass. No foreign fingers. She was in the kitchen, answered a ring at the door presumably, and probably he backed her in with the gun before giving her the works. He didn't stay long, and handled nothing. We're making you a scale plan, of course."

"Keep me informed . . . Janet, get me Ballistics in Amsterdam . . . Hello, Sam? Get my message?"

"I got your message; it came on the telex. But not the goods yet. I'll look after it as soon as I get it." Van der Valk was slightly indignant; a lot of time seemed to have passed, but no, it was barely an hour since the messenger had left, and he had fifty kilometres to go on a motorbike.

"Ring me straight back. Something of an oddity, I suspect."

"Right, Mister." Sam called everybody Mister. He had wanted to go to Israel last year, and had been restrained with difficulty. Said he was sick of air-pistol bullets.

He had his duty inspector and two plainclothes detectives working on the building in the Van Lennepweg, but they had not rung in yet. Which meant that they had nothing to tell him.

He had Esther's handbag on his desk. It had been lying on the coffee table, had been fingerprinted, photographed, and he had told his driver to take it. A handbag could—should—tell you a lot about its owner.

Ordinary. Neither tidy nor untidy. Imitation leather but good quality, fairly expensive, label of a large store, comparatively new, whether modish or not he didn't know. Her clothes had told him nothing either; she had been in the kitchen and was wearing a nylon overall.

Usual women's things—perhaps a lot of eye make-up, but he had not noticed her eyes. Ought he to have? Purse with average amount of shopping money—forty gulden or so. A diary with shopping lists; the last read "Beetroot, coffee, milk, R. socks." Ruth needed socks; he must tell Arlette. No identity papers, no papers or letters at all, not even envelopes. Had she no family? A credit card from a shoeshop— "Mevr. Zomerlust." The usual seawrack of soap coupons and cash-register bills, buttons and stocking sus-

18

penders. No hairgrips—she had it cut short. His telephone rang. Van Lennepweg.

"Nothing, chief. A few vague reports of a stranger but all the descriptions differ. One woman thought she saw the husband—but from the back. Fair hair, sturdy build, fawn raincoat—and where does that get us? She couldn't be sure. They've lived in this building a year and a half. Nobody has much to say. Kept herself to herself. Inoffensive, quiet. No close friends known. Went out a lot by herself, though. Husband away a lot, natch. You know he's a soldier?"

"Yes. Keep at it—neighbourhood, shops, you know."

A funny death. The assassination had been so smooth—over-smooth. When the neighbour rang after hearing the shots, the man had opened the door, hidden in the lavatory next to it, waited till the good soul got as far as the living-room, and quietly slipped out. Easy? Yes, but needing someone used to moving quietly and thinking quickly in the circumstances. Not like an emotional killing. And the husband was a soldier . . . Rather sadly, Van der Valk asked the switchboard for the commandant of the army camp.

"Lieutenant-Colonel Bakker," said a deep stern voice suddenly in his ear.

"Town police, Commissaire van der Valk, Criminal Brigade."

"What can I do for you?"

"You have a soldier there—not a conscript, a regular soldier, sergeant of some sort, name Zomerlust. You probably know him."

"Correct. Weapons instructor." Weapons instructor —it only needed that!

"On duty at the present?"

"I'd have to check—but you'd better tell me."

"His wife has died, by violence. I want to be the first with the news. That kind of word travels fast. I should like to ask you to find out where he is and keep him there an hour."

"Can do. I'll ring you back." Mm, he would have to be a bit tactful. The military authorities liked to look after their own laundry, and were not always terribly enthusiastic when the civil police arrived with the kind of news that got into the evening paper. But it took less than five minutes.

"Commissaire? He's here. I've asked him to be at my office in half an hour. If you care, you can be here in twenty minutes or less. I would like you to speak to me first—fair enough?"

"I'll be with you then—don't have any sentries asking me for the password."

"Very good," said the deep voice curtly, and rang off. Van der Valk buzzed his intercom.

"Car and driver straight away. I'll be away an hour to hour 'n' half. All reports and messages on my desk."

The usual wire fences and bricky blocks of a parsimonious military administration. Rows of lorries and half-tracks parked meticulously in line to white paint. Inside, old-maid fussiness, all cream-glossy and shiny red linoleum, corridors full of notices, over-polished boots and badges. Usual administrative sergeant-major with moustache and medals. Knock-knock. Bullshit came to a merciful end in a blindingly highly-frictioned office with an unexpectedly sympathetic-seeming officer of fifty or so, stomach kept down by much hard exercise. He lost no time in getting to the point.

"Commissaire—good afternoon. Sad errand." Van

20

der Valk, unsure of the difference between a lieutenant-colonel and a full colonel, wasn't taking any chances.

"Afternoon, Colonel—I'm afraid so."

"Our man won't be here for ten minutes. You said violence?"

"She was shot with an automatic weapon, this lunchtime."

"Shocking. You aren't thinking . . . ?"

"No. But I have to be good and sure. It would be a relief to me if his movements were thoroughly accounted for."

"Then be relieved. He's been here all day, and a dozen men can vouch for that. I may tell you at once, he's a good man. Private life's his own, no doubt, but a good man—I hope I can say it with pride: know what I'm talking about. A—how's it put?—hypothesis of criminal designs, since his being here doesn't or mightn't prove anything particular one way or the other, meets, uh, or would meet a pretty rigid barrier of incredulity." He paused, decided he was not very good at wrapping it up, smiled with good, even teeth, and said, "I'm trying to tell you, Commissaire, in a clumsy way, that if you entertain suspicions of this man they'd better be good, and it is certainly my duty to protect and defend his interests. You'll forgive me, I hope, for putting my thoughts so badly."

"That's quite fair. I'm glad you did. You'll be glad if I speak as plainly? Good. I've no presumption whatever against your man—that he did it, or had it done. I've got to question him, which I'll gladly do in your presence."

He had decided to be very relaxed, and was slouching in a military wooden chair, his legs crossed, playing with a cigarette he didn't want, of a kind he didn't like, being winning.

"It's a bit traditional, Colonel, that the army gets touchy at the thought of a man of theirs being involved in any way with the civil arm. Someone killed this man's wife. Why was she shot with an automatic weapon that could be of military origin?—I haven't had the ballistics report yet."

"Certainly I won't oppose your questioning him. I don't recall," the colonel sounded a thought pained, "that the civil authorities have ever had reason to think we here have failed to cooperate—when it was called for."

I'd like to look at his personal record—I don't think that would be an infraction of Nato security, would it?"

The colonel frowned, as though he thought it would.

"As you know, an officer of police is under oath and has to observe professional secrecy, exactly like a doctor."

"But once you've interrogated him, and satisfied yourself that he cannot have had a hand in this dreadful crime . . ."

"The Officer of Justice, you know, would call for all papers before seeing the man. I prefer to see the man first, that's all."

The colonel picked up his phone.

"Sarntmajor, Zomerlust's file, please." The voice must have said "He's here now, sir" because he added "Send him in" in an artificially jovial way. Van der Valk got up, not wanting to sit there being delphic and shrouded in importance as though he were the FBI.

A man was ushered in and stood at attention with

professionally incurious respect. Van der Valk, looking at him, felt quite sure that he did not know his wife was dead. Either way, it was a beastly moment to go through. Such an honest face. Eyes level, face muscles relaxed. It was a rounded, chubby face, very Dutch, with a shiny bumpy nose and a high knobbed forehead under fair curly hair. The man might not be conspicuous for intelligence but he would be good at his job and he would be a good friend. The colonel cleared his throat.

"Zomerlust, this is an officer of the civil police, who has come with an urgent message. I have to add that it is not a piece of news I like to bring to any soldier." The man's eyes stayed steady on his officer. There was a nasty pause.

"My wife?" he said at last. The tone was as level and disciplined as the face, but even in those two words, thought Van der Valk, who had brought news of this kind to quite a few people, there was a sort of resignation rather than disbelief or even anxiety. It was as though the man had expected all along that sooner or later . . . But don't go reading meanings now.

"There's been a serious accident," said the colonel with horrid banality.

"She's dead?" Hardly any note of query.

"I'm speaking to a soldier—she is."

The eyes came slowly round to Van der Valk and stayed there as though committing his features to memory. A muscle showed in the jaw.

"What happened?"

"She got shot."

"Yes . . . I see." The face slid a little, and he concentrated on getting control of himself. "I see," he said again, in the voice one has when one doesn't see, but wants to test if one's voice is steady.

"We have to have a talk," said Van der Valk. "Nothing formal, no provost-marshals or anything."

The colonel hadn't liked his man sounding so surprised: he got up in a jagged, worried way.

"I've no objection to your presence, Colonel."

"Yes. But I think it as well to leave the two of you alone for just a while. You can use this office." But loyalty came forward again. He held his hand out. "My very deepest sympathy and sorrow, Zomerlust. And I know well that you had nothing to do with this unhappy event. Don't worry. We'll see to everything." He looked back at Van der Valk without either sympathy or hostility. "I'll be just outside." It sounded appealing; it was almost a capitulation. Going to check up on the man again, thought Van der Valk.

"Sergeant Zomerlust, your wife has been killed, by someone who shot her at your home. She was killed instantly, and I would say totally unexpectedly. She did not suffer at all. There was no struggle, and no argument as far as we can judge. This is homicide. You can help me very much, and I intend to get the fishbone out of the throat straight away. Can you establish past question where you were—all today?"

"Why here—working."

"People see you all that time? I'm not talking about five minutes for a cigarette?"

"My whole section."

"So you could prove, you feel sure, forwards, backwards and sideways where you were, the whole day?"

The man did not protest at all. "Yes," he said, very calmly, and Van der Valk heaved an uninhibited sigh of content.

24

"Nobody's thinking of wholesale perjury in your section," he said dryly. "You aren't under suspicion. But it's very important to me to have you clear. I have a lot of questions, you know, that it will give you no joy to answer."

"That's your job, after all," said Zomerlust with sad patience. Something was worrying Van der Valk, though; he knew what it was.

"Your little girl's all right, you'll be glad to know. I'm looking after her for the present. She's at home, with my wife."

The man flushed; his open Dutch face was the kind that flushes easily.

"You hadn't mentioned anything happening to her. I didn't think she could have been there."

"It happened in the lunch break—but I hadn't told you that."

Zomerlust did not protest that he hadn't known it. "I'm very fond of her," he said awkwardly. "She's my sort of step-child, you know."

"There wasn't any secret about that, I think. She carried your wife's name."

Had he said it too smoothly? The man's face flared up with resentment and suspicion.

"No, I've never made any secret of it. Why should I? I've never—I offered to give her my name. I'm her guardian."

"Your wife was married before?"

"I don't know. I don't think so. Sounds daft, I know. But I never asked. It was a sort of pact—I never asked. Christ, what a mess," he said miserably.

"Ruth's all right where she is for a while. She knows her mother is in hospital. Would you be content to leave her that way—till we know more?"

25

"I suppose so. What else can I say?"

"I have to ask you what your wishes are. She won't be questioned or worried—you can rely on me."

Zomerlust was now looking harried and flustered. "I don't know—I have to think."

"Have you no family who could look after her?"

"Yes—but they wouldn't want to," he said at last unwillingly.

"I see. Well, she's all right for as long as you want."

"I don't know who her father is," said Zomerlust again. "I don't—I didn't want to know. We—my wife and I understood each other. Questions weren't asked. It's better that way."

"Were you happy with her?"

"Yes. She was a good wife."

"Was she happy?" And the answer came without hesitation, or aggression:

"Yes."

"I have to ask these things."

"You mean I could have shot her. That I didn't because I couldn't, but that I could have got it done somehow? That's what you mean, isn't it?"

"One of several very remote possibilities, but I'm not thinking of it that way."

"What way?" suspicious again.

"Was your wife friendly with many people here at the camp?"

"She wasn't friendly with any of them. She hated those army-wife cliques. Why d'you ask?"

"She was shot, probably by someone who knew her and whom she knew, since she let him into the flat. She was shot by a peculiar kind of gun—several shots and shells looked military calibre. We don't know yet —could be some kind of sub-machine-gun."

Zomerlust looked flabbergasted.

"You mean we have such things here?"

"I don't know. I've been told you're a weapons instructor," delicately. But Zomerlust appeared bemused. Perhaps he was bemused—shock took odd forms. Van der Valk tried again.

"We look first for what is likeliest. Something idiotic —not really a crime at all. Act of passion, say. But who in Holland has a weapon like that or access to one?"

"You don't think soldiers do?" He was utterly incredulous, as though this were some sadistic fairy-tale.

"Both ideas look equally silly, don't they? That you killed your wife in unpremeditated passion, not caring that the choice of weapon might seem to point to you —or that someone killed her in cold blood, choosing a weapon that might be thought to point to you."

His voice, light, unemotional, seemed to bring the man's feet to the ground.

"A machine-gun—of course we have them here— but you'd never got it off the camp. Controlled— counted, checked, signed for—every time."

"That's right—go ahead and eliminate the whole silly notion."

"Nobody here even knew my wife." Harshly. "She never came here—had nothing to do with it—didn't like it."

"She didn't like your being a regular soldier?"

Zomerlust rocked his head from side to side like a man bothered by flies.

"She didn't mind that, but she wanted nothing to do with camps or soldiers or my life here. Our life was— was a private life." Lamely, a little desperately.

"Well, that's all," said Van der Valk. "I'll be seeing

you again of course. I'll keep you in touch. And I'll hang on to Ruth for a while, shall I?—till you get things straight."

"Yes," dully. He still hadn't assimilated it altogether.

Van der Valk opened the door. The commanding officer was sitting boyishly on the edge of the desk, on which lay an ochre-coloured file.

"Sorry to have kept you from your desk, Colonel."

"You weren't long." The voice sounded so genial that either he had phoned the War Department and been told to go easy on those civilian police, or the office was bugged—who knew what Nato Security would get up to next?—or (likeliest, on the whole; he was now as convinced of his man's innocence as Van der Valk was.

"All right, Zomerlust. Just a minute, will you—I'll be needing you . . . Well, Commissaire?"

"Very nice fellow. Didn't kill anyone."

"Yes. Likeable chap. Not always an advantage for a noncom—but he's good at his work."

"Got an archbishop's alibi—I have to send a man to take short statements from the men working with him. Clear him formally; I'd be grateful if you could arrange cooperation on that. I suppose you give him compassionate leave, mm?"

"He's in the Army. We'll stand by him."

"I'd like to study this file if I may. I've no lingering suspicions but it may help me with background."

"Yes—well—it's military property—but you'll treat it as confidential matter?"

"Sign for it if you like," thinking of the military way with weapons.

"No, no but uh—your eyes only."

"I'll ring you up, Colonel, very shortly, and in all likelihood I'll return this by messenger, tomorrow."

"If you would. You know your way? Sarntmajor! . . ."

CHAPTER FOUR

Van der Valk's office desk was full of pencilled messages. He disliked tape-recorders.

"Piet Hartsuiker reports all negative on intruder in flat-block Van Lennep."

"Rik and Gerard have neighbourhood pattern on Zomerlust/Marx. Negative on unusual circumstances or particular friendship."

"Labo much interested by weapon reported Uzzi s.m.g. what the hell?"

Indeed. What the hell?

"Get me Amsterdam, Technical Services . . . Lab? Ballistics there? . . . Sam?—Sam? What is this animal?—a Japanese motorbike?" Jewish snickers came down the line.

"Now you've come to exactly the right shop, Mister."

"Huh?"

"Israeli, very nice, extremely simple, remarkable little weapon."

"Sammy, sonny, don't go technical. Guns bore me. Would it go under a raincoat without being noticed?"

"Go down your pants leg if you want it to, Mister."

Since the only possible answer to this was an obscenity, he obliged, put the phone down, and asked himself who the fornication walked about in Holland with an Israeli army sub-machine gun. It remained a simple, neat, thoroughly professional killing, but this rococo flourish of childish melodramatics irritated, intrigued . . . Nobody Dutch did such things. Professionals, anywhere, used ordinary, unglamorous medium-calibre guns from national arms factories, simple to supply, maintain, exchange, or dispose of; difficult to notice, trace, or identify. Fancy guns were for musical-comedy spies. To soothe himself he picked up Sergeant Zomerlust's dossier. He at least was a good sound Dutch boy who never did anything surprising. And to his amusement he was quite mistaken.

Forty years old. Origin Brabant. Religion, Roman Catholic. Father's profession, sheet-metal worker. Parents living. Career army man, re-engaged. Good technical man. Armourer First Class. Relatively low rank explained by a common phenomenon: promotion went largely nowadays by written examination and he was a poor examinee. Education had not gone beyond primary. His handwriting was unformed and laborious; he would always be top on practice and bottom on theory. Intelligence slowish. Turn the page. Medical history. Physicals perfect, eyesight twenty/twenty, hearing . . . aha, been wounded. Well well, he had served in Korea. And there was the first spark: the man had a thumping medal. Wounded by shell-fragments in the face and arm, ran the citation, had rallied section of badly-shaken infantry. Wounded again (abdominal), long stretch of hospital in rear area (Philippines). Mum-mum-mum, turn page. Service Dutch forces in New Guinea. Back to Europe, posted Nato training camp La Courtine, France. Wounded in leg and foot by grenade splinters in accident caused by nervous recruit—commended for saving said imbecile's silly skin. Six weeks in French military hospital. Van der Valk was turning pages back and forth by now, piecing together the man's life. Another flash of originality. Met—in the hospital?—and married a woman of vague antecedents.

But there was not much about Esther Marx. Jugoslav origin, nationalized French, born in the Pas de Calais, father miner. Profession nurse.

A woman who had refused to talk about her past. And the marriage had been disapproved of by Zomerlust's commanding officer. There seemed to have been some sort of incident. The episode had lain heavily on Sergeant Zomerlust; he had been punished for it. He hadn't been court-martialled or anything—clean record, wounds, a medal had helped him there. But promotion was slow, and scattered through the dossier in coded annotations and military jargon were various incomprehensible sanctions. Not suitable for tactical atomic-weapons training. Suitable for coordination with English troops but not with French or German.

Was it all just Nato bullshit? There was a lot more stuff—posting on manoeuvres with Scandinavian elements, some work on tanks, a belated promotion to his present rank and the posting to his present unit, a mechanized infantry depot; Van der Valk's attention sagged. It was all too ambiguous. What did "Not recommended for advanced ops in Central European theatre" mean? A thread ran through the dossier sounding almost like politically unreliable. Had the marriage with the dubious Jugoslav antecedents anything to do with it?

Van der Valk reflected that dossiers had always an unreal quality. Dangerous to read between the lines: half of this might well be the stupidities of owlish clerks.

The technical report, with huge numbers of glossy photographs, now appeared on the desk. Discouraging. No prints of foot or finger signalled a mysterious intruder. Esther Marx had been peacefully cooking the dinner when interrupted and massacred, and that, behind reams of exhaustive analysis, was all there was. This business was uncomfortably like a nasty mess.

Knocking-off time arrived and with it the Press. The sensational aspects had attracted an ususual crowd, milling and cat-calling in the waiting-room: two or three hopeful photographers took shots of him as he arrived.

"Statement, statement."

"You all know the rules. The Officer of Justice will allow no comment that may prejudice the investigation, which, I need hardly say, has barely begun and may be lengthy. We possess few valid indications."

"This sergeant . . ."

"Has satisfied me that he could not possibly have been present."

"She wasn't Dutch."

"She was of Jugoslav origin."

"Has that anything to do with it?"

"I have no idea."

"What about the weapon?"

"Automatic."

"Of military origin?"

"Possibly, but not Nato issue."

"Russian? Czech?"

He wished he could knock their silly heads together.

CHAPTER FIVE

Neither of his children lived at home, now. The casual insolence with which schoolchildren popped off to Tunisia or Turkey had first appalled and then entertained him. Since going to their universities and vanishing from ken they had become more and more far flung, and the elder, supposed to be doing engineering at Besançon, spoke offhandedly of Leningrad and Montreal as though they were next door. Their extreme sophistication and bounding self-confidence had a charming innocence: their father, who had never been to America, was on this account treated as the most circumscribed of peasants.

Arlette was disoriented and unoccupied; her instinct

for activity, described by her husband as the wish to "take cabs and go about," was now harnessed by outside work. Two afternoons a week she worked at the local orphanage, and three evenings at the hospital. Having no "diplomas" made her tetchy: other people were allowed to do things she could have done so much better!

"Get a few diplomas then," Van der Valk, who had dozens of the idiot things, suggested. "They aren't hard."

"I refuse, I'm like Malraux's grandfather—too old to pass examinations or change my religion."

"Well, then, eat it and like it. Valuable lesson in humility."

"I try to," said Arlette humbly. "But I lose my temper rather often."

Tonight was not a hospital night. Goody—nice supper instead of something-to-warm-up. He recalled that she would not have gone anyway, because of the child. This child . . . was Zomerlust telling the truth, saying he had no idea who her father was? It had had the accents of truth. But why had he married Esther Marx in so uncharacteristic an outburst of quixotic romanticism? She had been a nurse—military nurse. Had the father been some comrade, perhaps in Korea? Who had perhaps been killed or something? He decided that he was constructing a tale he could shortly offer to a women's magazine, and opened his front door upon a nice smell. Arlette, aided by Ruth, was making supper.

He was blunted by the day, and used to her talking French at home; she always did, to keep the boys bilingual. Undoing his shoelaces, he heard that the child not only understood but was replying. He rose as though he had sat on a pin and stumped into the kitchen.

"Have you seen Mamma?" asked the child at once, but he was prepared.

"We're both going to see her, tomorrow morning. But she may not be well enough to talk to us." Ruth, flushed and excited, seemed to be getting on well with Arlette.

"I'm tired, thirsty, and want a glass of vino."

"May I get it for you?"

"Sure, in the fridge, and take a kitchen glass."

"Madame talks French."

"Madame is French. So do you talk French—I hear."

"You do too! So am I French."

"Are you really?"

"Is that all right?"

"Pour one for me too," said Arlette. "You may have a small one if you like."

"I do like."

The child had bad table manners and was over-excited. After supper Van der Valk conveyed by violent sign language that she must go to bed. Arlette made a teach-your-granny face and was away for a long time: a lot of noise came from the bathroom. Finally Arlette appeared, said she was mangled, and asked for a glass of port.

"She's had a rotten time. Needs a lot of warmth, a lot of affection, a lot of spontaneous enthusiasm. Been left alone a lot. She's used to bottling it all in, and she has to learn to flood it all out. You can't do that in three days. Do you know anything about it?"

"Very little. The woman was killed by X with what appears to be an Israeli army sub-machine-gun. Her name was Esther Marx. Born in France of Jugoslav parents, it would seem."

"Israeli—Esther—Ruth—Jewish, you think?"

"I don't know," dully. "Has it importance? Did Jews shoot her?"

"More likely Arabs—they ran away so quickly," said Arlette frivolously. "I think she guesses that Mamma is dead—they're so sharpened to that. You saw the husband?"

"A nice man. Says Esther never talked about the past and that he made a point of never asking. Now that I think about it I'm sure that it's the truth and that what's more it was damn sensible of him."

"No doubt, then?—something or someone out of the past?"

"Perhaps—if only because she had so oddly little present. What did she do all day? We'll hear from Ruth—eventually."

"Have you plans, for tonight?"

"I want to have a look at the flat. The technical report tells me nothing. But I won't be late."

"What are we going to do with the child?"

"Keep her, for the moment. You don't mind?"

"I think I like it. You may find me asleep—she takes a lot of concentration."

"The husband's family is hostile. He doesn't know what to do with her."

"A very lucky thing that she speaks French. Does the poor little wretch get shoved off to the orphanage? I could help there, but so little.

"I wonder whether one could adopt her," she went

38

on vaguely. She looked at him, waiting for him to sort his mind out.

"I don't know—it seems to me that we could. This Zomerlust—he's her legal guardian, of course."

"Think about it."

"Sleep on it."

CHAPTER SIX

Raining again—the thin stinging rain of Holland that blows in across the North Sea in gusty draughts that go up our sleeve and down your leg, the cold fine streaks of wet slashing at his ears and eyelids: he felt old and disheartened at having even noticed. How many nights had he not spent in the open, professionally armed against cold and damp, boredom and fatigue? But now he was sick of it, and counted the years before he could retire. Ten years?—unless the doctors threw him out first. This weather hurt his bad leg and made him limp; it was a struggle to get into Arlette's deux-chevaux and even more to get out of it again in the Van Lennepweg. Ach, work kept one young.

He didn't have to run around draughty streets at night; he was the Commissaire, desk man, executive, armchair strategist, and for running about he had active healthy young men at his disposal. But there, he couldn't taste with their tongue.

The Van Lennepweg at nine thirty on a wet autumn night was deserted as an Andalusian village at two on a July afternoon; the leggy streetlamps poured their dirty orange light upon a total silence that blew to and fro in the curtains of ran; wind whistled over the tall grimy blocks of concrete but did not touch a silence as whole and heavy as the silence of the forest. He had never seen a forest until a year or so ago; Arlette had laughed at him—forty years old and never seen the forest. Well, there weren't any forests in Holland. But after his accident he had learned to walk in the forest country where Arlette had taken him. Forests of beech, of spruce and pine—now he had them in his blood. Mile after mile of silence, until one expected to come upon strange shapes in the clearing, scrape away the moss and find an Inca city unseen and untouched for seven hundred years.

Not a cat on the Van Lennepweg, and in the café were only three dispirited men bleakly drinking beer behind the uncurtained window with its sour potplants. And the young were not going to hang about this dragsville boulevard, but went into town to the steamy snackbars: enticing smells of *patates* not only fried in ignoble oil but smothered in mayonnaise— just the medicine for adolescent acne.

Three hundred two-bedroom flats as like as the spruce trees in his forest, tremendously overheated, spotlessly clean. A smell of hot dust from the glowing valves of television sets, a sickly waft of artificial vanilla from the biscuits that were being munched. He climbed steps, his stick under his arm. The man he had posted to watch the building materialized behind him.

"Hallo, chief."

"Been here long?"

"Took over from Gerard an hour ago. Not a mouse. No husband, no lover, no nobody."

"He hear what the neighbours were saying?"

"Ho yes: full of it, but flummoxed. Nobody knew the woman. Nice little girl, they say, but a different name, foreigner, ja, so that if your husband is away a lot, even if one can't say for sure, you very likely lead a loose immoral life, what?"

The neighbours did not seem to have been startlingly original; Van der Valk shrugged.

"I'm going to look about for an hour."

An hour later he knew nothing positive. A few negatives, like finding no photo album. Everyone has a photo album, no? Not even a photo of Ruth, as though, as though . . . no, no conclusions. Esther Marx was neither tidy nor untidy. Her clothes were expensive, but there were not many of them. She wore trousers a lot, but she had a very nice frock of Chinese silk and a nearly new jersey cocktail dress with the boutique label of a couturier, and two or three pairs of fragile high-heeled sandals. Mm, one would have to show her photograph in hotels and bars, but he felt instinctively that it was a thin idea.

The furniture was dull, conventional; she had had dress sense but no taste. She brightened her day with whisky, it would seem; there was an empty bottle and another a third full. She liked peanuts and a lot of fruit. She cooked a lot of Indonesian rice dishes—so did half Holland. She had no jewellry—a few pairs of earrings. She seemed to get no personal letters and there was no sign of any family or friends anywhere. Her pockets and handbag held several ticket-stubs from cinemas, but only one at a time. No, there was nothing odd or irregular in the pattern, for a woman who lived much alone. The television set was well used, there were no books, but plenty of magazines— *Match, Express*— ordinary French taste.

Personal papers were in a cardboard shoebox. A savings book for Ruth, extract of marriage certificate (the French functionary had had some difficulty with Dutch spelling), Ruth's birth certificate, dated three months later and baldly saying "Father Unknown." No passport or identity card for Esther. There were social security papers, rent receipts, odds and ends that meant nothing.

Ruth's clothes were like her mother's, simple, good quality, and not many of them. He found a suitcase and packed, shoving a few thing that needed ironing on top, but whatever was forgotten could easily be picked up later. Damn Esther Marx, why did her home tell him so little? What had the killer come for —to find something, recover something? It was such a dull story. Esther Marx, French woman of Jugoslav origin, Dutch subject by marriage, had earned her living as a nurse in a military hospital, married a Dutch soldier, and lived placidly without passions or dramas, for ten years, and then had been shot. Why should she be shot after ten years? What had brought the upheaval about? And killed with a machine-gun! Brutal, efficient, but reckless. How the devil was it that nobody had paid any heed to the shots? Mrs. Chose had talked about a crashing noise, but nobody else appeared to have thought anything of it!

Outside, he picked up his policeman.

"I can't see any real good in your hanging about here—I'll give you a lift back to the shop."

"Thanks, chief."

"How is it that in a soundbox like that nobody notices shots? Even assuming he fired all seven together —the woman across the passage thinks someone maybe fell off a stepladder—what are you sniggering at?"

"You never look at the television, chief?"

"What have I missed now?"

"Of course you haven't had Gerard's report yet. She was done in in the lunch hour—very cleverly, right in the gangster serial."

"Oh no," light dawning.

"There's always a terrific din—car crashes, broken glass, tommy guns—it's a send-up really: Perils of Pauline, 1970. Fifteen minutes."

"Once a week or every day?"

"Every day. You must know the theme tune—that drummer. You're standing still, dad—Rich Starr."

"Why not Rick Shaw?" resignedly.

"Yesterday they packed the police car with dynamite and it went off when he turned the starter key. Boy, poor old Rick, sticking plaster on for nearly three quarters of an hour and the girls hysterical about his eyebrows, cutting bits off their own hair and sending it into the studio."

"Just as a sacrifice, or intended to replace his?" interested.

"Don't ask me, chief, I've got no daughters, thank God."

"A pro who times his jobs to the television—well well. Not original, but effective."

Arlette was asleep. As he screwed the cap back on the toothpaste, a thing she was quite incapable of doing, he found himself humming a little song. With a little recollection he traced it to the hero of a television serial—words adapted by French urchins ...

> *'Thierry-la-Fronde est un imbécile ...*
> *Avec sa fronde en matière plastique*
> *Qu'il a acheté au Prisunic ...'* It was him!

He levelled a sub-machine-gun at the bathroom glass and said, "You've ten seconds to live." Wasn't his style. He needed a leather coat and a cigar, like Colonel Stok of the KGB. He tried to see himself as Colonel Stok, but his orange pyjamas, bought by Arlette, with *"Oui à l'amour"* in midnight-blue script across the bosom, quite spoilt the effect.

CHAPTER SEVEN

He nearly turned into Colonel Stok again next morning; it was colder than ever, the wind had risen, and was dashing the now much heavier rain against the panes in a rhythm like automatic-rifle fire. He put on his leather coat and hat with a wide brim, but forgot his cigars—he had to take Ruth to the hospital and was preoccupied.

"Those shoes are too thin—put on your gumboots." Luckily he had packed them last night. He watched Arlette biting her thread; she was sewing a button on Ruth's raincoat.

"Her birth certificate says 'Father Unknown.' Our sergeant offered to give her his name—she was born three months after they married."

46

She seemed not to be listening; she had pulled Ruth's red woolly beret out of the raincoat pocket and was regarding it, twiddling it about in an absent way. "Arlette."

"What?—sorry."

"If Zomerlust is not really keen to concern himself about this child—and I wouldn't blame him. . ."

"Bring her back to me," with unexpected vehemence.

"So you would be in favour—you want me to ask him whether he'd agree?" But it was cut short by Ruth coming back.

"Better," said Arlette, buttoning her up. "Rain won't get into you." She pulled the beret on the child's hair, laughed suddenly and tweaked it forward on her forehead, tilting it to one side. "Now you're a paratrooper." To her consternation Ruth broke into violent sobbing.

"I was being silly," said Arlette, cuddling her. Van der Valk could see the child making efforts to be docile and reasonable, not to throw herself about and howl. Be courageous before strangers.

"I know," hiccuping and snuffling. "You were making a joke."

"Silly joke."

"Mamma used to do the same." Van der Valk took her hand. Sure enough, she had a metal badge on the beret, military insignia, something of Zomerlust's.

"Come on, we have to go to the hospital and see what these doctors are getting up to." He had a car waiting.

"Will Mamma be long in the hospital?" Ruth had been silent for some time, staring out of the window

—rush hour, and they were held up at all the traffic lights.

"It wouldn't surprise me. She was badly hurt. We'd better be prepared to be told she's pretty ill." He had stage-managed a little scene at the hospital, asking them to put Esther's body in a bed in a private room. He was wondering why Ruth had never asked what it was exactly that had happened. Did the child know? Or had she decided she didn't want to know?

"Wait here a moment, Ruth, while I ask which way we have to go . . . Commissaire van der Valk. I have the child here; I have to break it to her. Where have you got the woman who was brought in yesterday?"

The woman leaned over with odious complicity to whisper: "You understand, Commissaire—it's in the paper—we didn't want people asking questions. Corridor B, and you go right along and turn to the left, and it's 11A. I'll ring up and tell Sister you're coming."

"Has the autopsy report been sent me?"

"I'm afraid I couldn't say."

He walked heavily back to where the child—how good she was—sat waiting. His leather raincoat squeaked as he sat down heavily beside her. Nobody else around, God be thanked.

"The news is bad, Ruth, I'm afraid. She was too badly hurt. But she didn't have any pain." The child looked at him with a face that told him nothing.

"I knew."

"Ah."

"She was shot. Like on the television."

"People do get shot. Not as often as on the television, perhaps."

"Mevrouw Paap said such silly things. She thought

48

she was hiding a secret, and all the time she was giving it away." Van der Valk knew that this calm would not last. Luckily a child had very little idea about "being shot." Thanks to the television! One fell down—it was probably a lot better than "being ill." So quick, so clean an ending, in a child's eye.

"Now I've no one."

"Yes, you have. One always has. You don't know the story of Cosette and Monsieur Madeleine?" said Van der Valk, realizing with a lucky stroke of humor that Colonel Stok had turned into Jean Valjean.

"No."

"Cosette was a little girl who had nobody—and who was very ill-treated. Dreadfully ill-treated. I'll tell you about her. Do you want to see your mother?"

"No," said Ruth firmly. "I've said goodbye."

"Would you like the car to take you home to Arlette? I have to go to work."

"Yes, please." How perfect she was.

As he stood up a voice blared at him from fifty centimetres away: "Going to go on keeping secrets, Commissaire?"

Van der Valk brought his heel very hastily across this clown's instep, said, "Oh I am sorry" and took the child's hand. She had started to cry, which was the best thing she could do. He sat her next to the driver, and said, "Take her back to my wife, Joe, and pick me up here." Ruth did not want to say goodbye to Esther, but he did. It was time that Jean Valjean changed back into Colonel Stok.

The pressman in the hall was holding his foot and looking both physically and morally pained.

"You," said Van der Valk. "You interrupt me when I'm working just once again and I'll unfit you for fatherhood. Six o'clock at the bureau is when I have time for you."

Esther was in a sort of anteroom to the mortuary where they put relatives; they had screened a corner off. There was nobody there. They had arranged her quite nicely, with a pillow and a hospital nightdress; her hands lay quiet along her body. He didn't want to look at her body; there would not be much left of it. He picked up her hand. A nurse's hand, competent and muscular, with two or three fine white lines from old cuts, but well cared for, a little roughened by housework, very clean, one nail slightly misshapen from being crushed at some time, no sign of her habitually wearing other rings. The forearm was strong and tanned; she had been out in the fresh air.

The face was an empty shell, like all dead faces, but the marks of her character were there upon the smooth surface, a clear skin still youthful but with the lines of an older woman around the eyes and mouth. One could read resolution and courage—he wished he had seen her alive. She had not been a conventionally pretty woman but her looks had been striking, with a well modelled forehead, a wide and beautiful mouth, a long supple neck. Her hair was brown and straight, cut short, that of a woman caring nothing for fashion and knowing well what suits her. He looked at her with respect; Esther had known how to keep her secrets. He walked slowly back to his car.

"She just kept crying," said the driver. "She made no fuss. Went eagerly to your wife. Rough for a little girl. The father not want her? What will you do with her?"

"Keep her," said Van der Valk, surprising himself at sounding so natural.

The office was very spry and brisk; with the national Press paying such close attention his staff appeared unnaturally bright and as though fresh from their New Year resolutions. He found it all slightly absurd—poor Esther. Had she had a talent for getting into theatrical situations? It didn't look like it, but what could one read on that dead face with closed pages?

His desk was full of paper; he glanced over it while picking up the telephone.

"Commissaire van der Valk—morning, Burgomaster. Yes, decidedly. No, certainly not. Likeliest, but it's quite hypothetical. A job for the archaeologists—no, I mean we go digging in the past. Yes, naturally we're checking all that but it's all very quiet and decent and frankly I doubt it. Naturally, Burgomaster, you can rely on that. Right, sir, yes. I'll do that, of course. Yes—'bye."

They would not be too worried. Congratulating themselves on his experience, on his knowing how to handle the Press even if it turned nasty. He would get criticized on every side, and there was a large and vocal group just dying to make trouble for him, but he was lucky in his burgomaster and did not worry.

Little in the police reports he did not know by now. Zomerlust's time was accounted for to the minute. All agreed that he was conscientious and loyal. No women in his life, no queer behavior, no debts or eccentricities—almost depressingly virtuous, this man. Liked a beer and a joke and a session with the boys. Sociable and popular, a bit over-familiar with subordinates. But sound, dependable—and an excellent craftsman.

Zero from the Van Lennepweg. Neighbours, shops, bars—nobody had much to say about Esther Zomerlust. Calling her "Mevrouw Marx" was a faintly spiteful way of underlining Ruth's name. Polite, but never forthcoming. Never noisy. No gossip. Rarely smiled. Low, fatigued-sounding, hoarse voice. Smoked a lot, drank a good deal, but never showed it. Several people had wondered whether she were Jewish, but she didn't look it, and certainly didn't say it. No stranger or intruder even hinted at. And no one believed that Sergeant Zomerlust had anything to do with her death. A quiet model couple. What everybody did say was, "Of course, she was a foreigner."

At Ruth's school they said much the same. Quiet well-behaved little girl. Solitary—"a foreigner." Lowspoken, unaggressive. Average pupil, quite bright, sometimes careless and lacking in concentration. No close friendships. A "poor mixer" but an easy docile child enough. Van der Valk resolved to change her school, if the decision got left to him. He had not known Esther Marx, and this made him the more resolved to know Ruth Marx.

Last on the list was the hospital autopsy, which had taken the whole evening and the report of which had only just arrived. He knew it would be thorough and unpedestrian—he knew the doctor, and had been wondering whether Esther's mutilated, torn body would prove talkative. But like every other line of inquiry, it was disappointing.

Robust health. Muscles firm and well-developed. All organs present and in good condition. Small scar of healed tuberculosis on one lung. No recent sexual intercourse, no sign of assault or struggle. No broken bones, no surgical interventions, no apparent lesions. Death due, predictably, to grouped perforated wounds in vital organs including pericardium, spleen and liver:

decease irremediable and virtually instantaneous. Teeth all her own and nearly all present. Blah blah— Haversma had written into the typescript above his signature—"Never saw a healthier physical specimen in my life."

"Tell Joe that I won't be needing the car, but I'd like him to go out to the camp and ask Zomerlust to come in for a talk. No obligation of course, but I should think the military will be agreeable about co-operation."

And now for half an hour he had to think about his administration; murder or no murder, the little trot of police business went on.

"Where are you getting on the hit-and-run?"

"All we know is the car had an American look. Opel maybe? Not a real American he says, not a Great Big Long one. We're showing him photos—he thinks he'd know it if he saw it."

"Thought of that thing Renault make for the Americans?"

"A Rambler?—an idea that. Garages all negative to any suspect paint or panel jobs, so far."

"And the pay-packet fiddle?"

"Bart got it—she was cooking the books, she said, to pay her doctor, whom the social security refuse to reimburse."

"Good . . . Van der Valk . . . right, shoot him up . . . Right, that's Zomerlust—I want you to take what steps you see fit about that factory where the pilfering's going on . . . Come in: sit down and make yourself at home . . . Bear in mind, Jack, I may take off suddenly and leave you landed with current affairs, mm? Handle that last thing on your own . . . Well, Sergeant. I can't keep calling you Sergeant; I'll feel happier calling you Bill. To get it clear—everyone's happy that you have no connection with your wife's death."

Everyone but me, Zomerlust appeared to think; his fresh face was glum and drawn.

"We'd have preferred it to be you—we're quite upset it isn't you. Would have meant a sight less trouble." Van der Valk, hamming away, saw this sink in; he was given to crude remarks in downright bad taste and every now and again they helped. He went back to the offhand tone.

"More trouble for me means less for you, but some, none the less. Somebody killed your wife, somebody whose identity I don't begin to guess at, about whom I know strictly nothing. I have to know a great deal more about Esther's life. Yes—sort of familiar, calling her Esther, and it irritates you. But understand that I have to become familiar with her: as familiar as I can get. I have to ask you questions that will embarrass as well as irritate you, and you'll just have to keep reminding yourself that I have one purpose only—to find the man who killed her. Better for you than its being thought that you'd killed your wife—in which case you'd be asked these questions anyway," dryly.

"Like what kind of questions?" Honest and a bit puzzled.

"Like for instance why did Esther not give you a child?"

The fair skin flushed at once, but he answered readily, woodenly: "We were against it."

"We or she?"

"She—but I agreed. Too many—here—everywhere. What sort of world are they born into anywhere?—hunger, napalm, you name it and we've got it."

54

"A man's instinct is to found a family."

"Less, when he's seen something of the world."

"Esther had seen a lot of the world?"

"My idea as much as hers," stubbornly.

"What made a bond between you, in the first place?"

"She nursed me when I got some grenade splinters and was in dock."

"In France, yes. And you found her attractive and took her out—that's straightforward."

"She was lonely. She'd been played a dirty trick by some man."

"Ruth's father?"

"Maybe. I suppose so."

"Don't you know?"

"No," simply. "She never told me."

"He'd deserted her? She was bitter?"

"I don't know. She told me she was pregnant. I told her that made no difference to me. It didn't and it hasn't." Life had crept into his voice. "She was a good wife. If she was killed it wasn't on account of anything she'd done and that's something you'd better get clear."

"A good wife," repeated Van der Valk ponderously. "How?"

"How, how?"

"Put it in military language—she was a passionate woman?"

"You mind your mouth."

"I told you it wouldn't be pleasant."

"She was a good wife every way and that's all I'll tell you. She never cheated, never lied. She was a fine girl." The simple phrase had a dignity Van der Valk hated to attack.

55

"Did she drink when you knew her first?"

"She liked a drink. I never saw her drunk."

"One couldn't ask for a more loyal person than you." The man looked steadily, turning it over. A slow mind, but firm. He would take his time about making it up, and once he had there would be no budging him.

"Not more than she was, Mister."

"She stuck to her loyalties?"

"Someone cheated her once, badly. I told you I don't know who. Maybe it was that man. But I never heard her say an unjust word to the child."

"I'd like nothing better than to leave things the way you did, and not even ask, believe me."

"Esther's dead. I can't change that and no more can you. Leave her in peace. That's what she would have wanted—and asked."

"As a man I agree. As a servant under oath—like you, I'm a servant of the state and I do what I'm told —can't be done. I do my best; I'll show you. What have you decided about Ruth? You've spoken to your family?"

Zomerlust flushed again; he seemed to be begging Van der Valk not to humiliate him.

"They wouldn't have her," painfully. "I'll have to see what I can do."

"You could marry again."

"No," slowly. "I couldn't ask another woman to accept—the situation," he ended lamely.

"Do you"—it was Van der Valk's turn to speak hesitantly—"want me to make you an offer? If you were to allow me, I'd like to adopt Ruth." He hadn't thought of coming out with it so roundly. It had only been a vague notion. He was a good deal astonished, and so was poor old Zomerlust.

"How do you . . . How would you?"

"My wife is French. I have two boys—they're more or less grown up. Away from home. It could be done."

"Mister—you don't know what you might be letting yourself in for. You don't know . . ."

"Neither did you."

"I did it for Esther."

"Put it that I am too."

"You're not what I thought, altogether."

"Meaning a bastard? Little do you know."

"No—you're a good man."

"Can't have that. In this job you see that there are very few good men. And perhaps even fewer bad ones."

"I'll have to think about this."

"Yes. Back to Esther. Born in France, up in the coal-fields somewhere—of Jugoslav origin—you know anything about that? Whether she had a family?"

"I don't know—she never talked about it. Never mentioned any family. She thought of herself as French. I've asked these things—it's no good. You have to take her as you find her. Take me as I am, she'd say. Just a camp follower."

"What did she mean by that?"

"I suppose that she'd always worked among the soldiers. She was a special kind of military nurse—airborne ambulance, ipsa or something they called them. She'd done parachute training. I served in Korea—you know? Well, she'd served in Indochina. You asked what was the bond between us; well that was, sort of. She had a uniform, had some kind of military insignia—French: I wouldn't know what."

"This camp—there were French troops there?"

"The camp was on loan to Nato—everyone used it. But there were lots of units of all kinds, engineers, paratroops, a cavalry squadron—it's a place the size of Holland, kind of desert. Not farming country. Good for nothing much but manoeuvre terrain and such—rocky."

"You liked the French—got on with them?"

"No, couldn't stand the sods." Van der Valk grinned inwardly. The Dutch never could stomach the French.

"Not good soldiers?" blandly.

"Oh they're tough enough—I've talked to a few, who'd served in Algeria, Indochina. They're all a bit cracked. I just don't like them."

"And Esther?"

"Well, she was used to them," defensively.

"Esther spoke French to Ruth. You think her father was French?"

"I prefer not to think about it. What good does it do? I respected her wishes. She'd had a hard life. What good would it do me to know? Or her? Ruth, I mean."

"So it boils down to this. You know little or nothing about Ruth—or about Esther—because you deliberately made it a policy not to ask. You stick to that? You'd tell the judge that?"

"Sure. It's the truth, whatever you think."

"Oh, I accept it," said Van der Valk. "I guess that's all. I'll get my driver to take you back."

Zomerlust got up slowly.

"Speaking of that matter? You mean it? Really? You see, I'm thinking of what would be best. For her. She owes me nothing. It would be best—for her, maybe—if she never saw me again. She'd soon forget me," without bitterness. "Course, I could only agree if I knew for sure. Not that she'd be looked after, I mean more that she wouldn't be let down. I don't know how to say it."

"You're her legal guardian. These things need lawyers. There are formalities."

"Damn the formalities," muttered Zomerlust. "If I trust you I trust you. Go ahead."

"This inquiry will take some time," said Van der Valk, well aware that this was something of an understatement. "We'll have the opportunity to see something of each other. It can be worked out."

"I'd better get back. My section commander . . ."

"You want to meet my wife?"

"You won't want me sitting drinking tea in your house," said Zomerlust with a ghost of a smile, "and neither would Ruth."

"See you soon, Sergeant."

The man picked up his beret; metal winked in the sun.

"Ruth has a badge on her beret," said Van der Valk idly.

"One of Esther's. She had a lot. Ruth asked for it." Of course. Nurses collected such things, souvenirs of boys they had nursed, been out with, slept with, very likely. There might well have been many, but it was a fruitless thought.

CHAPTER EIGHT

Van der Valk, who had been thinking for some time without its having brought him much further, was scribbling on a piece of paper. It seemed to be a draft for a telegram.

Department?—Tarn, Lozère, one of those.

"Military Hospital. Pray write all known details known Marx, Esther, born one, six, thirty-four—no. Pray send urgentest all known. Victim homicide stop. Official inquiry opened stop."

He scribbled it out.

"Marx, Esther, born one, six, thirty-four, victim homicide assailant unknown. Official inquiry opened. Pray furnish all known life and service urgentest." He rang for his secretary. "Get this into officialese. Find out the Préfecture for that camp and the district. Copies to Police Judiciaire, the military hospital and anywhere else you think of that might be of some use."

He took another piece of paper and scribbled some more: "Commissaire de Police. Personal. Parallel official request received," he had to make this a bit enigmatic, so that it would not arouse any curiosity in the wrong quarters, "would be pleased know your unofficial mind stop does bottle champagne interest you stop if desired phone home number after eight stop greetings downtrodden confrère."

He had known such little letters to succeed before now, childish as they were. Official messages advanced upon their appointed ways, through the bland and anaesthetized digestive systems of official bureaux, and in due course produced bland, tasteless replies. It was lunchtime; he went home.

"I don't understand this message," said the post-office clerk, worried.

"Where does it say you should? Just count the number of words, son, and spare the intellectual effort."

"There is bouillabaisse," said Ruth with open eyes; she had just learned the word and was pleased with the sound it made.

"Good—I've been getting anti-French demonstrations the whole morning."

"I am delighted," said Arlette, beaming.

"I know how it's made—Arlette taught me."

"Very very good; we will exchange lessons. Words in -ou make their plural with an s, except bijou caillou chou . . ."

"Genou hibou joujou pou. May I tell you? One big

onion, three tomatoes, six potatoes and six pieces of garlic."

"And a stone covered in seaweed," said Arlette with a straight face. The week before, she had come upon a recipe in an English Sunday paper, and laughed till she cried.

"Where do you go to school, Ruth?"

"On the corner of the Van Lennepweg and the Oosterkade."

"Would you like to change? There is a school where there are children from several different countries, and they do things in other languages."

"Oh yes. But it's the middle of term."

"We will say you've just arrived from Madagascar."

"But then I'd be very cold and I wouldn't speak Dutch."

"There you are—just think—you have an enormous advantage."

"Aren't I going back, then, to the Van Lennepweg?"

"If it's all right by you, no. You stay here with Arlette."

"And have bouillabaisse every day?"

"Except Saturday, when there is cassoulet, because of the rugby players."

"Official?" asked Arlette.

"No, not official—but from the horse's mouth."

"What horse?" asked Ruth, already alarmed by the rugby players, who sounded menacing.

"Dinner, children. Ruth, take off your apron and wash your hands."

Official channels being what they are he was surprised to have a telephone message before the office closed, giving him an answer to his inquiries. The answer had come on the telex, was very brief, and not very enlightening. It said, "Our representative will call upon you tomorrow morning," and was signed with a code number. Van der Valk studied this laconic phrase with interest. He felt as if he had thrown a fishing line into the Volga and come up with an enormous sturgeon, and got a colleague in the Hague on the phone.

"I read you a code number."

"Aha."

"Am I right?—is this DST?"

"It is. What have you been doing—joining the Secret Army?"

"No no, I like the French."

"Be very quiet and very innocent," advised the colleague, who had dealings now and then with the French police. "They're terrifyingly polite, like the General."

The second message pleased him more, though it was equally laconic. It was a civilian telegram delivered by a bicycle-boy, and said "Stand by your phone Mazarel."

Van der Valk was vague with the Press when they asked about progress.

"Now let's see," he said to Arlette when he got home again, "DST—that's counter-espionage, hm?"

"No, that's SDECE. DST is surveillance of territory, but I think it's a question of not letting your left hand know about the right. What interest have you in them?" She sounded a bit anxious.

"I don't know at all. They seem to have an interest in me. They propose to call tomorrow disguised as a traveller in groceries. The password is 'How do you stand for cornflakes?' "

"Very funny."

At five minutes to nine the telephone rang.

"France is calling you."

"Put them on." There were bangs and snaps, and the gabbling of exchange girls far away in the rugby players' country—the medieval guts of the French telephone system. Van der Valk suspected them of doing it on purpose. They could build a variable-geometry jet fighter in half the time it took the Americans, but were not going to allow the population to be contaminated by advanced technology like telephones. Civilized of them, on the whole.

"You're through," quacked several ducks.

"Through what?" said a male voice suddenly in his ear.

"The Mont Blanc Tunnel probably," he said politely.

"Go on," said a duck impatiently.

"Come and give me lessons," went the male voice. "Am I really talking to you?" in a voice without the sweet reasonable tone.

"Myself, confrère, to my pleasure."

"Good. The champagne is a good idea."

"It's a promise—I have a feeling I'll be in your district shortly."

"I'm not going to talk on an open line, of course. This may not interest you, but I'm doubtful, you know, whether your official inquiries will meet with much enthusiasm." Van der Valk digested this news for a minute.

"You think I'm going to hit a big dull echoing silence, do you?"

"I just thought of giving you a bit of a hint. So you wouldn't think I was just being obstructive." That, thought Van der Valk, is reasonably clear and cer-

64

tainly familiar, but one would like to know what he was talking about, even so.

"My customer's name rings a little bell, does it?"

"Oh yes. No particular surprise will greet your news. Nothing's known of course. I have nothing on paper. In fact I don't have anything for you at all."

"I didn't suppose you had. Would have been a great deal too much to hope for."

"It might strike sensitive ears in some quarters," went on the voice in a do-you-understand-me way, "turn them a bit red."

"I see." He didn't but hoped he might, with perseverance.

"That's all, really."

"Give me a clue to the crossword, though."

"Yes, of course—you couldn't possibly be expected to grasp it. Let's see—you talk any English?"

"Some."

"Think about a dee, a bee, and a pee, and then use your memory."

"When I get a tiercé in the right order I'll order two bottles of champagne." Chuckles sounded.

"Drop by any time. Yes, mademoiselle, but don't panic me."

"Are you finished with your correspondent?" asked a prim Dutch voice.

"Yes, miss, thanks." A dee, a bee, a pee? His mind was a perfect blank. "Di, bi, pi, and do I understand English?"

"What?" said Arlette.

"It's the police boss where Esther used to work in the military hospital. I sent a routine wire for anything known—I mean she might have a police record or something. I sent a civilian wire just asking casually whether he knew of anything that wasn't official. He goes extremely enigmatic, hints that my request may prove an embarrassment to persons unknown—I have no clue whatever who or why—and ends up giving me something and do I know English? Di, bi, pi—now what can that mean, in English?"

"Why English?" asked Arlette, puzzled.

"Well, he's spelling something out so he does it in English to throw the phone girls off—they use that Lucien Arthur jargon."

"And you don't understand?" asked Arlette, in such an odd voice that he looked sharply at her.

"You mean you do?"

"Certainly I do," in a dry, curt way. A red light, he thought. She's not going to say any more. It's something that affects her, which she refuses to talk about After a minute's thought he looked at her but she was deep in her book. He thought he understood but he was still no nearer the meaning of the dibipi.

Arlette was a handicap to him. A policeman, more particularly an officer in the detective branch, is in a sensitive profession. Just as a diplomat who marries a Russian wife runs a considerable risk of being sent to the Bahama Islands and left there, a policeman who makes an unconventional marriage stands an excellent chance of having thirty years in which to look at the four walls of the Bureau of Records. Van der Valk, who had occasionally brought off showy, nearly brilliant performances which had attracted the notice of his superiors, had been noted down as a useful tool, but he would never be thought altogether sound. He knew this and had accepted it. In more recent years there had been graver troubles. Arlette knew of this, and it burned her. She had done her best, but had never forgiven herself. She was still bitter, whereas he was no more than faintly cynical.

It had been a humiliating episode, with characters from the security police asking questions. Arlette had shown one the door and he had been very nasty indeed. When Van der Valk came home to find her crying and trembling but still refusing to be bullied, he had gone straight back to the office and slammed his resignation on the table. He had waited three weeks—suspended—to learn whether it had been accepted or not. He had some reason to believe that the refusal to accept it came from high up, higher than political police riffraff, at least. Arlette had been suspected of OAS sympathies, and the sad thing about this was that she did have OAS sympathies. She came from southern France, from the Department of the Var, had a brother in Algiers, and had, very naturally, been as vociferous as most about *"Algérie française."*

When the Armée Secrète proper was formed, when plastic explosive got stuck to the houses of doctors, lawyers and liberal administrators, and when she understood—before the day of the barricades—that Algeria belonged to the Arabs after all, she fought a battle between her emotions and her conscience and her conscience won.

It had no importance now. She no longer had any illusions about the admirers of General Salan, but she knew that a few years ago she had blocked her husband's promotion and had been close—within the thinness of her skin—to destroying his career. It had left scars.

CHAPTER NINE

He thought he understood. Esther Marx had served in Indochina and had been mixed up with French soldiery. She had been assassinated with a sub-machine-gun, and there was something in her past that was known to the French administration. It was easy enough to believe that this was something to do with the Secret Army, but how in heaven's name did Esther, peaceably married for ten years to a Dutch serving soldier, come to have importance to the Secret Army? Still, he realized that Sergeant Zomerlust's promotion had been blocked for exactly the same reasons as his own.

What should he do? Plainly, ask the political police whether they knew anything about Esther Marx. He was rather badly placed to ask anything of the political police. Ask for another man to do the job—himself feigning ill-health? Would be tactful; the Dutch would like that. No—he hadn't any tact. If there was a problem, for Arlette's sake he was going to meet it head on, and damn the consequences. But was there really a problem? Was that really the meaning of the French policeman's cagey behaviour? He had known nothing about Arlette, of course. He had only meant, possibly, that Van der Valk might do well to be wary of asking questions that might involve him in politics.

Esther Marx was—had been—might have been—involved with a movement for which many French functionaries had felt—and stifled—sympathy. If Esther Marx was now dead by violence, went this message, better not embarrass a number of officials in a small town in the South-west of France—perhaps not too long ago they too were being thought of as "security risks." Their promotion might have been blocked too. There have been magistrates for whom at one time the way to Versailles lay open—perhaps even prefects—who found themselves unaccountably left sitting in Rodez or Mende.

It does look, thought Van der Valk ruefully, as though I have stepped on a wasps' nest.

It is too late to withdraw. I got a telegram this afternoon saying that a "representative" would be calling on me tomorrow morning, and the telegram was signed DST.

And Arlette has proposed adopting Esther's child. Knowing her, she will now be more determined than ever.

"Arlette."

"Yes."

"I have understood some things."

"In that case," with a sideways smile, "I can go to bed."

"But I think we'd better reconsider this business with the child. *Que Zomerlustse se dérouille, non?*"

"By no means," said Arlette standing up—there, he had known it!— "If Zomerlust is agreeable, and I gather he is, I keep Ruth. Say it's my bit for the war effort."

"We don't know who her father is." He could see flame run through her, see her opening her mouth to say "He could be General Salan for all I care" but all she said, mildly, was, "Perfectly true, we don't."

"Very well, then that's settled."

"By the way, I don't suppose that badge means anything to you?"

"Badge?"

"On Ruth's beret." He looked at her, and went and got the beret to look at more closely. A blue cross of Lorraine, on a grenade.

"Isn't the grenade the Legion?"

"It is. Specifically, it is the badge of the Thirteenth Half-Brigade—the same unit that was at Bir Hakeim."

"Oh."

"You weren't to know. You weren't brought up in Toulon. Are you coming to bed?"

"Not for a little while."

"You'll forgive me if I go to sleep?"

"Of course. Goodnight—and don't worry." He heard her go upstairs. Now what was the meaning of the Bee Dee—no, the Dee Bee Pee? It sounded like I came—I saw—I conquered.

Di Bi Pi. Sounded like Vietnamese. Could it be a person—or a place—in Indochina? But the man had said it was English. When he saw it, suddenly, it was so ludicrously simple he could have kicked himself. Of course, the English alphabet: it went Ay Bee Cee. Translate into French and you got Day Bay Pay— Dien Bien Phu.

He went and looked in the cupboard and found that there was a bottle of whisky. Bravo Arlette— twice. He poured out a large glass and went for a hunt in the bookshelves. The plastic binding of *The Battle of Dien Bien Phu* was broken, and large blocks of brownish cheap print were falling out, covered with annotations in Arlette's handwriting. Tucked in were a lot of newspaper clippings and photographs. On the flyleaf was Arlette's maiden name. He understood—it had not been the woman married to a Dutch police officer who had read this book. It had been the little girl from Toulon.

A sad tale, this tale of political hedging, of half-hearted indecision and compromise. Of military vanity and obstinacy. Who had spoken for the world? Not Eisenhower or Congress. Not Churchill. Giap had had the last word; nothing new under the sun.

Yet the tale had nobility too, that of sacrifice and beauty and catastrophe. The suffering on the hillocks named Huguette and Eliane balanced the suffering on the hills, where the People's Army had hauled artillery by manpower.

Halfway through he could read no further, even helped by whisky. He glanced at the photographs; there were all the star actors, so vividly contrasted— Giap and Navarre. And the colonels—the courtly mannered Castries and those two harsh-handed, hard-mouthed peasant noblemen, Langlais and Bigeard.

Arlette had fallen asleep with the light still on, a thing only a woman can do. A man could never fall asleep with the light on; wryly he realised that his own light was turned on: so be it, he would not sleep. He got his jacket, and a beret; he was limping from fatigue and he got his stick, and hobbled out on to the silent streets of two in the morning in a provincial town. One hundred thousand persons, an area for which a paratroop lieutenant with under a hundred men would be responsible.

It had stopped raining but the wind still tore harsh and implacable through streets overhung by inky ragged cloud which parted now and again to show a livid moon, three-quarters full, waning. This was Holland, not the jungle. He was not a paratroop lieutenant, but a colonel, an administrator. He limped and carried a stick, like Castries. The commission of inquiry held to inquire into the catastrophe had been flabbergasted to learn that Langlais, a mere lieutenant-colonel with no field training, had been the sole responsible field commander of the French garrison, and that Bigeard, a lowly major commanding a parachute battalion, had been his "operations" second.

"What was then the function of Colonel de Castries?" asked a puzzled general.

"He transmmitted our messages to Hanoi," replied Langlais, simply.

Van der Valk had better be careful. He had been parachuted into a wasps' nest, a *merdier,* and he must be as careful of his career as of his skin! Avoid massacre, boy. Perhaps he was like Gilles, the paratroop general who was the first commander of Dien Bien

Phu, Papa Gilles of the bad heart and the glass eye, who made his first jump at forty and who had seen what was waiting, wise old man, and grumbled to Cogny, "Get me out of here—I have lived long enough like a rat." It would be wiser to be Gilles than to be Castries the cavalryman, swaggering *sabreur,* champion at jumping horses, bedding the girls and charging the enemy, who left his career for ever as the transmitter of messages to Hanoi.

So Esther was mixed up with this legend, this traumatic disaster that had bewitched the course of events in Algeria as well as in Vietnam, whose echoes had not ceased rumbling round the world. They had lost Beatrice, Gabrielle, Anne-Marie and Dominique with hardly a fight, and it had been too late for the incredible courage shown on Huguette and the Elianes. Van der Valk walked steadily through the harsh streets. Like all great catastrophes this one was encrusted with myth, that nobody could now disentangle. Tenacious, however stupid. The myth, for example, that the *pitons* of Dien Bien Phu had been named after Colonel de Castries's mistresses. Why, the original dropping zones for the first paratroop strike had had girls' names, long before Castries took over. Bigeard and Gilles had landed on Natasha. He—he had landed on Esther! A Dutch peasant, son of an Amsterdam carpenter. Well, Langlais had been a Breton peasant, Bigeard son of a Toul railwayman, and the nobleman had been Christian Marie Ferdinand de la Croix de Castries, a family of dukes, great seigneurs, Marshals of France. No; he had been parachuted in, and he would stand and fight, and if he lost his career there was the little cottage waiting, in the forest, in France.

Had Ruth's father been at Dien Bien Phu? There

had been everything there—it was another legend (sedulously fostered by the Dutch) that the defenders had all been ex-Waffen SS Légionnaires of German blood. Well, of course there had been Legion units; they had occupied Beatrice and Isabelle. Now that he thought of it, the unit on Beatrice had been the Third Thirteenth—the very same that wore Ruth's badge. Did it have a meaning? There had been Germans of course—far too young, naturally, to have been in any SS—and Spaniards, and Jugoslavs! And French officers, and Russians, and lord-knew-who else . . .

One part of the crossword was solved. Esther had been involved with troops that had fought at Dien Bien Phu—those troops who formed a freemasonry. Whatever happened, even now years later, soldiers who had been at this Vietnamese Agincourt which they had not won—but neither had they lost—knew, recognized and supported one another. And he rather thought that his telephone call from France had less to do with the Secret Army than with that magic bond, the private solidarity of men who had crouched in the mud on Eliane and looked out on Giap's hills.

Once could not, of course, place too much trust in the badge. Esther had been a nurse, Esther had had many soldiers in her hands and in her arms.

Arlette had seen it all.

Van der Valk stopped dead. Had Esther herself been at Dien Bien Phu? Zomerlust's words echoed in his head.

"Called ipsas or something—airbourne nurse; she'd had parachute training."

A nurse had won fame at the place—Geneviève de Galard, who had been unable to leave when the airstrip came under the direct fire of Giap's artillery. She had stayed throughout the siege, at Dr. Garuwin's side. But she had been alone. What other woman had been there? Brigitte Friang, most celebrated of women war correspondents, who had been under fire more times than he had had hot cups of tea. But she had left before the siege, and had been forbidden to parachute into the camp once it had started. Paule Bourgeade, Castries's secretary, had been flown back to Hanoi on the second day of the siege, at Castries's express order.

There were to be sure the Ouled Naïl girls, but about them both legend and—unsurprisingly—official accounts were vague. Certainly there had been no nurses, apart from Geneviève de Galard, but nurses had continued to fly in and out as long as they could.

Why was the name of Dien Bien Phu a talisman that should surround the doings of Esther Marx, in France, with a feeling of embarrassment? More important, were these people who proposed to call on him tomorrow there to tell him the truth, or to tell him lies? Everything to do with Dien Bien Phu attracted lies, and there were still too many unanswered questions. Why this, why that, like the other list of strange fatalities that had lost Waterloo.

At home he put his stick away, with a secret message of sympathy for Colonel de Castries, in whom something had broken that first day when Beatrice fell and the first of his "mistresses" changed her lover.

Esther, did you too change your lover? Why were you shot down, so abruptly and efficiently?

Van der Valk, before he slept, tried to recall the little rhyme about the matador. The fickle public in the tribunes, as ready to scream coward as to acclaim a hero. "But there is only one who knows, and he's the one who plays the bull."

CHAPTER TEN

He woke up bleary, result of all this juvenile prome-
nading in the small hours. He had to forget any irrita-
bility; Arlette would accept it ordinarily as part of life,
but this morning she would be alert to any signs—go
and have a hot shower. He had the hot shower, reflect-
ing that she must have found the book, which he had
left lying, and understood that he had solved his clue.

It was agreeable how simply Ruth had found a
place in the household—already she had her own
place at the table and an old silver napkin-ring of Arlette's. She knew that dressing-gowns and uncombed
hair were frowned on at breakfast, that it was not allowed to read the paper, and that the washing-up was
done and not stacked.

"I have a lot to do this morning, unfortunately. Perhaps you could see about Ruth's school? She mustn't lose any more days than she can help." He looked at the little girl, eating toast with that quiet air of wisdom. Too quiet, too good; she had accepted the whole break with the Van Lennepweg without a murmur, obediently falling in with the new life as though she had made up her mind to forget Esther. Had Esther done something of the sort? Why had she married Zomerlust, and gone to live ten uneventful years in a municipal flat in provincial Holland?

"Which do you like best—coffee or cocoa?"

"Coffee."

She called Arlette "Arlette" and him "Monsieur."

"Can't have coffee every day. But definitely on Sundays, birthdays, fêtes and the Fourteenth of July."

"Have you brushed your teeth? In that case get your coat," said Arlette. "I'd like to catch the headmaster before school begins."

"Is there any more?" asked Van der Valk pushing his coffeecup hopefully forward.

"Yes, petit père, but you have to get it for yourself. Ruth and I will clear away when we get back."

"Petit père," repeated the child giggling.

"A phrase," said Arlette.

"I'm all for it," he said behind the newspaper. "I propose to become a father in my old age. Ruth, you can keep the Monsieur for your new school. See you both at lunchtime."

"Yes, Meine Herrschaft," said his wife. The door slammed, followed by the door of the deux-chevaux, followed by the wheezing noise of the starter, always unwilling in the early morning. He drank a cup of coldish coffee, said "Houp-là to push himself, and struggled into his coat. There was really little point in bothering Ruth with her mother's funeral. Drizzle this morning, and car windscreens covered in a thin greasy mud.

There was only himself and Zomerlust; he detected a press photographer and sent him packing. But there were plenty of loud large floral tributes, from the neighbours of the Van Lennepweg, from the Army, from the sergeants' mess, from him. He had written a card saying "Ruth." Zomerlust brought a large simple bunch of bronze chrysanthemums. "She liked them," he said. You're a good man, thought Van der Valk again. The burial was brief and unceremonious.

"Come and have a drink."

Zomerlust looked dubious; was it the thing, after a burial?

"I'm in uniform."

"I can't stand chatting in the rain; I've a bad leg."

In deference to the bad leg he said he'd have a cup of coffee.

"We're a bit further," said Van der Valk, stretching a damp trouserleg towards the radiator. Zomerlust shrugged.

"What good will it do? You're only doing your job, I realise. But all I ever want—all she ever wanted—was to be left in peace."

"She is, now. I go on from here. Tell me, did she ever say anything about Indochina?"

"That's Vietnam? All that French mob had been there. I suppose she might have been too. I never took much notice. I told you—we didn't see much of the French troops. They had their Algerian thing going on. No affair of ours. I don't pretend to know anything about it. I mean it's still going on, isn't it?—I mean the Americans are there now. But it's all politics, isn't it? I do remember I said something about it one day." His voice trailed off as he recalled a live, vivid Esther.

"About Vietnam?"

"She told me pretty sharpish that I knew nothing about it. Well that was true enough. I suppose she might have been there."

"You've no interest in who killed her?" Zomerlust looked at him as though he had made a very stupid remark.

"She's out there underground. She'd had a rough life and precious little luck. Now you've got to go routing about with her bones."

"She may have had a rough life," mildly. "Which doesn't mean she was ready to die. Someone thought she was. I'd be interested to know who."

Back at the bureau there was curiosity in the air.

"Man to see you, chief. Says you're expecting him."

" 's right. Twenty minutes to read my reports. Give him my apologies and say I'll be at his disposal as soon as I can and I'm sorry to keep him waiting." It raised eyebrows among the staff; he wasn't as a rule one to bother about keeping people waiting. As for him he was curious as hell, which was why he throttled his curiosity with a quarter of an hour's paperwork.

"Sorry to be so slow. I had to go to the funeral this morning." He hadn't had any idea what to expect, but there were no dirty raincoats—more like somebody from the Embassy. A slim young man looking no more than thirty, with a well-fitting dark-blue suit and a sober silk tie, protected from Dutch weather by a leather raincoat, it was true, but not police style:

sportive, supple thing with a tie belt. His briefcase was black and expensive like the raincoat, and slim like him, and didn't look as if it had a gun in it, but doubtless it was more polite not to inquire. Fair hair cut short, greenish eyes trained not to be mobile, a candid look that—who knew?—might be genuine. He looked—as far as that went—what he doubtless was: bright young French civil servant with a political science degree. He spoke fluent Dutch with little accent.

"Sorry to be a touble."

"I hope I won't be telling you the same."

Soft smile, American cigarette, flick of a gold lighter, white intellectual's hand but a muscular face looking unafraid of fresh air: could be a judo tiger for all Van der Valk could guess.

"I have come from the Embassy, Commissaire, hoping that we may be of some use to one another. I won't make any bones about this—we do have an interest in this woman. Unusual circumstances surrounding her death."

"You're not going to tell me she was connected with any secret armies!" making an act of throwing up his arms to heaven.

A laugh.

"I'd be most surprised. We keep a close eye on our secret armies, who are very respectable and discreet—they have to be, you know, or the Dutch Government would not be at all pleased. They don't run about with any sub-machine guns."

"What do you know about this?"

"What I read in the press," blithely.

"Where there was no mention of machine-guns—very well, you have your ear to the ground and we are all thoroughly infiltrated, and I have no complaints about that."

"I know," unperturbed, "that you asked the French authorities for any facts they might know, since she had lived in France. The request was passed on to us, since we are better placed to cooperate with you if need be." Mm, he was not going to say he had received a hint that any facts might be conveniently mislaid by the famous authorities. Instead he burst out laughing.

"You have some facts these authorities don't possess?"

"I have no reason not to be candid. When she arrived here we did look at her with some curiosity, but we have been convinced for a long time that she had nothing whatever to do with any illegal organization. Her death is as much a surprise to us as it is to you; I can't say to her since I don't know, do I?"

"No, I don't either." They both laughed in unison, pleased to be understanding each other.

"You're trailing your coat a bit, which is a thing I do myself, but I'll be candid too," said Van der Valk. "We can take it, I think, that she knew her murderer. Any other supposition is contrary to all common sense. Your offer, I take it, is to pass on anything you know or come to know, and that I in return should do the same. It's a deal; I need all the help I can get. She was killed by a professional. The gun is an Israeli army model and I am told a very sweet job. So was this a very sweet job. Nobody saw any intruder come or go. There was no disturbance, fight, argument, or rape, and the noise was covered by a gangster television serial, a simple trick, but which shows smooth timing. Her husband knows nothing. We learn that she was a military nurse—Convoyeuse de l'Air of sorts. She married a Dutch soldier in France down there in the training camp—who is also a professional—and came to live in Holland quite a few years ago, with a child that is not his. One might suppose that to be out of tune with her temperament; her husband says she wanted peace and very likely that is true. I think that's really all I know of her, save that quite likely she was at Dien Bien Phu." He threw it out to see whether any bombs went off, but this fellow was well trained: didn't jump at all.

"Really—you know that? You're quicker in your mind than many would be."

"Not really—I have a French wife."

"I know," with a sudden charming smile. "I had the pleasure of meeting her yesterday." Bomb for bomb.

"Well, well—you're quicker in your mind than many would be." The double laugh was quite spontaneous.

"Let me try to help, Commissaire. I know, I think, anything the préfecture or the police down there are likely to, which will save you some time wasted. Yes, Esther Marx served in Indochina, and was at Hanoï in the spring of fifty-four, and she was a girl who liked the soldiers, liked the life. A woman, perhaps, who had had unhappy episodes in her life further back than that, who had reason to be disgusted with human beings, and who appreciated the simplified kind of ideals she met among soldiers in the old colonial army. It might or might not have importance—I wouldn't know. Nothing is known for sure except that she had love affairs, and on the bounce from something married your Dutch chap, who had qualities of heart that perhaps she appreciated." The white hand waved it aside. "To the point—perhaps, Commissaire, you might think you had reason to be wary of political entanglements, and we would like to reassure you. If I may put it even more simply—you might wonder whether investigations were going on parallel to your own."

"The idea had occurred to me. Of course I'm not very politically minded. I'm probably the only person in Holland that likes both skiing and rugby." The other laughed outright this time and Van der Valk leaned forward to get rid of cigarette ash. "But since you've met my wife—I should be very unhappy at walking forward along a path that made her bite her nails. Being pro-French has no importance to me; it's neither here nor there. She's outside her own country and that much more sensitive on the subject. I myself don't care a rap if a French security organization—or a Dutch one—makes an inquiry into this death. I'm only interested as the chief of the criminal brigade on this territory."

The man shed his former manner. He seemed anxious to be friendly.

"I'm not holding any tricky cards, Mr. van der Valk. There is no inquiry projected, or even envisaged. Esther Marx was not a member of any illegal organization, nor did she have any contact with such. You asked for a check on her past life in France: routine request, of which we get given a copy—as we do of any action of the sort originating outside French territory. The woman was killed in an unusual, formal way that could be described as assassination. You mention Indochina and her service there, and I infer that something has led you to suppose a connection of some sort. Then the machine-gun—unusual because unnecessary."

"Yes. Good. I start by saying that of course you're right and that it had the flavour of a political assassination. You tell me that makes no sense and I'm very pleased to hear it. You came closer still in suggesting that this formal, mannered killing is an execution, perhaps, and deliberately intended to appear so. That could start one on any number of hypotheses, which however amusing would be a waste of time because we know no facts. My mind worked parallel. What facts are there, and what kind of basis do they give me to start any inquiry? That she'd lived her adult life among soldiers. I made a routine request to the French authorities—I don't really expect to get anything at all; why should I? Even if she did have a police record—unless she shopped somebody. But it is in France that I should look, it seems to me, because there is one thing bizarre about this woman, and that is her marrying a very ordinary kind of Dutch boy and coming to live in Holland in so plain and unexciting a fashion that it seems deliberate. As for Indochina—the woman worked in a military hospital and collected badges the soldiers gave her. She kept a few—among them badges of units that served at Dien Bien Phu. And the dates are right. I haven't done any research—my wife, who has made a kind of cult of the battle, noticed the fact. Perhaps Esther made a cult—for the same sort of reasons. Relatives there, perhaps? She was Jugoslav in origin—there were plenty of Jugoslavs among the Legion units. It seems a poor line of inquiry, but I may tell you—it's about the only one I have. We've no description, hint or thread of knowledge about whoever killed her."

The man sighed a little, perhaps out of sympathy. Perhaps he was just feeling sad.

"A coincidence, that. That your wife had relations in Indochina. Don't look at me like that," laughing. "Your wife's name is not written in any of our nasty little black books."

"It is in some of the Dutch ones, though," sourly.

"Yes, I knew that."

"I rather thought you did," dry. "It cast a slight shadow here, at one time."

"On you? Professionally? These Dutch . . . So you're a scrap embarrassed at this Marx business, are you?"

"Yes. And the more determined to see it through. For Esther's sake—and my wife's."

"Perhaps you are even thinking of going to France?" so suavely that Van der Valk knew at once that something was up.

"If my kind superiors will kindly allow me, I rather think I will. You know the old saying—nothing pro-pinks like propinquity. One makes requests through official channels and the answer is a lemon. Go and talk to people, face to face—like us—and one might just barely get somewhere."

"I think you're wise," unexpectedly. "Perhaps I'm talking out of turn, but you've been very open with me and I appreciate that. I'd like to help you in any way I could. Don't get the idea I can open any doors—I don't know where you intend to knock and I'd be none too sure of finding the keyhole. We aren't too popular in some quarters. In fact," blandly, "as you certainly know, the petty jealousies between different subsections of the same administration can be quite staggering. Nor am I exactly a large puissant wheel even in my own little organization. However, I'll try to ensure that if you knock on the doors of our friends the draught coming through the keyhole won't be too chilly. If you'll permit me, I'll add a tiny word of caution."

Van der Valk smiled; he thought he knew what was coming.

"The days in Indochina—and the days that came after, in Algeria—caused a good deal of trauma, sometimes in the most unexpected places. Not only among soldiers. I dare say it won't surprise you if you run up against a certain reticence—even a good few lies." Van der Valk smiled some more.

"I've had experience of that already—with my wife."

CHAPTER ELEVEN

He spent the rest of the day thinking about it. Arlette was a clue to Esther; perhaps not a very good clue, but as he had told the man, it was the only one he had. Both women had married Dutchmen, and had deliberately renounced a good deal of their past. It could be a painful thing. The significance lay in the difference between them. Arlette had been an innocent girl, with a romantic attachment to the soldiers. Esther was a very different cup of tea, a woman hardened and embittered by experience, who had been a soldier herself.

He knew about the "trauma" for he had experienced it. He had made the effort to understand—not that difficult, in Holland, where for a long while something of the same mentality had prevailed, among those that had seen Indonesia—there was something about the East that got you. He had never been there, himself, and rather regretted it. Dien Bien Phu was a special case but there was plenty of literature on the subject and it took no great powers to understand the "slight reticence" that the DST man had mentioned with such delicacy.

The soldiers who were there spent some months in Vietminh prison camps—those that survived the march there. It all made a powerful bond, strengthened by each new layer of experience. They were the defeated, but they had not surrendered. They had been isolated, but they had not lost heart. Betrayed as they thought by Paris, they had stayed faithful. Dysentery-ridden, hardly able to stand, they had supported, even carried wounded and dying comrades over the stumbling unending kilometres to the prison camp. Many died. A sort of mystique grew up, of truth to a lunatic ideal of sacrifice and death. They came back to France, where they found that nobody very much cared what had happened to them, increasing their sense of embittered isolation. When what they regarded as the further betrayal of Algeria was borne in on them, many would regard themselves as freed of any allegiance to governments who sent them to die in a wilderness and then bargained away all that they had died to hold. The secret army mentality was plain to grasp at that point.

Of course, it would be a mistake to think that the secret army was all formed of the Dien Bien Phu survivors, few of whom took the turning that led to trial and condemnation—or escape and exile. But the whole affair had two conclusions that one could rely upon. Anybody with secret army affinities or sympathies who had belonged to the old Indochina group would get a wide tolerance. And anybody from the same group who got into trouble as a result of lawless attitudes—with the civil, military or police authorities—would meet an indulgent, even blind eye; whether he had robbed a bank or merely fiddled the Sécurité Sociale they would leave the stable door unlocked and know nothing when the gendarmerie came to inquire. They were honest people, who would rarely defend or even condone crime, but they would not denounce or help to hunt down. An immensely nuanced and confused double-think. Van der Valk bit on a pencil with his big, slightly horsy teeth, threw it down, and turned to more mundane things like shoplifting.

A little before lunch he decided to take the bull by the—had this bull horns? No, not unless his wife was a much misunderstood woman, but the Chief Commissaire of Police for the province of North Holland could make himself disagreeable upon occasion. He decided to telephone first to the gentleman in question.

"Ah, Van der Valk. I've been wondering when I'd hear from you. What's this machine-gun nonsense— Bonnie and Clyde come to town, hey?" Van der Valk laughed heartily at this wit, delighted that the old sour puss was in a jovial frame of mind.

"Well, it's liable to be tricky. It's certainly something out of her past, and her past is quite something."

"How are you so sure of this?"

"When she married—that's this sergeant, Zomerlust; he's a good man with nothing against him whatever—she made it the one condition that the past should never be spoken of. She had a child, true. She was also a French military nurse. Served in Indochina. Crowd that might have something to do with the secret army. However, I've just had DST in to see me, who assure me that such is not the case. But since they come at all, it's obvious that there's something. What, exactly, remains to be seen. We're making no headway. It strikes me that the best way would be to go to France, find out just what this famous past of hers is, and thrash it all out. It also strikes me that you may not be very keen on me doing that."

"What on earth are you talking about?" sounding a lot less jovial.

"Well, there was a time when our worthy equivalent of DST had a madcap idea in its tiny pointed skull that my wife was in the secret army."

There was a growling noise down the telephone, as though the old lion was keeping itself in trim with a few leg-of-mutton bones kept lying handy on his desk. Presently this noise resolved itself into the words "Nonsense, nonsense."

"I'd far rather be left on the job."

"Yes, yes," tetchily. "But I didn't say you could go to France. I don't like the sound of this at all. Still, Van der Valk, you know better than to try that on with me. You know me—loyalty upwards, loyalty downwards."

"I felt sure of that," very bland.

"Yes—well, I have to think about this. I'll have to ask The Hague before I can authorize you to leave the country, as you know. I'll let you know."

"Yes, sir."

Just as he was about to go home for lunch the telephone rang, that maddening way it had.

"Oh—Commissaire van der Valk?" said a bright shiny girl's voice.

"Yes, speaking."

"Oh—I was to tell you—secretariat of the Ministry of Justice, here. The Minister would like to see you. He's very tied up and he would be glad if you could be here at his office at one-thirty precisely."

"Oh God."

"I beg your pardon?"

"I said yes, thank you."

"Then I can tell his secretary?"

"If you would be so good."

"And we can count on you? The Minister's very busy and has an appointment at two."

"Yes, Miss."

"Thank you," all crisp and efficient. He put his hand on the hook, said "Oh go and get stuffed," lifted the hand, got a click from his switchboard, and said "Ring my wife, would you" in a gloomy tone.

"Arlette? What's for lunch?"

"Cassoulet."

"Oh God. Is there goose?"

"Of course there's no goose. Where d'you think you are, Toulouse?"

"Why are there no geese in Holland?—and don't come with that one about all the geese being human; we've had it before."

"I've no idea; I'm a poor illiterate barefoot Provençal peasant. I am the chèvre de Monsieur Séguin."

"Except that you ate the wolf. Well, I won't be home for lunch. I have to go to the effing Hague. Sandwich in snackbar."

"Well I'll keep you some for tonight. I fixed Ruth's school."

"Good. Well I'll see you this evening—I hope."

"Toi-toi-toi," said Arlette in German; a slightly politer way of wishing one good luck than the classic "Break your neck and your leg" so cheerfully used by sports reporters . . .

He was agreeably surprised, all the same, when at *exactly* thirteen minutes to two he was sitting on an overheated chair, having already said his little piece, and the gentleman across the Empire desk in a very pleasant airy Empire room—the overheated chair was strictly his own fault: central heating was under control, for once—was meditating.

"I can't quite see what this French security lot . . ."

"That's it, Excellency; they're being enigmatic—their way of tipping me off and wondering if I'm bright enough to catch on. They won't give us any cooperation, naturally, because they're the soul of tact and wouldn't dream of dabbling in our affairs. The message seems to me plain. No secret army, but something there. They may not know, or be unsure, or it may simply be something they prefer not to touch. They may be using me as a stalking horse. But it appears to me crass to overlook it."

Fingertips were pointing at each other in too clean shiny rows like chessmen; a green onyx pen set occupied neutral ground between.

"At all costs we must avoid anything political," said a quiet voice. "If you go, the newspapers will lose interest. I can see to it that a discreetly-worded release goes out, after you leave. I tell you frankly that if I agree it is to the least of evils, possibly. The French . . . charming, brilliant, delightful, and diabolical—not always in that order . . ."

"I have a confidential tip that they may smooth my path."

"At least you're well placed. You're familiar with the language, the people. If I remember aright your wife is French?"

"Quite correct, Excellency."

"I spoke to the Procureur-Général about you. Once you were called on to undertake an inquiry in France on behalf of a family. It appears that you made a good job of it. But you got shot. We don't want any of that." He reached out and drank a half-glass of milk that was on the corner of his desk. "Forgive me—I had no lunch."

"I sympathize, Excellency—neither did I."

There was a slow wintry smile. "Very well, Commissaire. Your experience in these matters is perhaps a treasury. Will you be cross with me if I repeat that under no circumstances must there be conflicts and scandals with these official and unofficial French watchdogs?" The avuncular manner did not ring false. This is a simple kindly man, thought Van der Valk, who liked to "be cross with me."

"I won't be silly," he promised.

"Well, well," sighing. "I'll have a word with the Chief Commissaire. You'd better go and see the Comptroller about currency and so on. I'll see that it's cleared with him."

In a dingier office he got a sub-Comptroller, who haggled for a long time about expenses.

"Don't come back with any notes for taxi fares or the Comptroller will take a very dim view."

"Fancy that."

"France is a very expensive country, you know."

"I had no idea. I'll try not to enjoy it."

"Rather you than me," said this dogfaced baboon, stung.

"Is there a choice?"

There was rather a nasty silence while a lot of paper got shuffled about and signed. When it was all over Van der Valk clutched a great mass of it, raised pious eyes to heaven, asked "Where do they get them from?" bowed and closed the door softly behind him.

In his own office, half an hour later, he asked for coffee, called for his senior inspector and gave him a cunning grin like Talleyrand going off on the Stock Exchange and leaving Foreign Affairs to run themselves.

"As I told you might be probable, I'm going to be away a few days. Maybe a fortnight, maybe less. Simple enough; you make a brief résumé of the daily report and shove it over by messenger."

"What are you going to say to the press?"

"I'm going to eat the press with those lovely little baby garden peas."

"What, at this time of year?"

"No, I'm not cockeyed—I've been drinking milk with the Minister of Justice."

"A short statement," said Van der Valk surveying the press assembled. "There are a few misconceptions floating about. This machine-gun—you can enjoy yourselves with it, but don't let's lose sight altogether of the truth, children, however boring. I recap. Esther Marx is not Jewish, nor is she Arab. I beg your pardon—was. She was not, repeat, not, a refugee, political or otherwise. Married regularly to a Dutch citizen, her status was regular. No political motive for her killing has been uncovered or is likely to be. So much for that." His voice took on the ritual drone.

"No particular friendships or suspect associations have been found. Her personal life was quiet, retired, and free from any hint of scandal. Since there are no gangsters, there is in consequence no gang. Full stop. Paragraph. The killer—we don't know him, we have no picture of him. He is certainly mentally deranged, which does not mean that he is dangerous or a criminal lunatic. No danger exists for the population and you can print that. This man has disappeared without apparent trace. No details can or will, repeat can or will, be given of actions either afoot or envisaged to find him. Lastly, no spectacular developments can be expected in the near future. Patience and a long, boring checkup of several lines of inquiry. Very well, questions."

"Are you yourself conducting the inquiry?"

"Yes."

"Leaving the country?"

"If need be."

"Had the woman Nazi sympathies?"

"Didn't you hear me the first time?"

"What about her past?"

"Being looked into, naturally—that's routine."

"She met her husband in France—is that a pointer to your future movements, Commissaire?"

"Not necessarily."

"What about the little girl that your wife is caring for?"

"No mention of the child will be made. Contrary to ethics, and has no bearing or relevance—get that clear."

"Has her husband produced any constructive ideas?"

"He has no idea whatever why his wife should have been killed."

"Commissaire, you've ruled out gain, sadism, politics, passion. What motive in your opinion is the right one to base your inquiry upon?"

"None at all."

"A meaningless murder?"

"I said the man was certainly deranged mentally if not actively certifiable."

"You're sure it's a man?"

"No. The gun makes it a probability; that's all."

"Your theory of yesterday—a professional killer—it doesn't stand up in the light of what you now know?"

"I'm heaving great patient sighs. It looked and looks as if we have to deal with a man of calm, skill and quick wits, who is probably used to handling firearms. The rest remains to be seen."

"Commissaire." A last effort at tugging. "Are the military authorities helping you in your inquiries?"

"When I see any need I'll ask them. At present. And now if you'll allow me I'm going home to supper."

He was in the outer office when he was called back.

"Telephone, chief. Shall I say you've gone?"

"Who is it?"

"The French Embassy, it says."

"Give it here . . . Van der Valk . . . Thanks."

"I hoped I'd catch you," said a light rapid voice in French. "I only just heard myself. She was in Hanoi at the time. Convoyeuse de l'Air. She certainly made trips out there to the high plateau. Wasn't of course present at the siege. I give it you for what it's worth."

"Thank you."

The house was as still as it usually was at this time. Arlette had gone to her hospital and Ruth was drawing.

"Hallo. How did you get on with your school?"

"I can go tomorrow. I'm weak on history and geography, and Arlette says I'll have to do extra and you can help me."

"What's she going to do—sit back and criticize?"

Ruth had been instructed to put the supper in the oven at half past six; at twenty to seven Arlette's deux-chevaux made a loud noise outside.

"Her arithmetic is passable, Mr. Thorbecke says, and her French is only fair because her grammar is poor and he made faces at her written work. But he is quite reasonable. She knows nothing about history or geography at all, but he says generously that that's no fault of hers. She can start either German or English next year. What do you think—is Latin a suitable subject for a girl? Since her French is fluent mightn't Spanish or Italian be better?" It was a problem they had not faced before; they had only had boys!

"Arlette—oy." It was nine; Ruth had gone to bed.

"What is it?"

"I saw the man from DST today."

"Oh." There was a silence, perhaps a scrap embarrassed on both sides.

"She was at Dien Bien Phu, you know. I've been grasping some of the implications, though all this is of course pretty intangible."

"If they're intangible how can you grasp them?" asked Arlette pedantically.

"I floundered about—I'm only a poor Dutch peasant. No, you aren't in the secret army, and Esther wasn't either and there's something peculiar about Esther all right, but he may not know it himself, but the ground is clear, so I can go off to France and try and find out, against a barrier of double-talk because Esther—whatever she did—got covered-up for."

"You're not making an awful lot of sense."

"No but neither does she. Now I don't want you persecuted by this. This child . . ."

"Stays where she is."

"Good—that's all I want to hear. That we mustn't be disloyal to Esther. I think I see—you have quite a lot in common."

"This woman," said Arlette very slowly, plainly determined to stand no more nonsense, "she was at Dien Bien Phu? Convoyeuse de l'Air? But she didn't stay. De Galard was the only one who stayed."

"Hanoi, I gather, filled up with people who wanted to get in, some of whom succeeded. Has it occurred to you that something might have happened—that she did something—which has been covered up? I got a hint that that was it, today. She did something. Maybe later it leaked out and that's why she left France. Somebody might have taken this length of time to find out where she was. Consequently the machine-gun—but what the hell did she do and how am I to find it out?"

"She may have done something that the world calls a crime but the army doesn't," said Arlette.

"What do you mean?"

"I don't know. Other women joined that life, feeling —how should I know?—disgusted with life, with the bourgeoisie, with cowardice and envy and petty dirty filthy ways to turn two cents into three—I only know that I could well have done the same. Brigitte Friang asked to parachute in and they refused her permission. I understand. If Esther was like that, and I somehow have inherited her child, all I can say is that it is a mercy of God. Find out what you can about her. For me. I have to bring this child up; it's important to me."

Van der Valk searched for and lit a cigarette in silence.

"Yes. Well, I'm going—I have a green light from the Minister."

"The Procureur?"

"No—this is an administrative thing: what standing I have professionally in France, what expenses I'm entitled to. They want it kept quiet, not to upset the French, not to alert the Press, a call costs nothing political. Like the Marschal time."

"Where you ended up getting shot."

"Oddly enough, that's just what the Minister said. Don't worry, having eaten Anne-Marie's rifle bullet I'll be very cautious of this maniac with the submachine-gun. The thing is, how to go about it. I go to the spot, I get dusty answers. That policeman—champagne or no champagne—he's a last resort. I have to have something to go on, first. I can't trot in and ask what it was Esther did and why it got smothered. I have to make a more indirect approach. The thing is, perhaps, to find people who were in the battle, and try to find someone who knew her. It was a relatively small group—how many, about?"

"The good ones—who survived the camps too? About two thousand. There are plenty around." She hesitated. "Those who were there . . . why don't you ask Jean-Michel?" Her brother, who lived in Toulon and sometimes lent them his country house. An engineer, very prosperous. When he had had his wound, in the Pyrenees, they had stayed a fortnight in Toulon after he was half convelescent. He liked Jean-Michel.

"He wasn't there, was he?"

"No, but he was in the delta. Another one who tried to get in. But he was a bridge engineer—at that stage they'd no use for the likes of him. Why don't we ring him?" reasonably.

The simplicity of the solution appealed to him.

"Go ahead."

As she was dialling, his impulse, suddenly reversed, was to put his hand out to strangle the purring throat of the chat-machine: did he really want to bring her further into this by introducing her talkative, clever family? Was there not something ignoble in thus baring Esther's private life, which she had fought so hard to keep secret, for the amusement and edification of the Toulon upper crust? Too late, now; she had composed several sets of figures with great care and her tongue sticking out, automatic long-distance had done its fell work, Toulon had flown towards him like released elastic and the little bip-bip was already sounding in Jean-Michel's living-room. She brandished the instrument at him in triumph.

"Hallo? Claudine? Yes, it's me. Yes, fine, yes, she's here. Me? Suffering as usual; how are you? And Jean-Michel? Is he there? Would you put him on a minute and then I'll get you Arlette. Hallo, vieux, how's life? Tell me, are you at home more or less, the next couple of days? I've a notion to drop in if that's not a horrible thought. I've something rather interesting on which I'd value your opinion. Yes—yes—oh, a long rambling tale. No no: professional. Something banal here and suddenly the shit hit the fan. Won't put you out?

Nor Claudine? But of course: over a long blissful drink. Tomorrow evening probably—what can I bring you—a smoked eel? Yes of course—hold on, here's Arlette."

There it was; he was committed now. Ach, the idea was not that bad. Jean-Michel was bright and alert and very modern. He knew how to operate the System D anywhere in the Var or the Bouches-du-Rhône. Better still he was a balanced person and no fool at all. One could do a great deal worse. Arlette was gossiping happily down the chat-machine; he went to the kitchen for some milk.

"Alors bye-bye," she was saying when he got back: that awful way French women had on the phone, using idiotic franglais phrases like "because le job" which he had heard in the doorway. It was the same when they were in France—the first day Arlette exaggerated everything, her accent, her appetite, her mannerisms, to show that she was "home." One couldn't blame her; it was human that even after twenty years in Holland she still cared passionately for the smell and sound and feel of her land. That was not chauvinism; it was right and proper. What had Esther felt? Had she too hungered for her "own" land while she sat in the municipal flat on the sterile Van Lennepweg? What was her own land? Jugoslavia, which she had quite likely never even seen? The Pas de Calais, where she was born? The arid, fiercely hot and bitterly cold uplands of the South-west? Or Indochina?

"Remind me to buy a smoked eel for them."

"And I'll remind you to bring back a smoked goose for *me*."

"I'll ring the airport."

Airports . . . do you think they had a flight to Marseilles next day? After an intolerable argy-bargy he got an Iberia flight that would land him in Paris and after some hours' delay an Air-Inter down to the coast, after rejecting two that would gain him one hour and land him (a) at Nice and (b) at Lyons . . . He would miss lunch again.

CHAPTER TWELVE

At eleven the next morning the Commissaire, clutching his smoked eel, was at Schiphol, with an official warrant authorizing Van der Valk, Peter Simon Joseph to proceed upon the affairs of the State of the Netherlands by air (tourist class). A bored ticket girl translated this into an illegible carbon saying Amsterdam-Schiphol to Marseilles-Marignane via Paris-Orly, with a great deal of small print all about the Warsaw Convention. Chauvinism showed; the morning paper was full of how the French were being very naughty and wounding to the Dutch about subsidized margarine.

"Rather you than me," she whined, unconsciously echoing the Ministry of Justice. Van der Valk—loyal to Arlette, loyal to Esther—was irritated.

"Just stick to the job, Sissi. Keep the home-thoughts-from-abroad for the distressed provincial lady."

Arlette was waiting by the registration desk with his case, containing, had he known it, cosmetics-for-Claudine, so cheap at airports.

"And duty-free whisky, so you aren't empty-handed."

"I should say not," he groaned, taking the case. "God, it's like lead."

"I packed your raincoat and a suit and thick shoes and a good shirt in case you go somewhere . . ."

"Oh, woman—all I need is spare underclothes." Women . . . always so bloody zealous when it came to packing!

"That's what you think. You don't know Marseilles —freezing cold and simply pouring—you'll see."

"Many thanks."

"I can't stop—I've Ruth coming home for lunch."

"What are you having?" full of envy. He would get an airport meal, as revolting as it was expensive, at silly Orly . . .

"Escalopes, as it's just us girls, with that cream that went sour—and grilled bananas."

"Oh—with rum . . ."

"Never mind—Claudine is a good cook. Look after yourself, my love—and don't worry. I'm on your side. Did you think I was against?"

"For a little while."

"My love to the family."

"My love to Ruth," She smiled, happy at this. She had high heels, to kiss without stretching.

"Alors bye-bye." He had found just the right phrase, before being sucked into the conveyor-belt.

* * *

Van der Valk had leisure to inspect Schipol, and would have even more to inspect Orly—and he loathed airports. No humanity. Railway stations were civilized; airports were not. The human was channelled and chivvied, stamped and docketed, squeezed through tubes like toothpaste and finally encapsulated in an abject little tunnel that cost the earth, so that a computer had calculated to the last milligramme the profit that could be made. The loss of dignity cowed one into accepting the conditions of a very bland, very humane slaughterhouse where one got a small gin before euthanasia. Worst was the fiction whereby airports pretended to set one basking in kissy luxury.

Airports always made him wish he were in Cuba.

In consequence he walked about Orly with a heavy forbidding step like Commissaire Maigret, looked at all the restaurant menus with a pouched and glaucous eye, had a meal that was all he had feared, found a corner so gloomy that even Americans in plastic overshoes slunk away from it, and settled down to read *Playboy* with an obscure notion that it was exactly suited somehow to his frame of mind. All that gigantic tit—took one straight back to the Zepplin age . . . At last he could stagger back into the eager bustle, even get a peppermint, and be squeezed on another worm of toothpaste all the way to Marseilles. At Marignane the rain was like a dogwhip across his face, but Arlette must have phoned because Jean-Michel was there to pick him up, in a DS with swivelling headlamps of iode, whatever that was, a radio-telephone and an invisible deathray in front to clear the rubbishy cars out of its flight.

He often teased Arlette about her brother. Jean-

Michel was so like "Monsieur-Tout-le-Monde" in television serials, rich as a walking safe-deposit box but always a good laugh; absentminded, gay, casual, irresponsible. Snappy clothes and a passion for toys and gadgets; the big engineer, slim and youthful in a bikini on the beach at Arcachon, blowing up the children's inflatable canoe to play with himself . . .

Jean-Michel had suddenly become middle-aged, but still in the correctly dashing way; his waistline had not thickened, he was beautifully tanned, but he had rimless glasses and a roguish little beard. Classically, ludicrously French, he ate noisily, talking through every mouthful, he smoked terrible tasteless cigarettes and drank whisky before meals busily "counting cubes" according to official anti-alcohol campaigns, was terrifyingly intelligent and thought writing letters a shocking waste of time, got on with everyone, and could play bridge with the examining magistrate or pelota in a lorry-drivers' pull-up with complete ease. He was pleasantly childish and got much innocent pleasure out of an engineer's diary full of useful data all in Russian, and a pen which had "With the personal good wishes of Dwight D. Eisenhower" stamped on it. His gigantic skyscraper flat in Super-Toulon amused Van der Valk intensely; more mirrors than the ladies' lavatory in a Hilton . . .

The bathroom was green marble, with lots of spotlights recessed behind copper portholes, the hallway was full of little buttons commanding things, but the living-room was a prehistoric cavern, with huge stones and guaranteed-genuine Greek amphorae. One entered through an irregular arch of rough concrete and found that all the furniture had peculiar foetal shapes. Here one could be sure of finding transparent sofas filled with water, tables like huge fungoids containing fountains, bars, and high-fidelity apparatus, and hallucinatory mural paintings.

Claudine went with this; a thin supple woman with pale-silver shingled hair, curled bonelessly in a chair like someone's left lung. She smelt delicious and loved giving people tiny complicated things to eat; there were quantities of hot ferocious bits of fried octopus and devilled chicken to greet him, together with ouzo, retsina, and frightful Macedonian brandy—hm, Claudine was having a Greek Week. He liked it here: spontaneous, warm-hearted, bursting with life. Claudine looked the total butterfly and was a kindergarten teacher. Every time he met them he remarked, staggered, how horribly rich they were. Yes, they agreed, beaming: stinking, madly rich, isn't it lovely—and so it was.

"And how is Holland?"

"Greatly upset this morning about the bastardly French." Happy shrieks.

"What happens if I stick a pin in this sofa?"

"I don't think one could, it's like elephant hide and it even resists a cigarette end, but one might try acid," said Jean-Michel, looking quite eager to start that minute.

"Shouldn't there be a naked woman?"

"Oh but there is frequently; Claudine leaps about naked as a ball-bearing."

He took a mouthful of something odd.

"What's in this?"

"No idea; they're communist. Something radioactive from the Sea of Japan, the tin said," replied Claudine.

"I'll tell you why I'm here," said Van der Valk when he had finished stuffing himself, and did, in bits.

"I want to know all about the battle of Dien Bien Phu."

"Good grief." Jean-Michel was getting serious in stages. "A wilderness of unanswered questions. I was Génie, you know. We calculated that if the Viet had one-o-five artillery the camp needed thirty thousand tons of engineering material for protection. They found three thousand on the spot, chopping wood. Two thousand in bits and pieces were airlifted in. The rest was an embarrassment so was hastily forgotten."

"No no, not shop statistics. The men."

"Langlais is a general, Bigeard finally is too. Brèche left the army and I see him from time to time . . ."

"Not now. Then."

"Then—everything was queer then. Double-think and let's-pretend. Looking at it now one can hardly believe that ten thousand men were dumped in that pisspot with no protection whatever. The Viet could count the aspirins in one's bottle—they knew every gun, every hole, every radio. That had no importance of course—we would massacre them with firepower the second their nose showed. What is astonishing is that despite everything we nearly did. In April, you know, after a month's siege, Bigeard moved out with a thousand paras and knocked them arse over tit off the Huguettes and off Eliane. You know that to the last day we held Eliane? When I think that I volunteered to jump in! If ever there was a *merdier* . . . The thing to remember is that everyone who was there is loony on the subject. If your woman was machine-gunned—by someone who was there—(a) I'm not a bit surprised and (b) you'll never find out."

"More or less my conclusion," murmured Van der Valk, "but I've got to try and get upstream to where all this started before I can draw any conclusions. I've nothing whatever to suggest that 'he was there'—my elusive pimpernel. She was in Hanoi—that's official sources. My first question is that she may have had a lover there. The thing is, can you think of someone who might know?"

"I'll have to think about it," said Jean-Michel a bit evasively, "I might."

"What does that mean, you might?"

"People are loony on the subject, as I said. People have elaborate explanations for things they did then which seemed reasonable at the time but which would now be thought damn stupid. People clam up. Admit your girl had a lover, admit she did something daft, admit the improbable and say you find someone who knows—you'll never get them to admit it."

"I want to go a very small distance at a time," said Van der Valk softly.

"Come with me to the office in the morning and we'll see what we can hunt up."

"But I don't want to leave too much time between the times."

Jean-Michel smiled.

"I ought to know you by now, digging away like a solemn old badger. Let me think. You don't really want someone who was there. The odds are that he was in charge of one small splinter like shoe polish and can think of nothing else. Somebody who was in Hanoi would be better." He looked for the phonebook, which was hidden inside a splendid leather cover with "The Complete Works of the New Novelists" on it in gold. He muttered and nodded over this for some time, before taking the top off a small fat leather pig which had been perplexing Van der Valk for some time.

"When the bell rings his eyes light up—green to starboard and red to port . . . Monsieur Marie? Stressed Systems, in Toulon. Listen, Monsieur Marie, I'd like to ask a kindness, if you'd permit me. It concerns my brother-in-law, who is a commissaire of of police, in Holland of all places, and who's here on a visit, well, business in a sense. He has an odd question, and since you're something of a specialist, I wondered if you'd consent to have a word with him . . . yes, of course; read it over . . . about seven thousand cubic metres, I'd say . . . no, of course they can't, that's out of the question . . . by all means, send a dossier along and I'll give you an opinion forty-eight hours from then. A pleasure . . . Yes? The bar? Yes, I know it. Right. And many thanks . . . Woof." He was smoking furiously. "Nothing for nothing and not much for sixpence. Old bugger. But he'll see you."

"He can have seven thousand cubic metres of my fresh air too."

"You're not kidding; he'll take them. He's a funny old swine but he draws a lot of water in Marseilles. No don't worry, it's a thing I can do in ten minutes, the forty-eight hours is bullshit. As I was saying, he knows everybody. Let's see now—you know Marseilles? Know Les Catalans? Know the coast boulevard from there? About two kilometres along there's a restaurant on the coastward side, sun-terrace affair called Le Clown Vert—be there at ten—little grey man. Was a logistics expert in Hanoi."

Claudine, admirable woman, had said nothing for an hour.

CHAPTER THIRTEEN

Jean-Michel's DS left him among the palm trees and policemen of Toulon station, in nice time to catch a commuter train to Marseilles. There was heavy continuous rain the whole way, so that the landscape of Provence was reduced to muddy ruts and pools of water, and a forest fire looked about as likely as Winston Churchill on roller-skates. Marseilles when he got there had a resemblance to Nottingham, and he was reminded of an airline pilot he had known, looking at the ancient historic town of Haarlem, simply reeking of Franz Hals and William the Silent, and saying thoughtfully, "Very like Staines on a Sunday." A taxi left him on the sea-boulevard; Le Clown Vert was a concrete blockhouse with Moorish leanings, one of a hundred such along the sea wall between the Vieux Port and the Prado beach. At the kitchen entrance a van was delivering potatoes; the front was shut and shuttered but a door surrounded by tourist-club emblems let him in grudgingly to a tiled floor being mopped by a cleaning woman.

" 's closed," she said, " 'n mind m'floor."

"I know," he said humbly, "but I've come to see Monsieur Marie."

"In the back—'n mind my floor."

"Can't fly," he said. He had a wish to add "no wings" like Mr. Jellyby, but she might hit him with her mop.

"The back" was carpeted, hushed, clean and neutral—a window had been opened facing the sea, to air out the clinging reek of anis and whisky. Piles of empty glasses stood on the bar, and a crate full of champagne bottles. Beyond the picture window was the dead concrete terrace, and beyond that the dark angry sea, a lot of rocks and islets, the Planier lighthouse, the Château d'If, a scruffy steamer plodding in towards the Joliette. On this side of the window, quietly drinking coffee, sat an old man reading *Le Monde* and paying no attention for the moment to anything else. One thing at a time. Before, it had been a croissant, eaten carefully without making any crumbs. When Van der Valk padded over he got the old man's full attention; the paper was lowered, and a broad intellectual face all peaks and hollows, blanched like a skull, with fine dark eyes and a massive forehead, was lifted towards his. Monsieur Marie did not speak, but waited for him.

"Ten o'clock," said Van der Valk.

"Sit down then, Monsieur Brother-in-Law."

"I'm disturbing your breakfast."

"No." A half-empty cup of coffee was pushed aside and the paper went after it. The old man took a long filtertip Française from the breast pocket of a plaid woollen shirt which he wore open-necked under a blackish-brown corduroy jacket, and put it carefully between firm yellowish front teeth which were his own.

"I haven't presented myself properly. Van der Valk, Commissaire of Police."

The weary experienced eyes showed no curiosity. He struck a match and lit the cigarette carefully.

"I am in the dark, Monsieur Fanfan. What can I do to be of service to you?"

"I am anxious to find out something of the past life of a former military nurse named Esther Marx, who was serving in Hanoi at the time of Dien Bien Phu.' And he had thought of being oblique! Pat, his question had flapped out on the plate like a fried egg slid out of the omelette pan. Did it matter? This man could answer the question or he couldn't. If he could he would or he wouldn't.

"Ah. Dien Bien Phu. A place of phantoms and chimeras and unmarked graves. The nest from which the eggs were stolen before the illusions hatched." A very short, abrupt, noiseless laugh. "Why do you come to me?"

"She was killed—in Holland. It is reasonable to suppose that in coming to Holland she left her past behind her, and that some shadow of that past came again to touch her. She wanted nothing, you see, but to be left in peace."

"So you come to Marseilles. It seems a long way round."

"Oh, you know, I think—better than most if I am any judge—that official sources of information tend to have one thing in common, which is to inform no one."

Monsieur Marie took his time. He looked for some time at the sea by his right hand, said, "Nobody any longer cares," and again studied the outline of the Château d'If as though he might be thinking of making a bid for it. Van der Valk decided he had better not interrupt. Finally the eyes came back to Van der Valk and the voice came dragging up out of the leathery throat.

"Back along the boulevard is a monument, of no great artistic value to be sure. Marianne in a helmet, soldiers, cannon, wreaths of corn and laurel leaves. And a dedication—to all who served the colonial cause. Those who left their bones in the empire. How many left Marseilles wondering whether they would again see these rocks, this water that we hear and smell as we sit? A lot of blood, a great deal of blood."

Seven thousand cubic metres, thought Van der Valk.

"A half-hearted monument in a dreary, dusty corner. It is of no importance, now, how many died. One more—and in Holland."

"People still care sufficiently, it seems, to prefer me not to come rooting about among the souvenirs—just as somebody cared enough to kill."

"Somebody in a subordinate position," suggested the old gentleman dryly. "I offer you a piece of sound advice—always go to the top."

"Like you."

"Yes, like me."

"Did you know Esther Marx?" He was rewarded again with that abrupt, noiseless cough of laughter.

"I recall her well. Not a pretty girl but vivid."

"What kind of a girl? I only saw her dead."

"Caring for no opinion, counting no cost—the right one for an empire. A nice girl." *Fille bien gentille*—in the old man's mouth the banal phrase had unexpected weight.

"And what happened to her?"

'How should I know? Our Indochinese adventure finished shortly afterwards."

"You never saw her again?"

The old man shrugged.

"I took up other interests. I entered politics. I reentered politics," he amended, so that it should all be quite clear.

"And did you know Esther's lover?"

The answer was so direct and so simple that he wondered whether Monsieur Marie had decided to rock him to sleep.

"Lieutenant Laforêt. A pleasant boy. You are interested? I do not think he was very interesting. Good-looking, dashing, brave—a little noisy. Like many other gallant and picturesque young men whom one got accustomed to not seeing again."

"He was at Dien Bien Phu? And got killed?"

'He was taken prisoner, if I'm not mistaken. He used to write poems, I believe. One of these young men who have visions."

Monsieur Marie gave way to a harsh little cackle of laughter. Having visions was plainly un undesirable trait.

"He survived the prison camp?"

"I think he died," with no great interest. "You understand that I took my place in a different world, somewhat more demanding. I ceased to have the time for sitting in bars and noticing the antics of young officers," indulgently.

"Some of these young officers later took an interest in politics."

The old man looked amused. "Not politics, Monsieur Fanfan, not politics."

"Visions, if you like. But you think Laforêt died? He didn't, to your knowledge, serve in Algeria?"

"I fear there is no more I can tell you. These people dropped—out of my sight." He stood up, neat and trim in the shabby jacket. "I regret that there are other calls upon my time."

"Je vous en prie," said Van der Valk with the same formal politeness.

The old boy walked with a brittle step, as though his legs were getting fragile, but the shoulders in the rough jacket were broad and resolute. He shuffled across the room; he was wearing woolly bedroom slippers. He took a warm-looking beige overcoat that might have been camel down from a hanger, a white silk scarf, and a black trilby hat. As he turned to say goodbye Van der Valk saw that the coat had a mink lining. Suddenly Monsieur Marie looked quite another person.

"Good morning to you. I hope you catch your murderer," he said very civilly. Van der Valk opened the door for him. On the pavement outside was parked an official-looking DS, black and shiny. It had not as many gadgets as Jean-Michel's but was even grander because a uniformed chauffeur was holding the door open. It went off down the boulevard like a rocket, reaching a shocking speed in five seconds. Van der Valk blinked. When he stopped blinking it had vanished. Perhaps Monsieur Marie did not exist at all but was simply a figment of his imagination.

The cleaning woman had gone. He walked back to the bar, where heavy silence greeted him. He felt like a drink, a cup of coffee, anything, but there was not a soul to be seen. He pushed the swing door through to the kitchen; a basket of mussels stood on a table and a pleasant steam came from a soup pot on the stove, but there were no human beings. He went through to a scullery full of vegetable boxes, a yard where empty bottles were stacked, past the dustbins to where he had seen the van unloading potatoes and still there was nobody. It was uncanny. Monsieur Marie was a little uncanny too. He went back in again through the front. Everything was as he had seen it; no spectral hand had cleared away the coffee-cup. He looked around. The bar was curtained halfway down: a little dance floor and a platform for musicians at the far end. Behind the curtains, doubtless, were Corsican gangsters called Fernand and Dédé, feeling their knifeblades with nicotine-stained thumbs. Enter those lavatories and you will never leave them alive, son. Still, one was only a human being and one had to do pipi from time to time. He fixed his hat to tilt against the direction the wind was blowing from, turned his raincoat collar up, and set out to have a nice walk back into Marseilles. He would find another horrid little bar, even if it were full of Corsican gangsters.

When he reached a café where there were quite real-looking persons standing dejectedly around a pinball table he had a nasty cup of espresso coffee in a smell of pizza and pastis and wondered what he was supposed to do next . . .

It was not worth the trouble of phoning for a taxi; he would go on walking. His leg, despite the perfectly vile weather, was giving him no pain at all—was that a sign of something? It was comic that a supposedly reasonable, logical person like a policeman—and he was a Dutch policeman, feet planted firmly on the ground—should get superstitious. But like Commissaire Maigret, repeating the same drink throughout a whole book, Van der Valk sometimes felt "obligations." Hostages to fortune. Thus, sometimes, one had to accept things, submit to a sort of ordained pattern. Accept little trials and discomforts as so many lessons in patience, humility, fortitude. Rain poured down upon Marseilles—so be it. And there was a violent wind, but not the mistral blowing away the clouds and the cobwebs, making the boats dance on sparkling diamonds of sunlight. A nasty Dutch wind, waiting to pounce on one at street corners, throwing one's hat into the harbour with the ignorant wastefulness of jolly polly drunk. Very good; so be it. And somehow he had to walk up all these lovely steep hills, and he didn't understand a damn thing: all right, all right. He plodded steadily back, past tall yellowing apartment houses, their skin squalidly peeling, past a little park, cramped and draughty, where in a gloomy pile the Faculty of Medicine trained budding dentists, apparently, to look out to sea with a keen windswept gaze—nice changes from teeth. Past a deflated Foreign Legion barracks where a sentry yawned horribly, past the old fort and the new tunnel, past the ragged fishing boats the whole length of the Vieux Port, as far as the corner of the quay, where his leg flatly refused to go further without nourishment. He flopped into a chair in a dimly lit bar that after midday would be full of whores but was now pleasantly empty, put his feet up, and had a hot rum and lemon.

Had he found anything out? Was he being told what was good for him to know? How was it that Monsieur Marie—who "knew everybody"—could recall with such clarity and precision an ordinary little girl in a gaggle of others, a young officer in a thousand more? Other girls had been gay and pretty, other young men good-looking, brave, dashing—others were now dead. Was he being manoeuvred? No, that was nonsense. Jean-Michel had thought of the old boy. Who was simply a local bigwig of purely local importance, an ex-intelligence officer with a talent for municipal politics, a good memory for faces, who had been clever enough to get out of the army before the Algerian affair. He might, of course, be by pure coincidence something to do with the DST. Van der Valk considered this, shrugged, and burst out laughing, causing a glass-polishing barman to ask whether he would like another drink. Yes, he said gaily; he would. He didn't give a damn for DST. This might all be some small but complicated intrigue—for all he knew Esther Marx might be DST herself!—and he just didn't care. He was going to go ahead and find out who killed her, even if it took him six months and then he found she had been killed by something out of Len Deighton.

Still, he did rather wish someone would suddenly say, "Mind if I share your table" and leave a lump of sugar behind with "Room 405" written on it. And in room four-oh-five he would find an exquisite ravishing creature with tumbled silky hair and a slow smile. Then he would be contented. Damn it, his glass was empty and he was sitting here having dirty daydreams. He asked for another rum and the phone book.

He meditated on the subject of Lieutenant Laforêt, whom Monsieur Marie rather thought was dead. How would one find out? Easy enough, one rang the Military District, or Les Anciens Combattants, or one could panic about the corridors of the Prèfecture, or one could phone the talking clock. If there was an agreement to observe a gentlemanly reticence about Esther Marx in the good old official sources, did that extend to a former boyfriend, who wrote poetry, and was a bit of a visionary? Some of those visionaries had got peculiar ideas in Algeria.

One could go and get a train and buy a bottle of champagne for a friendly policeman who hadn't wanted to see one made a fool of, the honest man. And one could go back to Toulon and have some more of Claudine's amusing food.

He stood up, and swayed slightly. He had had three large rums in quick succession, on an empty stomach, before midday. He decided he was a bit pissed. He had thought of Monsieur Marie's little aphorism: "Always go to the top." The barman gave him a telephone *jeton*.

"I want the Toulouse telephone exchange—the *chef de service*. Police!"

"Hold the line, please. Your number is?" There was hardly any wait at all: magic.

"Good morning. Police Judiciaire!" It must have been the three rums. "I want a military establishment, Army Group Seven. I don't know the number, the address or anything else. I want a personal call to the Commanding General. I don't want any secretaries. I'm at a private number in Marseilles; will you have the kindness to clear me a direct line—I will hold on."

Down the line he could hear the functionary struggling with the military administration. Gabbles, protests, the words "Police Judiciaire Marseilles"—he almost believed in it himself by now. The gibbering stopped, there was a dead silence. He thought the line was broken when suddenly a dry booming voice said in his ear:

"Colonel Cassagnac, *deuxième bureau*," very close and clear.

"Mon colonel, I regret that you have been called by error. This call is to the General in person."

A ferocious grunt, a series of clanks. A light crisp voice, very clear, very superior.

"Captain Lemercier." Bloody aide de camp.

"Mon capitaine, I have said and I have the honour to repeat—a personal call."

"State your business please."

"Is the General there or not there?"

"He is here, but I regret I must insist—your name and rank please."

"Van der Valk, Divisional Commissaire, criminal brigade, city of Amsterdam."

"I was told Marseilles."

"I am calling from Marseilles—an error of no importance."

He had as much right to say Marseilles as he did Amsterdam! But it was a place they would have heard of. He was gripping the phone so hard his hand hurt; he took a deep breath, flexed his fingers, and thought: feet first, boy—shit or bust.

A voice said a name, softly, but recognizable even on a telephone.

"Mon Général," said Van der Valk and swallowed hard.

"Well?" The voice had long been known for impatience with cretins, but had learned never to show anger, even with imbeciles on telephones.

"You have my credentials." Suddenly, he couldn't think what to say: damn that rum.

"I suppose it's a matter of life and death." He sounded as though hysterical little men from Amsterdam were a daily occurrence.

"Just a question of death."

"I am listening."

"I have no doubt that you know the officers who are or have been under your command."

"I have no doubt either. Well?"

"Lieutenant Laforêt, Operational Group Northwest, Hanoi, March nineteen fifty-four."

There was a brief, icy silence.

"Laforêt, I think you said."

"Yes." The pause was not longer than two seconds, which to a skier going downhill is a hell of a long time.

"I regret: I cannot help you."

Van der Valk clenched his hand again upon the telephone.

"Yes, *mon Génèral,* you can."

"By what right do you challenge my word?"

"By right of a woman called Esther Marx, found shot three days ago, whose death this department is investigating."

"Put your request in writing; I will examine it personally."

"No, *mon Général;* requests in writing are never examined, especially this one."

"You have tried it?" flatly.

"I have," flatly.

"Listen," said the voice, very slow and very cold. "I cannot speak with you—do you understand that?"

"Yes I do."

This time the silence lasted fully fifteen seconds, while fifteen litres of sweat crawled slowly from Van der Valk's shoulder-blades to his belt.

"Where are you calling from?"

"Marseilles."

"Very well. Listen carefully. You will go to the Legal Department. You will ask for Colonel Voisin. You will be given a form to fill in. On this you will write your name and function, which will be checked. You will write, further, that I have spoken to you. That is all. Do not come here. I will not receive you." The phone went dead and he was left shaking.

"Are you finished, Marseilles?" asked an indifferent voice.

"Yes, thank you," he said and staggered out into fresh air.

"You had a long-distance?" asked the barman chattily. "Have to wait a bit, before we know the price. Another of the same?"

"You drink it," said Van der Valk, mopping a pale and sweaty brow, "but give me a couple more *jetons;* I've a local call."

The Military District of Marseilles was peopled with the regulation strength of Ostrogoths.

"Legal Department? What legal department?"

"The one that will shortly be preparing your court-martial."

"Oh, you mean the Legal Department? It's in Clermont-Ferrand."

"Thanks. Just tell me how I go about joining the Foreign Legion."

"Well you can do it in Clermont-Ferrand. Or here, of course," helpfully.

"This is the police," bellowed Van der Valk. "Be funny with the girls back home in the village."

"No no, it really is in Clermont-Ferrand. The whole Southwestern Command."

At first he could not remember Jean-Michel's number, although he knew it by heart.

"Hallo."

"Hallo there."

"Things are moving fast. Too fast. I'm a tired old man."

"That old pest Marie help you at all?"

"Too much. I made a dive for sixpence and found a sunken Roman galley—or some damn sunken thing anyway that's about eighty metres long and full of corpses."

"You sound as though you were a bit pissed."

"I'm more than a bit pissed—I'm stocious as a tourist."

"Lovely," said Jean-Michel sympathetically. "What are you doing about it?"

"Going to Clermont-Ferrand."

"Dites, are you all right?"

"No, I'm perfectly serious. On second thought can I get there overnight?"

"I should think so. You want your case? No strain, I can get it sent over. Leave it for you in the luggage office."

"But you must make my apologies to Claudine."

"No no, she'll be delighted about the sunken gal-

124

ley. But let me get this straight—you're going off into the jungle tonight but what are you doing now?"

"Going to have a bloody big lunch. After which I'll probably go to the cinema. Raining like hell. After which I reel into one of these half-hour hotels and have an unaccompanied sleep."

"After which a bloody big dinner. Listen, Claudine and I will come in, and we'll have dinner together, and you tell about the galley unless it's a state secret—I'm curious about that old Marie; he's sly as a lynx—and we'll take you to a train and tuck you in. And we'll bring your case."

"For God's sake don't let me forget to buy a smoked goose."

"Meet you seven o'clock at the Surcouf—get the brothel-keeper to wake you up."

"Understood."

And now for a bloody big lunch.

"Is there a place around here where I can have a sleep for a few hours, or do the whores take up all the space?"

"Thank you," said the barman pocketing a lot of change. "I'll fix the whores. You an American? I know, you're a journalist."

CHAPTER FOURTEEN

He had a big lunch. He had a red mullet, with its liver taken out and spread on a piece of toast, and then he had a bass grilled in flames—altogether a very fishy performance but well, one was in Marseilles. It cost a fortune and he put it all on the expense account.

Feeling a great deal better he wanted a big cigar. They didn't have any big enough and the piccolo was sent to buy a Big Cuban Cigar. What a loss of dignity, he thought, contemplating a massive Punch locked in a nasty aluminium coffin, just like himself in an aeroplane. He extracted it out of a sense of pity rather than hedonism.

"Not good?" asked the head waiter anxiously. But he didn't want to hurt their feelings.

With the cigar came contemplation. He was certain now that drawn inevitably by some magnetic field, he was approaching a tragedy. No dramas, there wasn't anything dramatic. Esther Marx had been involved with a soldier, and he knew the name, and knew there was something about this soldier that made generals freeze in their tracks. He himself—he was the smallest of bit players, with an unimportant role in the last act. For the first act, surely, had been played at Dien Bien Phu. The second act had culminated in Esther's death. He was only on in the last act, but it was possible that he had been picked as the small unimportant bearing upon which wheels turned massively, and that without his being able to do a damn thing about it a tragedy was in the offing.

He took his cigar back to where a hotel had been found, for now he had nothing but a crushing need for sleep. The whores were all just out of bed, fresh and skittish.

"Get a load of him," they giggled when they saw the huge cigar.

"Later, girls, later." He felt like Baron Ochs looking over the latest batch of kitchenmaids. Dear dear —putting half-hour hotels on the expense account— the Comptroller would take a very dim view.

He woke up as it was getting dark; the Marseillais were going home, all the drivers making an infernal din with the forbidden tooter and leaning out of the window to yell at one another. The French! What was it the Minister had said?—"the best and the worst"— something like that. Not far wrong, and in war the same, their most showy and theatrical victories alter-

127

nating with disasters so extravagant as to be unthinkable anywhere else. The French made a cult of such, quite indifferent to battles that could as easily be a defeat as a victory—Wagram or Waterloo, who cared. But they cherished their calamities; Agincourt or Pavia. Dien Bien Phu combined the lustre of a superb feat of arms under impossible conditions—like the passage of the Beresina—with a horrible great defeat. What had happened there to the dashing young Lieutenant Laforêt, who wrote poetry? Was he going to learn the truth from Colonel Voisin? Some military hairsplitter, no doubt, a uniformed and bemedalled attorney who could reduce any drama to orderly patterns of dusty yellowed paper? It was, he reflected a little sadly, only too likely.

In Clermont-Ferrand it was snowing, though it was not yet December. Van der Valk had never been in Auvergne. High plateau, he said vaguely to himself, thanking God and Arlette for solid shoes and an extra pullover. Massif Central, big ancient block of extinct volcanoes, bare conical peaks, fiercely hot in summer, full of wolves in winter. He would be learning it all with Ruth, no doubt.

It was not inappropriate to his task, this oppressed yellow sky and the dark grey slush in the streets. Some detective work was needed to run the Legal Department to earth—as in all French provincial towns there were narrow alleyways lined with high blank walls, close-shuttered grey façades, enormous buildings in the really blood-boltered bad taste of the mid nineteenth century. The Legal Department, full no doubt of Provost Marshals and Judge-Advocates and lord knew what military vultures, was housed in one of these, a building that could as easily have been a lycée from the eighteen-eighties named after Alphonse Daudet or Prosper Mérimée. But the concierge had the unexpected, charming courtesy that is also to be found in France.

"Could you tell me, please, whether Colonel Voisin has his office here?" Monotonous tone; he was quite prepared to be sent to four buildings in turn, and to be told in each and every one that nobody had ever heard of Colonel Voisin: rudely into the bargain.

"You wish to see Colonel Voisin? Nothing is easier. But it is a vile day—why not leave your coat here by the pipes where it can dry?"

"That would be most kind."

"But come in—you can warm up while I get through to Colonel Voisin for you."

It was just like a French village post office. Cacti in pots, a smell of radiators and onion soup, a wilderness of official forms and where-has-that-rubber-stamp-got-to. Ashtrays were full of cigarette-ends and paperclips, a blackened enamel coffee-pot stood on the radiator; a musty old raincoat and a greenish beret simmered beside it. Next to the telephone switchboard stood a floor-polish tin full of bits of wire and three pairs of pliers. He stood steaming happily.

"Now let's see; Colonel Voisin—he's expecting you, no doubt?"

"Vaguely—I have no definite appointment."

"Not to worry; he's not busy today. What name?"

"Van der Valk."

"Good good." He wound at his handle. "Mon colonel, a monsieur Ven der Venk. No, a foreign gentleman. Yes, mon colonel. Yes, mon colonel . . . Colonel Voisin asks you to be good enough to give him four minutes and he will be happy to receive you. No no, truly—when he says four he means four. Not like some. A gentleman. Perhaps you'd like a cup of coffee—I'm afraid it's a bit old?"

"Gladly; thank you."

It was bitter and muddy, but tasted strongly of coffee and almost as strongly of rum, and it did him the world of good. The hairy old boy watched with approval.

"You won't be offended?" with a five-franc piece in his fingers.

"My dear monsieur—in France nobody is ever offended at being offered money. Now let me give you directions: up the stairs, second landing, turn to your left, not the first door, that's the broom cupboard, but next door, that's number twenty-nine, and I thank you wholeheartedly. Can I be of any other service?"

"What's he like?"

"Him? Very nice," without hesitation. "Very polite and hates to give trouble."

Greatly refreshed, he fairly bounded up the stairs and had no trouble with the broom cupboard. A sign said "Knock and enter": he did.

A large bare room, with nothing in it but a flat desk at an angle with the windows to get the best light, and plain unpainted wooden bookshelves full of grey cardboard files lining all the walls. Behind the desk sat a heavy man with short grey hair and gold-rimmed glasses which he took off to greet his visitor. He stood up; he wore a plain grey suit. His waistline had thickened in the way of middle-aged men who have been athletes in their youth, but he would look all right in a uniform too. His right sleeve was tucked in his jacket pocket; the square shaved face was full of kindness as well as intelligence, and unsurprised; Van der Valk saw that the concierge had not exaggerated to please him. A nice man.

But a stern man: the voice was low and pleasant, but gave every syllable its exact shape and weight, with a sharp edge. Henri Matisse, cutting out paper with scissors.

"Good morning. You are welcome. Be pleased to sit down." The left hand was offered naturally. This man had no use for furry phrases like "And what can I do for you?" "I had a message from the general. You rang him up, as he told me. You are an officer of police, from Amsterdam—I understand? Will you believe that there is no hostility in my asking you to prove your identity?"

Van der Valk rummaged in his pockets, and produced this and that. Colonel Voisin put his glasses back on, and showed considerable deftness with his one hand. He patted the papers together, pushed them across, picked them up, and handed them courteously to their owner. He uncapped a pen effortlessly and made a brief note in minuscule handwriting on the pad before him.

"Monsieur le Commissaire, the general was obliged to make a rapid decision upon very slight knowledge; that is his job. Mine is to examine briefs presented to me. You have a brief; perhaps you will do me the honour of outlining it."

"Five days ago a young woman named Esther Marx was shot and killed in her apartment in Holland. I am the officer responsible for the inquiry. She was married to a Dutch noncommissioned officer, a marriage legalized here in France. He was serving here in a Nato force; she was a military nurse. Gathering routine information from various authorities here seemed to bring to light only one fact and that, naturally, much distorted. While something was undoubtedly known about this woman—possibly something shameful or even sinister, and perhaps criminal—there was a reluctance to talk about it. First point.

"I had a visit from DST—or perhaps SDECE—it is not always easy to tell the difference. The woman was assassinated in a neat and tidy fashion, with a sub-machine-gun; it did look as though it might have been a political killing. The visit was to assure me that this was not so. Second point."

The points were being briefly noted in the neat minute writing. "One of the persons I spoke to, realising that I would not be satisfied with the meagre information I was getting, gave me a friendly, unofficial hint—roundabout I may say. For me to make of what I could or would. Obscurely, the name of Dien Bien Phu was linked with this woman. It happens that I have a French wife. She has relatives in the south—some of whom fought in Indochina—and in Algeria. Her thoughts and reactions aroused my curiosity. The fourth point is that shortly after her marriage this woman had a child whose birth certificate states 'Father unknown.' I came to Marseilles to talk to some of my wife's relatives. As the result of some good advice I met a man who told me without concealment that Esther Marx had indeed served in Indochina in 1954, and had been linked with a young officer. It seemed natural to ask the authorities for some news of this officer. However, I have learned that aspects of these episodes—the war in Algeria—sometimes inspire reticence. It is no part of my business to comment upon this."

Voisin nodded coolly.

"Among the pieces of advice I received was one very good one," went on Van der Valk in his colourless functionary's voice. "To apply, when one wishes to find something out, at the top. It is common knowledge that the general commanding Army Group Seven was an officer prominent in the defence of Dien Bien Phu. An officer without the slightest stain on his name. I rang him up, after some considerable thought. The result is my introduction to yourself, mon colonel, and now you know as much as I do."

"That is very clear. I understand better why you made that—surprising—phone call. A bold thing to do."

"For anyone who knows the general? It took, I agree, all the impudence of which I am capable." Voisin didn't smile. On the other hand, he didn't exactly look furious, either.

"The impudence—since you yourself use the word —was no doubt a grave offence to protocol." One couldn't tell whether he was amused. "To anyone who knows the general," a pause, "possibly an astute step to take."

"I don't know him," with regret. "I was thinking more that things put in writing get so covered in caution—ach, mon colonel, you understand."

"I do indeed. Have you more to add?"

"Perhaps that in my position it is important to avoid delay. I have a criminal inquiry to conduct. This woman—now that I can no longer protect her, it is my duty to defend her."

Colonel Voisin turned this remark around awhile, to study it under different lights.

"Yes," he said at last. "It is certainly your duty

to ask some of these questions. It will be my duty to answer some of them. Others . . . Well well, you have a right to probe. If I am not mistaken you wish to know more about Lieutenant Laforêt . . . I do not ask you how you come by this name; it is probable that you prefer not to tell me. But tell me how you come to have grounds for supposing that a man serving in the army overseas in 1954 could have any link with a woman's death in Holland five days ago."

"This soldier in Holland," heavily, "a good man, an honest man. He offered to marry this woman, somewhat quixotically, and he—defied is too strong—he went against the social disapproval of his superiors to do so. It was the first hint that something might be known of her. He is a plodding, conformist, exact man of no very high intelligence. But once he performed an act of quixotic bravery, in Korea, and was decorated for it. I think that this was another such flash of defiance, of devil-take-the-consequence. I may may be wrong. But the woman was pregnant. Knowing her to be pregnant he offered to marry her. Knowing this she accepted. The implication is clear—she could or would not marry the child's father. She even went so far as to blacken herself by claiming that the child's father was unknown to her.

"And might that not be the exact truth?" asked Voisin mildly. "Might she not have had several lovers? Do you start with Lieutenant Laforêt as the first such name with which gossip happens to have provided you?"

Not really acid. At the most sub-acid. But Van der Valk was stung.

"I'm afraid you will find my last piece of reasoning unsatisfactory," he said mournfully.

"I will be the judge of that," in the voice that no doubt he had used to many soldiers who had robbed, raped or deserted, and were now suggesting that they might have had a blackout.

"This child—it happens that the dutch soldier we have spoken of is poorly placed to look after her, though he is quite ready to. His family, it appears, is opposed . . . Be that as it may, I myself have taken the temporary responsibility of giving the child a home. My wife is looking after her. I think I said my wife was French. The child has been taught to think of herself as French, and knows herself that this man is not her father. Esther seems to have decided upon this course. The child has a military badge in her beret—that of the Thirteenth Demi-Brigade. I attached no importance to that—I told myself that a military nurse might well have several such souvenirs."

"Lieutenant Laforêt," dryly, "did not serve in the Legion."

"Perhaps not," agreed Van der Valk. "It is a red beret. My wife, as a joke, putting it on the child's head, tipped it forward and said—frivolously—'Now you're a paratrooper.' The interesting thing is that the child burst abruptly into tears and said, 'My mother used to tell me that.'"

There was a long silence, broken at last by Voisin.

"You are an interesting man, Commissaire. You yourself are Dutch?"

"Nothing more Dutch."

"You described this soldier—this Dutch soldier—as a placid, phlegmatic man. What we think of as illustrating the Dutch, in so far as we know them. You detected two flashes—of quixotry you said—which illuminated this man's character. Does it strike you that with two such flashes of similar behaviour you have illuminated yourself—in my eyes?"

"It hadn't," said Van der Valk humbly, "though it does now. In a way. Will you be surprised, then, to hear that I thought I understood something about this woman because of my wife's own character? Now that you tell me I resemble her husband?"

"It is perhaps appropriate that you should have chosen to shelter this child, if you will pardon my replying to one question with another?" There was another long silence. "I will tell you about Lieutenant Laforêt," went on Voisin at last.

He felt in his pocket and produced a packet of Craven A. He offered it, got no-thanks, shook one loose, and lit it with an old American Zippo.

"Operational Group North-west," he said at last. "Contracted, in military fashion, to 'Gono.' Strangely naïve, is it not, the military mind? No one seems to have noticed that the official designation of the garrison of Dien Bien Phu was both comic in a vulgar way and also somewhat ill-omened." He drew on the cigarette, tapped the ash, looked for a moment at the burning tip, and said in his level steely voice that clipped words, "The first thing to know is that there isn't any Lieutenant Laforêt. He was dismissed from the army in the year Esther Marx married. I prepared the papers. There, if you like, is the reason why the name rang a bell in the mind of your informant. She acted in a fashion that led to something of a scandal. She shot him."

Van der Valk felt more like a bit player in the last act than ever.

CHAPTER FIFTEEN

"She shot him," repeated Voisin deliberately. "She was brought to trial but the tribunal, after mature consideration of the facts, was persuaded that she had acted in a condition of legitimate self-defence. You see, all the witnesses were in the army. It was," he concluded unemotionally, "a fairly grave miscarriage of justice."

"You mean it was hushed up. That was what was hushed up."

"Come, Commissaire. You are using a pejorative phrase about a due process of law. A civil tribunal, and I assure you an active prosecutor as well as competent judges. I cannot allow you to imagine there was corruption: there was no such thing. But it is true that all the witnesses were perjured."

"What—against their own comrade?"

"They all agreed that he was very drunk, dangerously drunk—this scene took place in a bar. That he was flourishing a pistol, that she courageously took it away from him, that he drunkenly resisted and was wounded in the course of the ensuing struggle. The proprietor of the bar was told very clearly that if he cast any doubt upon the word of French officers his bar would be plasticked—with him inside. It was the time," precisely, "when a street in Algiers was popularly known as the Rue de la Bombe. You see, Commissaire, that I am opening doors upon things that do me little credit. You see further that the decision which the general was called on to make was how best to defend the honour of the army. Not, however, a decision he has made for the very first time. The scissors-voice was more cutting than ever.

"But their comrade?"

"Are you acquainted with the French insult 'Faux frère?' "

"Yes."

"Esther Marx was regarded as a comrade. You will recall, since the Press gave it headlines, that Geneviève de Galard was decorated at Dien Bien Phu— with insignia borrowed from a paratroop officer? Esther was not there. But she had done the same job and was ready to do it again. She did her utmost to join her lover at Dien Bien Phu. There are legends on the subject. I have heard them, but I cannot vouch for their accuracy. I was not there, and I never knew Esther. She was certainly something of a wildcat. She was an expert parachutist. Myself—my Indochina was the bureaux of Saigon. I have never seen the High

Region." Was there a note almost of regret in the voice?

"But—then Laforêt had committed some treachery? What was his crime?"

"He deserted—in the face of the enemy. However, he was not shot for it."

"But she—she didn't have the child till two years after . . . Oh my God—you mean she hadn't known. And that she found out."

"You have hit it. Nobody knew. Certain strongpoints, particularly those on the perimeter of the camp, were overrun and never again recaptured. Officers and men were posted missing. It was not known till long after whether they were captured or killed. It was never known whether some died of wounds, or in enemy captivity. There was a legend that an officer of the Legion asked for quarter, on Beatrice. It has since been dismissed as Viet propaganda."

"Something in your voice, mon colonel, tells me that you are not totally happy with the legends of Dien Bien Phu."

"The remark is impertinent."

"In that case I beg your pardon."

Voisin got up, walked over to the window and stood looking out for a moment before turning back towards Van der Valk. His face against the light gave nothing away.

"I am a lawyer. I have studied penal codes, but I am also aware of more recent thinking. Are you, for instance, aware of the concept known as the penal marriage? The idea that there are two parties to a crime, the perpetrator and the victim, and that the two are linked in what has been called a marriage? If, for instance, a man goes to rob an old woman, and the old woman screams and agitates, so that the man takes fright, hits her with anything handy to silence her—kills her. A murder, is it not, and a crapulous murder into the bargain. Yet plainly it was the old woman's fault. I have taken the simplest example, involving two near-mentally-deficient persons. But most crimes of blood show the same strange bond between the murderer and his victim." The voice had no special warmth, but Van der Valk crossed his legs and got his behind more comfortable, aware that he was hearing two things from two people. A professional speaking on his own subject, and a man justifying himself.

"We are men of formulas, of congealed and codified rigidities. Military law . . . you, Commissaire, meet many persons technically, perhaps, criminals. Courts readily admit the mitigating circumstances you yourself put forward. You are not blocked by phrases such as dereliction of duty and military honour, for society is looser knit, and more fragmented, keyed more to materialism, quicker touched by a little loss of liberty or a blow to the pocket. Whereas the mystique of military honour makes almost all punishments aleatory, save the two great sanctions, death and dismissal, both tantamount to dishonour.

"He was heavily punished. Stripped of his decorations and dismissed from the army. But rightly punished."

"Nobody but Esther thought of shooting him?"

Voisin regarded him bleakly.

"I dare say you have heard that Langlais at Dien Bien Phu considered turing the artillery on the crowd of deserters known as the rats of the Noum Yam. But he did not. I dare say that Esther Marx had some notion of pity when she shot him."

140

"She shot him before—or after his desertion became known?"

"Before. I do not know the source of her information. It may have—must have—been Laforêt himself. Poor wretch—you see, he had got clean away with it. His fellow officers found him in Vietminh hands. The Viets themselves seem not to have realized. It seemed unthinkable that a paratroop officer should desert. Having told you so much," his voice was unchanged, "I may as well tell you that I was urged by many to suppress the charge of desertion and substitute mutiny. I refused, naturally. It was later that a perhaps unspoken agreement appeared to take effect, that Laforêt no longer existed."

"Then he didn't die?" said Van der Valk, startled.

"Oh no. She shot him. But he didn't die. He had the added punishment of a hospital staff making it clear they would have preferred not to save his life. And on top of that the spectacle of his former fellows perjuring themselves happily to give his mistress a self-defence plea."

"What happened to him?"

"How should I know? He disappeared—as well he might."

"I wish I could go on allowing him to disappear," with feeling.

"You think he killed Esther Marx?"

"I don't know. I have to go on turning stones over, finding things I would much prefer not to find. Raking up old enmities, bitterness—and injustice. There's not much doubt in my mind. But there's never certainty in police work. When there is, it's negative. If I know that her husband did not kill her it still does not allow me to say her lover did. I have to find the man and I think it probable that you can help me."

Voisin flexed the fingers of his hand as though to get stiffness out of his system.

"I am accustomed to unenviable situations," he agreed. "But I am reluctant to relaunch a hunt against a man who has been hounded once."

"He's a civilian now, mon colonel. He will have a right to his mitigating circumstances."

"Vision," said Voisin abruptly. "We have so little." He wrote on a scrap of paper and handed it to Van der Valk. "You started with a general—I send you back to a general. A partroop general." The scrap of paper had a name and an address in the Rue Saint-Dominique in Paris. Well, anyway, it was a step in the direction of home, he thought. It might well have been Pau . . .

As he crunched heavily down the last gritty stairs, the concierge stood beaming with his warmed dried raincoat.

"Good appetite."

"Thanks. The same to you."

And why not? Why not some warm and welcoming brasserie where he could eat solid Auvergnat food full of cabbage and sausage? Shoulders sagging he plodded back towards the centre of the town through uneven antique streets that turned and wound as darkly as his thoughts.

A voice behind him said, "How about some lunch. Commissaire?" He turned around, furious. Not poxing DST again!

"You know what Raymond Chandler said?"

That had him flummoxed.

"Who?"

"When you don't know what to do next, have a

man come in the door with a gun in his hand. And I wish one would . . . following me about like that. Shoot you my bloody self for two pins," bellowed Van der Valk.

"Oh Commissaire? Shoot a man who's just invited you to lunch?"

"Yes."

"Very well then. I'll pay for the lunch." He put his hand in his pocket, produced a handful of change, and started clowning. "One, two, three, ooops, that's a Swiss franc, what's he doing here, four, four fifty, four seventy, wait a bit . . ." It was like punching somebody under water—or in a dream, where you hit out furiously but your fist stops humiliatingly, just short of its target . . . "Oh very well, very well. Come on and be trickly. Do you at least know a good place or do you have to buy a guidebook?"

He was a brown man, with a face like pale wood, eyes as brown and shiny as an Auvergne chestnut, a brown raincoat and hat, and well-polished but saldly splashed brown leather boots.

"A lot of footwork," said Van der Valk with his eye on these boots.

"Yes," smiling. He had sunburst wrinkles at the corners of simian eyes, that went right back to his ears. The face was studded with tiny scars as though he had had smallpox, and there was a whitish look of surgical repair about the chin.

"Indochina?"

"Algeria," grinning as though it had been immensely funny. "Grenade fragments."

"Lucky to have your eyes."

"Very very lucky. Some hot wine, don't you think?"

"Now I know," said Van der Valk hanging his coat

up, "why a kind friend warned me I was heading for a horrible great merdier. Why did I ever leave St. Louis?"

"You weren't to know," said the brown man kindly, "that all officials would remember the name of Esther Marx and curse. But don't be mad at us—we didn't plan to make life a misery for you. Nor do we now. What you were told in Holland holds good here—you are helping us and we will help you. We wondered—I wondered—what Monsieur Marie could have been telling you. But he had the very good idea of ringing me up and asking what I knew about all this. He always wants to know a little more, you know —it's knowing a little more that makes him so successful."

"I don't see much sign of either of us helping the other much," said Van der Valk with a very lumpish Dutch irony.

"You do, you know. The general wouldn't have told us anything. Kept in the family, you might say. But he can't stop you. I was astonished—and full of admiration—when you went up against him like that."

"Handy for you."

"I give you my word—I'd never even heard of Laforêt. It is perfectly true that our people in Holland were as puzzled as you were. It meant nothing to me at all. Then I check up in Paris just in case, and lo, we have a file on him. File with nothing in it. Dead." The neat mouth mimicked someone blowing dust off a file, and dust was brushed fastidiously off the agile brown fingers. He took a swig of hot wine.

"What the hell do you want a file for?" asked Van der Valk, taking a swig at his.

144

"I completely agree but it's automatic, you know. Officer dismissed with ignominy—may harbour wicked thoughts. Nobody ever followed it up—we knew nothing whatever about Laforêt, in Paris or anywhere else.

Van der Valk's grumbling, gloomy rage boiled over stickily, like porridge.

"Five minutes ago I was telling myself that if I'd been five years younger I'd be taking a swing at you. Now you'd better get out of my sight, or call your judo expert—he can't be far away." He felt like a bear being teased by little yapping dogs.

"I see that you subscribe to the legends about us," said the brown man. "Get this into your thick Dutch skull—we have our share of crass stupidity. By yourself, not knowing a damn thing, you have worked this out. With all our resources of judo experts, with bits of information sticking out all over the place, we failed to make the connection. The old story—the right hand not knowing about the left. Do I have to map it out? Your story interested them in Holland and they thought there was something there for us. They sent a signal asking us here to look it up. The name Esther Marx rang a vague bell. By pure coincidence old Marie gave me a ring, thinking of nothing but securing his own rear. Since then I've been panting along breathless, trying to catch up with you. When I got here it occurred to me that we'd better try to tune our violins to the same pitch."

"The file on Laforêt."

"I didn't know it existed an hour ago. Tidy little minds in Paris would like to see it closed and concluded that you'd make an excellent last entry. We don't know where he is or even that he's really alive. All I succeeded in finding out is that there was a charge of violence—he was wounded in a struggle with Esther Marx but it was his gun. The charge wasn't pushed at the time because he'd been hammered and they were rid of him."

"Charge of violence my arse," said Van der Valk bleakly. "He was framed."

The brown man put down the drink he was sipping.

"The funny thing is that there's a note on the file suggesting just that, but it couldn't be proved. In fact you'd find it quite hard at this stage to prove Laforêt ever existed." He looked at Van der Valk and gave a little laugh. "You—you've really got the military eating out of your hand."

"Now tell me," said Van der Valk in a grating voice like a nineteen thirties gangster movie. "What is your real interest in this affair?"

"Yes," The man smoked a moment in silence, muttered "No very bad thing, telling the truth every six months," smoked a moment longer and decided to stop playing secret service.

"We're a standing joke here, like the telephone system. The seventeen different kinds of parallel police, and the little rivalries—each one determined to keep the others from knowing anything. Sacred tradition that the Sûreté Nationale came under Interior, and the PJ under the Prefect, and so on. All been changed now."

"Since the toss-potting that went on over Ben Barka."

"Just so—the right word. Didn't look good, did it? Two policemen getting bent—if ever I felt sorry it's for those two poor bastards—the chief gossip-centre at Orly blown sky high, did the principal witness fall or was he pushed?—talk about pigsticking . . . Well, it has small importance now, but ten years ago and more,

146

at the time of Algeria, there was not an awful lot of love lost between these silly little intelligence organizations. Specifically, not exactly a warm friendship between DST and some army units. Paratroops formations, mostly—there was a fairly well-known instance where a para unit raided an office in Algiers and quietly swiped all the DST files as a small aid in organizing their own intelligence.

"I see," said Van der Valk.

"Our interest in Laforêt dates from then. At that time, I emphasize, the paratroop mafia cast a long shadow. Now all this means very little. I think, probably, that they would never have allowed him to survive if we hadn't been barking at their heels. In a sense, you see, what has now happened is our fault."

"Do you know Laforêt's whereabout?"

"No. But I dare say we can find out. What d'you want to eat—duck?"

"Something with chestnuts in."

"Seriously," said the brown man with his mouth full of chestnuts, "they had to answer your questions. You're an officer of the PJ on a job, and they were profoundly grateful—so are we, though I'm not saying so—that you didn't launch a big official tra-la, asking the magistrate here for an interrogatory commission, sending the dossier back for supplement of information, the whole works."

Yes, Van der Valk was thinking, maybe those civil servants back in The Hague are not quite as stupid as we thought them.

"Who did you see back there—old Voisin? I thought as much. I'm not quite barefaced enough to ask what you got out of him, and unlike that old twister Marie he's not going to ring up and tell me! But I'd be interested to know how you're going to go about this."

"Since there's not a hope of my getting across Paris without a few of your squalid informers noticing," said Van der Valk pleasantly, "I got the address of a brigadier-general in the Rue Saint-Dominique."

"Really?"

"That surprise you?"

"It does indeed. That's not just an underdone steak you have there on your plate—that's a chop off a live lion."

"I have to look up the goddam train times."

"No need. Permit me to smooth your path."

"Huh?"

"I can get you on a military plane, and you don't have to make any parachute jumps at the end either. You can be in central Paris in two hours—have some coffee."

CHAPTER SIXTEEN

Arlette was waiting anxiously for some news. She was always nervous when the man was away. One controlled it, naturally. What would be the point of a police wife who came out with remarks like "Make sure you have regular meals and don't drink too much?" Even the time he was carried in with half his middle missing from a bare hillside near St. Jean de Luz, after being nearly blown in two by a big-game rifle, had not been the shock to her she would have expected; she had been waiting so long for something of the sort that she was more relieved than anything! As a young nervous wife, sitting alone in a creaky house after nightfall and starting at every sound, she had had to be merciless with herself to conquer panic. Now that she was an old bag she allowed herself, occasionally, a bit of fuss. But this was altogether different.

It was not just being "involved"—wasn't one always, in varying degree? One could respect rules long laid down, like never asking questions, and never allowing work to be discussed at home, but after twenty years of marriage one was telepathic, and instantly recognized a man frightened, bewildered, exhausted or frustrated. But this time, she felt, she was the origin of the whole mess. She had brought it upon him and herself with her silly hysteria. Just because she had been an embarrassment to him back in 1957 . . .

She had had no plan, no system. Everything had swarmed all over her, so that she had had to ward off the blows without time to organize a counter-attack. *"Boucher les trous,"* as she called it. Since the moment when she had "known" instinctively that Esther had been at Dien Bien Phu, she had felt an uneasy identification, as though she was herself Esther . . . no, she couldn't sort it out, she was confused and darkened she had no equilibruim, no sense. Her thoughts were like herself, fiddling stupidly about and not getting anything done properly.

"This won't be in the least funny," the man had said, standing around at Schiphol, his professional eye gliding gloomily over the senseless activities and the atmosphere of anxiety for which she hated airports, "just a mess."

She had wanted to be a support and an encouragement, and had of course only succeeded in saying something cretinous.

"But she had a dramatic past. It will be most absorbing to turn it up leaf by leaf."

"My poor friend, you've been reading detective stories again. It will be dull and flat like a restaurant on New Year's Day. Ice buckets full of lukewarm water, with dead flowers and disintegrated cigarette-ends floating. Broken paper streamers knee deep, and a frightful stink."

"Oh you're seeing things too black, surely."

"No, no. Sordid pathetic people, frightened and anxious, repeating themselves." She had crept home on her belly, feeling suicidal!

His telephone calls had not helped. A voice sounding drunken and slightly crazy had spoken to her from Marseilles, with Jean-Michel's voice being funny—so he thought—in the background, and Claudine unusually raucous and screeching, so that her teeth had been on edge throughout. Not just that they were all bibulous, but they had all sounded so silly. He had done something very stupid, or very clever—or both together—she hadn't understood what or why. She couldn't understand anything at all. And now he had rung up from Paris, terribly depressed, and had been in Clermont-Ferrand of all places, and it all seemed to be going from bad to worse from what she could make out . . .

Arlette sat in the still house alone, for Ruth, the only other person there, was in bed upstairs, terribly far away. The weather had gone foggy as a prelude to becoming warmer, and the whole of life outside seemed dulled and muted. Food had no savour. Even music had not helped. Whenever Arlette felt miserable she put on *Fidelio*—it never failed. Never did she miss feeling renewed and stiffened after the prisoners had sung, never fail to enjoy the sinister swagger of Pizarro's march, never stop her neck prickling and her eyes stinging as the voices join one after another in *'Mir ist so. wunderbar'—and* tonight she had been limp as a corpse throughout.

She felt besieged. She knew now, she felt, the sensations of a soldier in a little muddy hole on one of the *pitons* of Dien Bien Phu—and all around the ring of iron hills swarming with unseen silent Vietminh soldiers waiting patiently—for the kill. A thought struck her silent body and noisy mind. Esther, in that ramshackle, jerrybuilt municipal block—had she too not been besieged? Surrounded by a Dutch Vietminh! Was that too fantastic? She had not stayed limp, a stale cucumber waiting to be thrown in the dustbin; she had defended herself, inch by inch, bitterly, as the paratroopers had. She had not given up. But she had lost slowly, her hope, her child, her life, in the end . . .

Knowing nothing, able to do nothing. "What the hell are they playing at, in Hanoi?" had snarled the embittered and exasperated soldiers, crouched in the mud to watch the sky for the help that did not come.

Arlette had no idea of it—her man would have been amused, wryly—but she too was conducting a little investigation, trying to understand Esther Marx, trying to understand that for the first time she was not just touched by a criminal affair, not just tangentially or peripherally involved, but entangled to the neck at the very source. Through Ruth, she was trying to penetrate the darkness much, had she known it, as her man was through the jungle of passions and loyalties of which Monsieur Marie and Colonel Voisin had been distant, uncomprehending spectators. Arlette did not realize this. On the surface, she was trying to build a home, a warmth, a security and a love for this child. Within, she felt unhappily, she was herself clutching desperately at the child for relief from pain and anxiety. Much the same dichotomy, had she known it, was affecting Van der Valk; on one side a typically dull and wearisome police inquiry, further muddied and distorted by the ten-year-old petty jealousies between DST and the army!—while on the other lay the genuine tragedy of two human beings who had loved each other.

Arlette had been making efforts to use her sense and her experience in handling Ruth. Affection, confidence, reliance—twenty psychological clichés went trotting through her head. Luckily, the child was easy. They were getting on quite well together, in the three days that "Dad" (as the boys used to call him sardonically) had been away.

"Vous êtes gentille, vous savez."

"Tu sais, tu peux me tutoyer."

Arlette and Ruth were discovering one another. Both had much the same trouble: slight embarrassment. The woman was unaccustomed to girls of this age. The child had had little contact with women, knowing only her abrupt, uncertain mother and the over-bright, over-assured voices of elementary-school teachers.

They were both in turn brusque and effusive, elaborately calm and self-consciously undemonstrative, hardly able as yet to show spontaneous affection one for the other. They both had to play detective, taking hours to discover the obvious.

Arlette had to learn what she could without forcing the child's confidence: she was succeeding fairly well, she thought with some vanity. Ruth—on the lowest, purely physical level of communication—was accustomed to a silent, morose existence, and chattered like a jackdaw, and it was surely good, Arlette told herself, to allow this. Especially about her mother, for that way the pain and shock would be dulled most quickly. Nothing could be worse than Esther promoted into a taboo. That Arlette herself was passionately interested in all that concerned Esther was beside the point. Nor was Ruth old enough to have lost spontaneity; she chattered all day, however, disjointedly and inconsequently, and she seemed to have confidence, for there seemed to be no areas at the frontiers of which she closed up. Must be good, Arlette reassured herself again: the silent bottled-ones who creep off by themselves are the most difficult to reach.

She was lucky, too, she told herself. She had always been convinced that she was no good with children—excruciating boredom of the prattle of tiny tongues—and with astonishment she found she enjoyed the company of this marmot.

I suppose, she thought, that I am a fairly easy woman. Mum type; broad maternal bosom—oh yes, that reminded her, and she went into the kitchen and wrote "Bra" on her shopping list. At least I am still pretty even if I am an old bag. Comfortable—a bit overweight. A Bonnard woman. As the man says threateningly, "If you go on eating cake you will become one of those rosy uncorseted Renoir women. Down on your hands and knees and scrub the floor —good exercise for your belly and make you luscious in bed." Yes, yes, but keep your mind on work, you scoundrel!

She could take no credit for it, but she did have natural gaiety. She sang, she took pleasure in everything and got amusement from small things—like women with fat calves who wear boots, that familiar feature of the Dutch landscape in the winter months.

She loved food, and did the week's shopping with Ruth to carry the spare basket.

"While Petit Pére is away we're going to have especially nice meals. No cauliflowers!"

She found a bottle of cider and bought it happily; put her in a Norman mood.

"Such a pity that chickens do not exist in Holland."

"Do you like pancakes?" Of course; all children love pancakes.

Esther had been silent and dour; buttoned lip, pinned-back thoughts. She had smoked all day and drunk too much whisky. She had been bored by food, tending to open tins of corned beef or buy smelly *patates* as the Dutch call chips—or worse still, one of those ready-to-cook packets with everything all snipped fine and dehydrated in little plastic envelopes. She liked rice . . . Whereas Arlette loved rice too, but didn't at all mind—in fact enjoyed—the fiddly cutting of leeks and cabbage hearts in strips and making peanut-butter sauce.

"The reason why the Americans are a dead loss in Vietnam is that they don't like rice."

"Mamma liked Indochina."

"Everybody we know loved Indochina." Yes, it helped her being French. The child had been born there, and felt some sense of belonging; she knew no more than that about her parentage, but she shared a heritage with Arlette, who like Esther was an "exile."

"Esther found rice too much trouble." There—she

had stopped saying "Mamma." She had tried "My mother" once or twice, but had found it too self-conscious.

Arlette was shaking the vegetables in the large pan: Ruth alongside was shaking a pork fillet, cut in cubes, in the little pan.

"And she said in restaurants it was no good because they made it too long beforehand."

"Quite right. Sensible Esther. Don't let it stick." Arlette peeled two bulbs of garlic and smashed them with the flat of the knife, fried a banana with a bit of curry powder sprinkled on it, and coloured the sauce with a little soya.

"Don't let the vegetables get soft; they should be just transparent and no more. Yoohoo, the rice is ready . . . What did Esther do in the evenings?"

"She read lots. Newspapers and magazines and books—everything."

"What about when your father was home?"

"They used to play cards—can you play cards?"

"Belote . . ."

"Yes, that's it. Or go out—I don't know—to the cinema I think."

"Esther liked the cinema?"

"Yes, ever so much—often I came home and found a note saying she'd gone to the cinema. Then she'd come home and say how silly it was but she always went again!"

The telephone rang.

"Aha that'll be Dad, living it up in Toulon, the lucky boy. Hallo. What d'you mean my voice is funny. Well, my mouth's full of rice. Pouring rain?—I'm delighted to hear it. Oh, you're in Marseilles—even worse. What? Called a general up? You must have been drunk. Do

156

tell Jean-Michel to shut up. Is the general drunk too? You'd better go easy or you'll be a wreck—yes well, even if your raincoat was soaking, no need to go stuffing yourself. Ruth's here. I'll put her on in a sec. What? Yes, I see, a name alone doesn't tell one much. You're not making much sense, you know that? That noise like a parrot, is that Claudine? No, it's profoundly irritating and I'm anything but clear. Here, I'll pass you Ruth."

"Hallo," shyly.

"Like witchdoctory, isn't it—think, I'm in Marseilles. Don't let Arlette overeat, but give her my best love. What will I bring you back?"

"I don't know but you mustn't forget the goose."

"Leave it to me. I'll be back in a couple of days. Weather's vile; pity the poor policeman."

"Why don't you have a cape like French ones?"

"Yes, that is an idea, I'll have to look. Bonne nuit, ma fille."

"Bonne nuit, darling," said Arlette fiddling with the blankets in the female rite known as "tucking them in."

"Bonne nuit, m'an."

Arlette did not know whether to be happy or miserable, and went downstairs for some cherry brandy, which would serve either way.

CHAPTER SEVENTEEN

DST's transport was not especially impressive; a beat-up Simca Mille with no room for long legs, but the acceleration was impressive. So was that of the aeroplane, though there he had no room either—a jet trainer adapted for an extra passenger. The pilot was a nice round-raced boy who chewed gum with frenzy, and said things like "Grab your gut and lean on the toboggan." And at four that afternoon, just as the man promised, he was in the Rue Saint-Dominique, being intimidated by tall courtly doors and forbidding concierges.

"The Brigadier-General?" as though he had said something blasphemous. "Well, I suppose there's nothing to stop you filling in a form if you really want to"

"Bet you ten to one in francs I'm in behind the curtain inside ten minutes."

"Tuesday fortnight, my lord—if at all."

"Can you see it's delivered straight away?"

"Of course I can," indignantly. He put it in a shell, and pressed the shell into a metal tube. "I take your bet—only because I'm curious. Curious is all. And because you have an honest face."

"But I give you the money just the same—bribing the concierge went out with the Third Republic."

"I'd hope that a bribe would be rather bigger, myself." But the ten-franc note went into his pocket just the way Chandler once described it—"with a noise like two caterpillars fighting." The two of them smoked a cigarette, lounging but a bit stiff, like two gunmen in the same saloon. The pneumatic tube went *ffss* suddenly and the shell clonked in its metal basket. The concierge shook his head sadly, read the piece of paper, made a horrid noise with his teeth like wind among the rocks of the Khyber Pass, took a franc out of his pocket, wrapped the piece of paper round it, and passed both to Van der Valk, who looked with some curiosity. "Admit" it said with military brevity.

The concierge was laboriously filling in a green card. Where it said "Bureau No." He wrote "The General" in longhand. He date-stamped it at the bottom with a fierce metallic crunch that went right through and could not be faked. "Show that to the sentry—and don't lose it, even if you're taking the general out to a party—I'll want it back."

On the terrace across the courtyard was a soldier in combat uniform carrying a machine-gun, who looked at the green pass, said nothing, and motioned up the steps. In the hall was a porter, who took the pass, looked at it carefully, invited him to enter a little vertical coffin which photographed him and would let out shrill screams if he had any guns, cameras, or concealed microphones, smiled politely, and said, "First floor, to the left. You may use the staircase of honour if you wish." It sounded a great privilege, and indeed it was a very beautiful staircase, marble smoother than a girl's skin and a great deal whiter.

On the first floor he had only to follow his nose, for a soldier beckoned to him, looked him over politely but with a tendency towards unarmed combat in his eye, and stepped softly towards a door a few paces away. This soldier was in parade dress, with white leggings, but seemed an ordinary soldier, not a Zouave or a Senegalese, so that Van der Valk felt obscurely cheated. The soldier smiled very slightly and held the door open.

A brightly furnished, brightly painted office. A young man in his early thirties, very slim and dapper in captain's uniform of exquiste cut—cavalry no doubt—two young bits of crumpet, one dark, in burgundy red, the other blonde and in buttercup yellow, but both long-haired, long-legged, painty-eyed and delicious-smelling. No need of flowers with them in the office. Military princes were coming back into style, and perhaps this was the new look, thought Van der Valk greatly amused. Paratroop senior officers had gone through a Templar stage of religious austerity: hair shirts and no servants, together with remarks like "This is not a drawing-room" and "Soldiers are not lackeys." Now, apparently, there was a swing back to the flamboyance of De Lattre's day—but, alas, with no Spahi uniforms. Uniforms by Hubert de Givenchy, more likely!

160

"Good afternoon, Monsieur," said the captain politely, standing up. The two secretaries looked at him expectantly under carefully negligent hair to see whether he smouldered but alas, he was slow that day on animal magnetism. He felt lumpish and sweaty, as no doubt he was meant to. The heavy-breathing provincial, a bit pink about the ears, felt absurdly ashamed of his shabby clothes and trodden-down shoes. Should have had a haircut and bought a bunch of sweet peas! He wanted to think of something witty and only said, "Good afternoon."

"The general will receive you at once."

What have I got to be impressed about, he told himself angrily. Only a lousy brigadier-general, and staff at that! He could hear the voice of the brown man in Clermont-Ferrand, amused and malicious. "Not one of these bristly whisky-swilling ruffians in Pau. A Turenne, descended from the Marshal. He and Séguin-Pazzis are the intellectuals, highly sophisticated, apt to talk to you about structuralism and painters. You'd better go to charm school before you set foot there!"

The general stood up with the same princely courtesy as the captain, but the artificial feeling, of being in a literary drawing-room or an English country house, with echoes of the Duchesse de la Rochefoucald and the Cliveden Set, vanished immediately. True, the general's uniform was as fine in cut and cloth as art could make it. True, he was smoking a pipe and a tin of Three Nuns lay on a Louis Quinze map, but Van der Valk recognized at once that this was a natural person, through a small and ludicrous detail. The hand that the general held out was long and fine-boned, with beautiful narrow nails—but the nails were chipped and decidedly dirty, and the two first fingers of the right hand had squalid bits of filthy sticking plaster wrapped round the middle joints. The general put his pipe between his teeth, followed Van der Valk's shocked blue eye with his own, laughed out loud and said, "Terrible thing to meet a policeman who sees through you at once."

"I didn't mean to be rude."

"But you're not rude. I was painting the boat—mending little things. Do sit down." Every line spoke of breeding, of the flat in the Boulevard des Invalides and the Marshal as godfather, but he had no need at all to make capital out of such trivialities. The simplicity of a man who is brilliant, knows it—and knows how unimportant it is. Slim shoulders and thighs of steel—a slalom champion, who would efface himself before an obstacle the better to by-pass it. Wide mouth and formidable jaw muscles. Thin silver or platinum wedding-ring; the plainest of plain watches. Make no mistake about those feminine nails: a swifty.

"Since you are Dutch may I have the pleasure of offering you a cigar?"

A good start: I know who you are, I know your errand; if you wish to fence you will find me a fencer. Van der Valk examined the terrain and his cigar together. One was slim, greenish, Cuban and good, the other was plain and elegant as its master. Silver vase of chrysanthemums, model 1915 aeroplane made by a jeweller, black morocco desk set, ivory crocodile whose tail became a paper cutter, and a solid gold fountain pen much scratched and dented. Van der Valk slowly opened the small blade of his knife; the general smiled and put the cigar-cutter back in the drawer, puffed at his pipe: the smile got more concentrated and brilliant; the eyes were dark sapphire under silky blue-black eyebrows.

"There, we have settled the preliminaries. You have been having adventures, and you come to me now to learn about a man who was once a paratroop officer, and you are uneasy and a thought unhappy with the suspicion that you are about to be swathed in charm, twiddled till you are dizzy and thrust gently out stuttering excuses for having been misled. Error. I have decided that now is the time to operate upon an abcess that has paralysed far too many people for far too long."

"He was just a man."

"He was just a boy. He is a man, and cannot be obliterated. You wonder why we pretended he didn't exist and I am ready to tell you."

"You've spoken to the mafia and decided not to have me assassinated, I hope?"

"I could have you strangled by my batman," enjoying the notion, "but we are all respectable now—all generals. We were young then—almost boys. To be under forty seems pitifully young. And we were lowly. Even Castries was only a colonel. Langlais a lieutenant-colonel. Tourett—Bigeard—Clemençon—Thomas and Nicolas—majors. Pazzis and me—squadron-commanders: cavalry you know," gaily. "Such nonsense has been talked about the paratroop mafia of Dien Bien Phu—but look at the photographs and you will see excited schoolboys, dedicated as scouts. Keep fit and sleep with your sword.

"No; I am not trying to play it down. These men were freed very suddenly from the bonds of hierarchy. The place was full of colonels, of course—rear-échelon persons commanding typewriters and cans of vino-concentrate. And then—these youngsters found themselves free to conduct their battle as it pleased them, and they had all read Dumas. All for one—one for all, and their honour. Not the honour of France; that was too plainly compromised. Their own—and their men. There to fight but above all there to die. Hopped up —high on pot." A high ringing laugh of pure enjoyment.

"And they loved it. You see—Colonel de Castries . . ."

"Transmitted your message to Hanoi."

"Hm, yes, the phrase has made a career for itself. But can one forget the enjoyment—Langlais bellowing down the telephone at Sauvagnac in Hanoi—his superior officer . . . Now—it is important to remember —very junior officers indeed, mere boys, had loads in proportion thrust upon them. Platoon commanders— carrying the wreckage of a battalion scratched together from a dozen smashed-up units—Spanish anarchists and Moroccan bandits. Fox, Le Page, Pichelin—children! These children," the pipe stabbed, "wrote a very brilliant page in our history, of which we can be exceptionally proud. Whooping up their French and Germans, Jugoslavs and Vietnamese—what a salad!

"Not all those boys could be like Makowiak—you know the stories about Makowiak?"

"No."

"He was a sub-lieutenant—the last man out of Na San, which was another fortified camp in the High Region—the prelude and the precedent for Dien Bien Phu. A chopper picked him up and took him back to Hanoi. Where a reporter asked him what he would have done if the chopper *hadn't* picked him up— picture it, hundreds of kilometres of jungle, infested

164

with Vietminh. "I would have walked," the boy said. Well, that's just a phrase. Boy meant he had the *baraka,* Arab word, means aura of luck and invincibility. Came the surrender at Dien Bien Phu. All of us, hungry, head down, buggered, whipped. Hands tied behind us with phone wire. Makowiak just walked out. And walked back."

The general smoked his pipe, Van der Valk his cigar.

"Now nothing could bind these men together, coming from twenty different units, but faith—in one another—and truth, to themselves. Lots were killed, and lots died of wounds or fatigue or dysentery on the march to the camps. Some were overrun after burning the last of their ammo, in combat. Some, stunned by shell bursts, came back to life covered in blood and debris in Viet hands. None surrendered. None. One deserted—Laforêt. Poor boy, seeing it from today, what happened to him was the worst misfortune of all. He must have suffered a hell worse than any. You see, we had one another—and the Viet. He had nothing, not even himself."

"What exactly was it that happened to him?"

"We didn't know ourselves—and he never told. But reconstructing it with hindsight—this. I have to make you a drawing—you're familiar perhaps with the general layout of the camp?"

"Very roughly."

"Ah. Here is the central knot of the camp, a huddle of little hillocks. River running through the middle —the Nam Youm. Here to the left—the Huguettes. The other side to the right—the Elianes. Airstrip here in the middle. And Viet all round, closer every day. Now at the beginning, when it was thought that troops could

165

manoeuvre, there were outlying fortified posts. A few kilomètres off. Isabelle down south—cut off straight away and was never part of the camp proper. Up north-east, quite isolated on a hillock—Beatrice. The most lonely and vulnerable, so held by the Legion. Here to the north above the airstrip, on a ridge— Gabrielle.

"Now Gabrielle was held by troops thought of as a bit shaky, a bit substandard. So they were put in the strongest position of all—best natural formation, two complete rings of defences, covered throughout by artillery, and to get there a counter-attack only had to rip straight out along the airstrip. Right?"

Van der Valk watched the hands, holding a piece of paper flat upon the morocco blotter and sketching upon it with a pencil. The sketch faced Van der Valk sitting across the desk, so that the hands demonstrated upside-down, which gave them no trouble. He could see these hands working on a small sailing boat with the same rapid deftness, disregarding a scratched palm or a crushed nail, sometimes maladroit from lack of practice, but never hesitant. The hands would unpin and throw a grenade with the same automatic ease with which they uncapped the gold fountain pen.

"On the thirteenth of March, Beatrice was attacked with a violence and rapidity that stunned us all—yes, even us back in the central sector. The Legion, and it was the Third Thirteenth, was blitzed flat where it stood in a couple of hours, and our artillery was quite helpless. From that very first attack Dien Bien Phu never recovered. It broke Piroth, the artillery commander. It broke many . . .

"And on Gabrielle they stood watching this. It broke them, and can one blame them? When they saw the Legion submerged like so much sand they just ran. The officers stood where they were and died too, most of them, where they were. Now follow closely.

"No counter-attack was mounted on Beatrice; we were all dizzy with the shock and the bombardment. But one was launched on Gabrielle, a vital place to the camp defence. It was mounted by paratroop formations, and was a failure. The troops had just jumped in, they were tired and demoralised—the same troops performed prodigies later but that day, for several complex reasons, the attack petered out. Gabrielle should and could have been retaken—and never was. When Botella, commading the Fifth BPVN—para regiment—regrouped his men, he was so angry and humiliated that he threw half of them out, on the spot. 'I've no use for you,' he yelled. 'Go to hell or to the Viets—I've no use for you.'" The general bit on the stem of his pipe. "Don't let me see you again," were his words. Now Laforêt was commanding a company there. Was he there to hear his commander's words? We don't know. Some groups had trailed behind. Some had gone on but lay down on the slope under the Viet fire. Some perhaps had already run. What we know is that the ones Botella threw out joined up with fugitives from Anne-Marie and Dominique, the other two Northern posts which fell later, and hid in the cafes."

"Caves?"

"Yes—Dominique was the only post that had some quite high ground, and it went down to the Nam Youm in a fairly abrupt slope. It was sand, and had been tunnelled by the river bank for stores and engineering materials. They hid in these holes—between us and the Viet."

"The Rats of the Nam Youm."

"Yes. They could not escape. They spent the siege there, living on what they could find. They came out at night to steal parachuted supplies. They trafficked in food and medicine—medals—whisky . . . They lived the way deserters always live, despised and neglected by both sides. We left them to fend for themselves."

The general's voice had gained in warmth and was faintly throaty. Even now, thought Van der Valk, the tale has power to move him, nearly twenty years after. The pipe puffed; there was a slight hand movement as though to say "Pass the bottle."

"Langlais once considered turning the guns on them, but where would have been the point? Waste of ammunition—we could not even feel contempt, though they trafficked in what we held dear. We did not know that among them there might be a parachute officer."

"But did no one wonder what could have happened to Laforêt?"

"You must recall the shock and chaos of those first two days. The unbelievable happened—Beatrice fell. The next day, with what seemed the same astounding ease, Gabrielle fell. They did not all run—they fought and fought well. De Mecquenem, the commander, was wounded and captured in his own command post. But the world was collapsing about our ears. Gaucher, commanding the Third Thirteenth, was hit by a shell right in the underground command post of the central subsector. Our artillery was impotent—the next night Colonel Piroth killed himself in his dugout with a grenade rather than live with the consequences of his failure. The Thai troops on Anne-Marie watched the fight on Gabrielle and melted quietly away into the hills. It wasn't their war. We—we were struggling to reorganize ourselves, trying to close ranks, trying to hang on, gritting our teeth. Langlais took over from Gaucher as commander of the reserves at a second's notice. A day later he found himself superseding—unofficially—Castries himself. Can you be surprised that his first counter-offensive was ill organized and insufficiently thought out? These things need a time—however short—of cold, unhurried arranging, and he didn't have it.

"Can you blame Botella? Paratroops then as now have one mission and one only—not to fail. He was told to take Gabrielle—and he had failed.

"It was thought Laforêt had been killed—or captured—in that chaos, who knew? He was posted missing. That he might have deserted occurred to no one—not for a second. What happened—can one tell? He may have seen his soldiers wavering around him—or melting away behind him. He may have been ashamed to face Botella. He may have found himself alone behind a stone, there on the slope. I do not wish now to condemn any more than I wish to forgive."

"And after? At the moment of the surrender?"

The general shrugged.

"He was on the left bank of the river. It would not have been impossible, on that last morning, to see that the camp was dying. He could have worked his way down to our line. When the Viet found him, they thought nothing of it—other officers were alone in a trench full of dead and spent cartridges. We—when we finally caught up with him we naturally thought he had been taken prisoner two months before. He said he had escaped into the jungle, and had been hiding there for weeks before being recaptured. There was nothing at all intrinsically improbable." The voice had deadened and flattened; the general leaned back in his chair.

"Do I bore you with my military reminiscences, Monsieur van der Valk?"

"But it is precisely these hours, these minutes, that were missing for me. Without them I could not hope ever to grasp what happened to Laforêt—and Esther Marx."

"Esther Marx!" The tone was not sentimental, but it was indulgent. The same indulgence that had not recoiled before perjury, for Esther.

"I remember her well, in Hanoi; a thin eager little thing, all nerve and muscle, afraid of nothing. We heard afterwards that she marched straight up to the general, in Hanoi, and begged for authorization to jump over the camp—with a bottle of whisky for us down the front of her blouse. Chewing gum. I think of her when I see that girl, the skier, with the very white teeth and the wild hair, what's her name?"

"Annie Famose."

"That's her." The general looked wistful: a boy again . . . And Van der Valk was delighted—his own favourite skier.

"You realize, plainly, that justice was not done towards Laforêt."

The general stopped contemplating his youth instantly, and suddenly reminded the onlooker of the little joke made over the coffee-cups in Clermont-Ferrand. The underdone steak and the live lion . . .

"I care nothing for justice. I command to win. Anything that interferes with the solidarity of my men I hunt down, I extirpate. Justice does not exist. We talk about it—and who has ever seen it? In a Western film, and the pages of Victor Hugo."

"You have said, yourself, that the solidarity of the offensive had already broken down."

"The men were already tired and confused. Langlais had been blamed for not choosing another unit. You misunderstand. The formations that failed in front of Gabrielle, a few days after took part in a brilliant counter-attack in the west. Recaptured and held the Huguettes. Kept possession of Eliane to the very last day.

"What caused the man to break? I have asked myself many times. The Viet artillery?—surely it did much to weaken and undermine us. You will tell me that other officers had nervous collapses beneath that shellfire, and I will answer that they were officers commanding printed forms. Tell me that Castries himself, known as a man of bravery and dash, lost—or appeared to lose, which comes to the same—his will and capacity to react. Castries was an armoured commander, a man of the open country, and one of the worst mistakes made was to shut him up in that hole. We were thrown into that pisspot to leave our skins there—yes: Séguin-Pazzis, myself, cavalry men too. But Castries—he was there to become a general, Which—be it said in passing—he did. We were all raised a step in rank—some politician's notion of inflating our morale. Rank! We wore no insignia; soldiers and officers shared the same life and the same death. Rank was something they had in Hanoi, in Saigon—or in Paris. To us everything merged in the knowledge that we were soldiers and that we were going to die. Did that mean nothing to Laforêt? He was as good an officer as we had. The type to gallop till he dropped. Gay, good-looking, vital—very like Pichelin—who died—retaking Dominique.

171

"Did we fail him? . . . If only he had surrendered to the Viet! . . . He attacked us where we had no defence."

"Perhaps he believed in a Viet victory?"

"Tcha!" Bark of impatient amusement from the general at this naïveté. "Did anyone believe in a Viet victory? The Americans—do they believe in a Viet victory? Look at the incredible, bewildering number of stupidities that were committed, all the handicaps that were accepted, and then look at the course of the battle. As late as mid-April, after over a month of siege, after the airstrip was lost and no plant could land, after Beatrice, Gabrielle, Anne-Marie and Dominique had changed lovers—to use the phrase of the moment —even then the fight hung in the finest balance. The Viet was as ripe as we were—his best troops were cut to ribbons in the struggle for Eliane. They could no longer fight, and changed over to siege tactics— digging tunnels. Two fresh para battalions and we would have broken the ring. How could he have believed it? Later—afterwards—then, perhaps . . ."

"Afterwards there were others."

"Yes. Few. Was it not even more important then, after, after the surrender, the march, the camps to show our unity, our solidarity—our trust? The Viet tried everything to shake that loyalty. And succeeded— sometimes."

"And throughout that time nobody questioned Laforêt's tale?"

"He was determined to survive. Survive he did. He was thought bizarre. So were many others. Nobody queried his tale. Perhaps," the general laid both palms flat, upon the table, "perhaps we found that, afterwards, the crowning enormity."

172

CHAPTER EIGHTEEN

Van der Valk realized that he was clutching a dead cigar butt as though it were something precious, and laid it reverently in the ashtray. The general's pipe had long gone out, and had cooled enough to be refilled, which the fine hands were now doing. To look at them one might think that filling a pipe was the nearest they had got to manual labour for the last four generations, despite the sticking plaster there to prove the contrary. He had almost a feeling that the two dirty scraps of Elastoplast had been left deliberately, theatrically—a little symbol of the vulnerability and invulnerability—of paratroops.

What had he learned, from these so unreal-seeming fragments of military history? Why did the general give him so much time, and why was the general so talkative? Was it too crude and too simple to surmise a nagging guilt? No: yes: the man had settled his neuroses along with the rest of the army, and if he had been mixed up in anything dingy during the Algerian time he wouldn't be in the job he now held. But the bare mention of the ominous name, name deeply etched and ineradicable, threw up traces of the now-forgotten "para mentality," of the days between fifty-eight and sixty when they had walked slim and negligent in the leopard dress through the streets of Paris, balancing their hips ever so slightly, marked with the seal of "we are those who attack."

One had learned precious little—what one knew already, more or less. That the paratroops had come to regard themselves as set apart in an unhealthy and introspective way, that there had been a time when they held themselves openly above the law, that they had seen themselves as the saviours of the country, the nation, the Republic—and that to talk about Dien Bien Phu sent even a sophisticated cavalry staff-officer in a Paris bureau back into that walled-in world. He had had to let the man talk, if only to allow that memory of old tensions to unwind and dissipate itself. The general, he felt, had got himself back on the rails, and might now answer one or two simple questions without disappearing into the sweaty claustrophobic foxholes of Huguette and Eliane.

"So nobody found out—until Esther did. That, at least, is the story that I have been told."

"Exactly. The first accusation came from her."

"And she heard it?"

"Where but from the man himself?"

"Painful . . ."

"I imagine," glacial, "that he found it unbearable and confided it—in or out of bed—to the person he thought could neutralize this poison."

"And she betrayed him."

"Correction. He betrayed her."

"You think that's why he killed her?"

"It sounds as though that might be so."

Van der Valk was less sure. The military mind was fond of over-simplifications and dramatizing itself, but had Laforêt a military mind?

"We don't know for certain that he did kill her."

"That," said the general relighting his pipe, "is, thank God, not my problem."

"How cosy for you," acidly.

"Do not misunderstand. If he killed her, and I accept it as likely that he did or I should not have received you, I am far from going off whistling happily to wash my hands."

"Dien Bien Phu was at fault?"

"And who is to be blamed? Navarre given ridiculous instructions, Salan being cunning, the so-called government we had then—the Americans?—if they were responsible they've certainly paid for it, since. Cogny had to take the rap, of course. He was an artillery man—it was supposed that he should have known better

"It all sounds so unreal."

"So it was. Think—the Americans—a hundred or more aviation sorties a day, to protect a post of six men and a corporal. Whereas then—ten thousand troops in that pot, thinking themselves very lucky if the aviation managed thirty."

"One last thing about this garrison—why paratroops? The Legion I understand: ponderous, powerful. And old-fashioned soldiers—stomachs, beards, hung around with grenades and canteens full of vino. But paratroops! Supposed to be mobile, sudden—no?"

"Just so," tranquil, "but the longer one looks at it the sillier it becomes. The original idea was for an attacking base—Castries was to command manoeuvres—including armour! When it became apparent that this was in reality a besieged fort paratroops were still used—a mistake repeated in Algeria. It became commonplace to concede that the Legion and para regiments were the only really effective shock troops. They were held as the general reserve, and were too often wasted in little packets to block a hole. And lastly, of course, once the camp was sealed off the only reinforcements that could be given it were para units."

"Nobody noticed the stupidity of that—unless of course Laforêt did?"

"Paratroop units carry out the instructions given. The sillier those are, the more important that there should be no failure."

"They failed—did not forgive themselves—but were happy to pitch on any scapegoats there might be going."

"The camp was held for two months under continuous attack—by roughly two and a half thousand effective troops, commanded by a lieutenant-colonel with no strategic training, aided by half a dozen officers later abused as the 'Mafia'—including in a minor role your humble servant."

"The same mafia condemned a junior officer guilty of a nervous collapse to a living death, perverting justice to do so."

"You are mistaken," with a sudden impressive dignity. "The mafia was in no way responsible for that act. At the time he was my boy, under my command, and for what was done I take sole responsibility." As he spoke, Van der Valk had to admit, the general was formidable.

"I seek to judge no man," said Van der Valk. "Neither you, mon général, nor Colonel Godard, nor Lieutenant Laforêt. No one, perhaps, will ever understand."

"What went on in their minds—perhaps not. And perhaps you are right to make the equation."

"Laforêt had the fatal gift of imagination."

"You seek to exculpate him—to whitewash him," snapped the general.

"Nobody even tried to defend him." Van der Valk's voice was heating in its turn. "What did you do— send him a pistol in a Christmas-wrapped box—as legend suggested some officers did to Navarre?"

"What would you expect—that I go politely with my hat in my hand, inviting him to collect his gratuities and would he be so good as quietly to resign from the army? . . . In the camp, Langlais tore the beret off an officer he thought did not deserve to wear it. An officer of his own rank. The rule was universal. Nobody singled out Laforêt, as you appear to imply. History, Monsieur le Commissaire de Police, has forgotten those who did not enhance their reputation in battles. And we—I say we—do not submit ourselves to the judgement of a civilian—even a policeman."

"No," said Van der Valk lumbering to his feet, "and neither did General Christian Marie Ferdinand de la Croix de Castries, descendant of dukes and marshals, submit himself to the judgement of a Breton peasant. He just couldn't help himself."

"Sit down, Commissaire," said the general gently. "I beg your pardon."

"And I beg your pardon. He was your boy, and you suffered for him."

"Esther Marx put a bullet in him. She was one of ours. It was her sorrow and bitter regret that she was not here with us."

"Had she been with you, Laforêt would not have deserted."

"I never thought of that," said the general.

CHAPTER NINETEEN

"How many I's in intelligence?"

"One," said Ruth.

"There are two," said Arlette severely. "Which makes four large horrible faults in your dictation, which means you'd get a six at the very best and probably a five-and-a-half or even a five. Write it out again taking especial pains with the presentation, and if you really concentrate I'm sure you'll get a nine at least tomorrow."

There was silence for ten minutes, underlined by a faint muttering noise like a mouse in a wainscot.

"Bugger."

"Where did you learn that expression?"

"You."

"Mm. None the less it's a vulgar expression which you're not allowed to use. Don't lean so heavily on your pen."

Another minute's silence and muttering.

"M'an."

"What?"

"Esther was shot, wasn't she?"

Arlette had always supposed that a day would come when one had to tell lies to children, and in theory she still had a feeling that this must be so. In practice it never seemed to work out.

"What—have you finished your dictation?" to gain time.

"Yes."

"Oh. What gives you the idea?"

"I heard Mevrouw Paap telling her husband. She thought I didn't understand."

"Yes. It's true."

"Who shot her?"

"Père being a policeman, he's doing his best to find out. That's why he went to France."

"Somebody in France?"

"I don't know—maybe he does by now."

"Does it hurt, being shot?"

"I've never been shot but I'm told it doesn't. A bump and a fright—like falling down the stairs. She died very quickly and I'm sure she didn't feel any pain."

"Like on the television serial. Was it gangsters?"

Arlette, who was on her hands and knees on the floor, cutting a pattern, put down the scissors.

"Gangsters are a rarity. Luckily. Père thinks perhaps somebody Esther once knew. Somebody unhappy and upset, not at all well, who imagined somehow that he had to shoot her."

"Why?"

"One imagines things when one is ill. Haven't you sometimes been feverish and had horrible dreams, that you were being chased or something?"

"Yes, but I didn't shoot anyone."

"Which goes to show that you weren't very ill. Once when I was very tired and upset I threw a kitchen knife at somebody. That was just as bad."

"Who at?"

"That has no importance—I only wanted to show you that one could shoot people."

"Were they frightened, the person?"

"Yes—a bit."

"Esther wasn't easily frightened," with an implied contempt. "She was a parachutist."

"Would you like to be a parachutist?" rejoicing in a possible change of subject. "Pass me my pins; they're on the table in your reach—and screw up your pen; it might roll off."

"I could be. I know where one can learn."

"Really?" mildly interested but wanting to accelerate down this promising side road. "Where's that?"

"In Belgium somewhere. It's quite a long way. Esther took me once, in the car." Zomerlust's old dark-blue Simca Ariane; Arlette felt a slight pinch in her heart.

"When was that?"

"Oh, about a month ago. Esther said just for fun she'd show me how it was done."

"What is it then, a flying club?"

"What's that?"

"I don't know—a sort of little airfield."

"Yes, like that. You can learn to parachute—there's

a sort of gymnasium. But I don't know exactly because she didn't, after all."

Arlette had begun to prick her ears up.

"What made her change her mind?"

"I don't know—I think she had a row with the man there. Cost too much, very likely," with an air of familiarity, as though she knew all about making a row over something that costs too much.

"These places are pretty expensive, I believe," said Arlette cautiously. "Tell me about it though—I'd like to try, some time."

"I think it's not far from Hasselt. A long way. Be too far for you in the deux-chevaux, I dare say," with a superior voice. She was plainly pleased at knowing about something Arlette didn't.

"I'm sure I could—parachute, I mean. One has to conquer one's fear. I only hope I wouldn't get vertigo."

"Esther said one didn't get vertigo. You have to learn first jumping off a high platform, with a sort of line strung to you. Landing is the hardest part."

"I suppose it would be," humbly. "And this man —was he in charge?"

"I think so. He was all right. He was talking to me for a bit, and then Esther came out of a sort of office place, and she told me very crossly to go and wait in the car, and then a bit after she came and said she'd changed her mind. She bought me an ice, though —but she was very niggly all day so she was fed up about something. I wanted to go back another time but she shut me up."

Arlette did get a feeling of vertigo because she suddenly realized that she had understood.

"What's the matter?"

"I got a bit dizzy from bending over. Come on; bed-time."

"But it is only half past eight."

"I said bed and I mean it. But you can have an orange first."

Her heard beat furiously and she longed for the telephone to ring. She was sure he would ring, since he always did unless there was something very startling. Would he laugh at her?

She paced about nervously, looking at her watch all the time. I am in a trench, she thought, waiting for the signal to be given for a counter-attack. She made several feeble attempts to quieten her nerves, including a drink that was much too strong. I'm a bit pissed, she kept thinking. I am certainly imagining things. I wish he were here. When the telephone did ring, at the time it always did, between nine and half past, she was depressed and as though disappointed, and afraid to say what was on her mind.

"Hallo—oh, it's you. Where are you?"

"Who did you think it was—an unknown admirer who saw you buying a cauliflower and followed you home?" His voice sounded tired and tart, and none too sure of himself, which made two of them. "Where am I? I'm in Paris, and not enjoying it a bit."

"I thought you were in Clermont-Ferrand."

"I was. I left. I got a plane. It went very fast. I think I left my brains back there or something. It was snowing there. Here it's quite mild—Breton weather. Which is just as well because I lost a glove."

"Oh dear. What are you doing in Paris?—where are you exactly?"

"In a very odd little hotel near the Boulevard Saint-Germain. Queer things are happening to me. I'm being

183

buggered about by DST. I'm not at all sure how to act —I've got to try and think things out. People have been following me about. And this evening I met a rather peculiar individual—I've got to disgest him. I'm going now to get some sleep—alone, thank heaven."

"Are DST still mixed up with this?" anxiously.

"I'm damned if I know how much. I'm still trying to find out where Laforêt is. I have a suspicion they know but they won't tell me. I can't make out what they're at. Quite likely they're listening to me right now, and I'm damned if I care, either."

"Are they really?" asked Arlette, distraught. "I've got something to tell you but I'd better not if the line is tapped."

"No no, that's all nonsense. I'm pretty sure they've better things to do, though I sincerely wish I knew what. Tell me anyway—take my mind off my own clowning about."

"I think I know where he is," said Arlette in a tense whisper.

"Where who is? Your admirer? What are you whispering for? Where is he then—the bathroom?"

"Shut up, you fool—yes you are clowning. I'm serious. I think I know."

"Who?"

"You know who." There was a long silence. "Are you still there?"

"Yes yes—there was a little green man in here, but I sent him away. Is Ruth there?"

"She ought to be asleep but I want to keep my voice down."

"Let me try and concentrate. Has she said something?"

"Yes, she had a story about Esther going parachuting and changing her mind."

"Where, in heaven's name?"

"Belgium somewhere—over the border and I think somewhere near Hasselt. Isn't that roughly across from Eindhoven?"

"It is. Parachuting—you mean really jumping out of a plane?"

"Apparently. She mentioned an airfield. But she said Esther went there for fun, you understand, to show her or something, and there was a man there, and Esther changed her mind abruptly and went straight home and behaved oddly for some time."

"Did she talk to this man—Esther I mean?"

"Ruth talked to him. Esther sent her back in the car—and came herself a little later. How little?—no idea."

"What's he look like, this man?"

"Darling—a child. Even if one could ask she wouldn't know."

"Sorry of course. Parachuting. This is extraordinary."

"You think there's something in it?"

"I don't know. But it would illumine some remarks I have heard."

"You didn't know, though?"

"No, but I rather think you may have something."

"It's not very funny though, being a detective."

"You've taken rather a time finding that out. This may be most important. Does the child have any idea?"

"No, but she does have the idea Esther was shot. They know everything. She saw something funny in this episode, but she didn't get it worked out. What are you going to do—go there?"

"Of course I have to go there. You know this is a very strange thing—you know coincidence doesn't exist."

"A coincidence that you should be going to arrest Ruth's father for killing her mother," said Arlette, and burst into tears, and was immediately so angry with herself that she slammed the phone down without another word, and sat on the floor by the telephone table crying to herself for ten minutes and more.

CHAPTER TWENTY

Van der Valk stood heavily planted on the pavement of the Rue Saint-Dominique and looked about without joy. Impressive but wearisome part of Paris, the Faubourg. Overwhelming houses; humbling in their immeasurable wealth and pride. He supposed there were still more *hôtels particuliers,* last bastions of privilege, with enormous gardens, cavernous salons, hordes of servants: very nice too, and he was all for it: he hated nothing more than mediocrity. Most were the seats of the mighty in the administrative sense; ministries and subministries, bureaux for this and for that—very dull, jostling the dukes and the marshals in their Jockey Club entrenchments and making an agreeable meeting

187

place with ancient wealth where the First Minister perched luxuriantly in the Matignon Palace on the Rue de Varenne.

Some houses were divided into apartments just as in less god-begotten quarters, and behind these windows looking down on him there might even be poor: heartening thought. But the whole quarter stank of self-assured wealth from the puffed ministry on the Quai d'Orsay, staring arrogantly across the river, to the Ecole Militaire asphyxiated with rage at the sight of the Eiffel Tower, and at the centre was the Temple of Generals, Saint Louis des Invalides. Hereabouts, what generals said—that went.

Beastly quarter too, where there were no comforting little cafés. Where did the chauffeurs sneak off to? Surely they did not sit all day rigidly at attention behind the wheel of those huge glossy autos with flags flying from their wings. What was a poor policeman to do? Trudge an eternity back down to the Raspail crossing—or hunt around up by the Invalides; there was something there on the boulevard for sure, but one couldn't hang about here; be arrested for loitering and suspected bomb-thoughts as soon as winking. Oh well, he might as well trail off to that horrible air terminus; he had his case parked there in the luggage office. He crossed the Rue de Bourgogne with a sagging tread, like a worn-out mule in the stony Pyrenees, and was thoroughly cross with DST. Useless lot. Here if anywhere they should be swarming like busy bees. Here in this quarter where their honey burst and bulged from every stately window there should surely be hundreds of them to come swarming up—offering him a nice glass of champagne first—and tell him obligingly whom he should see next.

What! They had been busy enough already in Holland! In Marseilles they had been zinging with ambitious energy, in Clermont-Ferrand eager hawkeyes had even got their feet wet running through the snow, and here, right in the centre of the Seventh Arrondissement, there wasn't a peep out of them. What did they do nowadays, when there was no longer a marvellous nest of spies out in Fontainebleau, so that they could spend happy weeks grilling talkative colonels from Standing Group suspected of fraternizing with Americans? Crossly, he used a public telephone in the Invalides bus station.

"Monsieur Borza please." For the brown man had given him a name and number, professedly most interested in what the general would have to say, for some obscure reason of his own.

The voice at the other end was young and cheerful.

"Sorry, Monsieur Borza isn't in the office. Ring you back?"

"Yes, the bus station; he'll be thrilled. All aboard for Le Bourget, next stop Glasgow, thank God to be home."

"The gentleman from Holland?"

"Yes, Comrade."

"Where are you staying?"

"I haven't the least idea."

"Oh that won't do at all; must have somewhere to put your feet up. We have a ducky place where we keep friends, just round the corner so don't bother with a taxi. I'll ring them for you, shall I? Saint George and Saint James—we call it the English Martyr By-bye now."

It was perhaps not such a bad idea. He could do with a cup of tea.

Typical secret-service place; almost impossible to find. No vulgar notice boards on the street, but a dark little passage between the two windows of a flower shop, with chaste grey-velvet curtains and a card printed in gothic letters saying *"Complet"* to discourage the importunate. Inside was a mahogany cavern and an elderly page in a striped waistcoat.

"I'm afraid we have no rooms."

"A kind friend was going to make a phone call?"

"The Dutch gentleman—I am so sorry." He wasn't asked to fill in a form!

His spirits rose rapidly at sight of the lift, which lived behind rococo spirals of gilded wrought-iron flowers and whose doors opened with large polished brass knobs. Inside there was a large brass handle connecting one with the engine room; one rang for Slow Astern and behold one went astern, slow but splendidly reliable and in Edwardian comfort; it was like a very tiny 1910 Cunarder. He was shown into a small chocolate-box where even the telephone had been salvaged from the *Titanic*. The window had a view of the Palais Bourbon: aha, this was where those Third Republic Deputies had kept their mistresses. Plumbing like a Wedgwood Ivy tea service got under way with loud clanks; the water was pale rust-colour and deliciously boiling, and there were three colossal towels. This was the life—join DST and Get Aboard the Atomic Age. Wrapped in all three bathtowels he picked up the telephone and said, "I'd very much like some tea." And it arrived, in massive pot-de-chambre procelain with little roses on it and "Worcester" written in gold on the bottom. The chambermaid who brought it had an elderly musky perfume and a bunch of huge shiny steel keys.

"We thought you might like the paper. And would you be wanting a suit pressed?"

It was the London *Evening Standard*—he felt as though three large whiskies in quick succession were lifting the top of his head ten metres or so gently heavenwards. The tea was thick and dark and probably Fortnum and Mason's Darjeeling; he folded the paper to see how his shares were doing on the Stock Exchange.

The phone was wrong; it made a brief Parisian bleat.

"Aloo-allo."

"Comfy?" The voice, barely recognizable through his opium-eater's trance, was that of a bright young man with a leather raincoat who had "come from the Embassy" in another continent.

"Very. I am now going to have a little nap. Send me up the menu and a few mistresses about eight."

"Just tell me very briefly about the Rue Saint-Dominique."

"Confirmation. You heard about Marseilles?"

"Yes, we were given a sudden injection of interest as you gathered. Blowing dust off files, and generally doing our little exercises. Consensus of opinion last night was that it should be my baby, so I've been Beneluxing like crazy ever since."

"I'm feeling too bloody Beneluxurious just now for mental activity. What does all that mean?"

"It means that after frenzied activity in all that flat boggy country the gamekeeper thinks there must be a rabbit around somewhere. Thing is to find the hole.

One of the peasants thought he'd seen a shy little white tail."

"Yes," said Van der Valk alarmed, "but I don't want the rabbit chased with loud shouts and bangs—I haven't got my gun. I want this one tamed with lettuce leaves."

"Quite all right," soothingly. "We haven't the slightest interest in the fur coat industry. For us this is a question mark that's been pencilled in the margin and left there quite a few years. Our one very small interest is to take our little indiarubber and rub out the pencil mark. Now I may have something for you tonight, arriving on the evening plane from Brussels. Don't get nervous; it pays its own expenses because it thinks there's a quick profit to be made. It doesn't belong to us. Clear?"

"Clear."

"It flatters itself that it is deeply in our confidence because occasionally we have given it a penny in its sweaty little palm. It is for you to handle as you see fit; I hope it may prove useful. Enjoy yourself—enjoy Paris. Why don't you have dinner at Lapérouse—they have those nice creamy potatoes. Sleep well."

Van der Valk put the phone down, got underneath a magenta satin counterpane, and went peacefully to sleep after the porter had politely agreed with him that Lapérouse was a nice peaceful place where he would certainly be happy.

CHAPTER TWENTY-ONE

He got a table by the window, and pink lampshades and the kind of steak that sticks to one's insides and those nice creamy potatoes and the kind of Burgundy that comes straight from a Renoir girl's big luscious breasts and there was even a bit left over to go with the Roquefort. The coffee was nice too. And he had a view of the autumn night across the Seine to the Quai des Orfèvres and the Palace of Justice and the Prèfecture de Police, which gave him a nice homy feeling. Back in Amsterdam the local pub on the Prinsengracht had been nothing like this. It was a pity that this man had to come and spoil it, and worse still to waste the brandy on him. One had to be in something really squalid like DST to appreciate such people. He felt grateful for the two hours of delicious cocooned sleep before the chambermaid called him with his suit sponged and pressed, and for the really solid dinner that removed that lamentable clueless feeling.

Still, it had been well-timed, no doubt of that. He had been dallying over his second cup of coffee and had a cigar going, an Upmann that could have been made of tightly-rolled hundred-franc notes, the price the Ministry of Justice in The Hague had to pay for it. Well, he had saved them the price of a train ticket from Clermont-Ferrand to Paris/Austerlitz, hadn't he?

The man was smoking a cigar too, a tough dark cheroot from Holland by way of Sumatra, Brazil, and lord knew what other small unimportant places, and he was smoking it in a peculiarly horrible way. He put the well-wetted cheroot in the middle of his mouth, sucked a great gobful of smoke, spat it out and caught it again in two obscene serpents up his nose, and from there it came out of his ears as far as Van der Valk was concerned because he could not bear to look.

The man was big, as big as himself and fatter, but he moved quickly and softly on his feet and seemed agile. He had a head full of distinguished silver hair, very thick and healthy and expensively cut and arranged, and a pale grey suit open over a cream silk shirt. No overcoat unless he had left it downstairs. No pullover. Toughy. Swiftly. He might have been fifty years old and again he might not. He was talking to the waiter and as Van der Valk watched idly he came catfooting down the plummy carpet and leaned over with easy familiarity.

"Thought I'd catch you here—friends gave me the word. No, I had dinner at Orly but I'd like an ice-cream." The waiter was standing there with his finger-tips tapping negligently on a menu.

"With pineapple, and kirsch, and cream."

"Brandy, Mr . . . ?"

"McLintock's the name, Joe McLintock from the Far North. Don't suppose they've got any Glenlivet, but the brandy sounds good." "Two." The waiter bowed.

"Glad to meet a friend," said Mr. McLintock stretching luxuriantly. He had a chest like a barrel under that silk shirt. One could have taken him for an ex-heavyweight champion, or the manager of a very prosperous football team. He spoke a fluent thick French but had trouble getting his mouth round diphthongs. He could be from the Far North all right, thought Van der Valk, though himself he thought Mc-Lintock a poorish choice unless the man was fronting as a fur salesman for the Hudson Bay Company. "I just got in from Brussels—looks like I timed it. Say, that looks good." His voice was soft, low, and creamy, suitable for expensive restaurants and going well with the pineapple ice-cream he now began to eat happily. A scent of kirsch floated across; Van der Valk blew a fan of smoke. Brandy arrived. Not a football team—an ice-hockey team. "The friends have the word you're anxious to meet a fellow." His language, too, was something that Van de Valk could take a dislike to without any effort at all. It seemed to be culled from espionage fiction, and enlivened with catchwords learned from disc-jockeys.

"I'm looking for a man called Laforêt."

"Ah you spika de English too. Great, great. You say it, I'll follow it—Spanish, Norwegian, anything you like. Terrific linguist, McLintock. Well now, a chap called Laforêt . . . Yes, sir, I heard a little whisper about that this morning in Brussels, and I made a tiny teeny phone call because I reckoned this was where McLintock might make a tiny teeny deal. How teeny would that be, according to your catalogue?"

"Just for the address?"

"That's what we're dealing in right now or have I got out in Atlanta instead of in Memphis? Don't let me hustle you, natch—I haven't got this address right here on a bit of paper. But I can find it, yes man, I can find that bit of paper. Twenty-four hours?"

"Twenty-four hours from now—one thousand francs." The big man was very busy cleaning out the ice-cream coupe and licking the spoon with a large pink tongue. Van der Valk sipped his brandy. "Swiss," he added negligently.

There was a loud affected sigh.

"Holy cow, that sure tasted good. Just can't resist being lazy even if it does me an injury. 'Tisn't ezzactly a heavy rate for twenny-four hours' hard slogging, but in these handsome surroundings it's kind of cruel to be horsetrading." Certainly not American. As good as certainly not Canadian. Scots was out of the question.

"Now whereabouts?"

"The tables on the gallery in the Saint-Germain drugstore," said Van der Valk, rather pleased with himself. "They have good ice-cream there."

"Between eight and nine in the p.m.—I don't like making promises, Mister, but I'll see what I can do." He lit another of his phallic symbols. "I'd like to have a little insurance. This party—he's wanted? By the way, I guess I never introduced myself properly—Joe McLintock's in the commercial aviation business, but he likes to steer clear of politics."

"Balthasar—Arthur Balthasar. I'm in the legal business, Mr. McLintock. I don't have any interest in politics myself; in fact I'm a bit of a pacifist. But you know what they call us Swiss—the bankers of Europe. And why are we the bankers of Europe? Because people trust us. They bring us money, and they bring us secrets, and we have friends in the most unexpected directions, and we are trustworthy because we don't mix ourselves up in politics and fancy adventures. We like sober, careful investments that aren't too insecure. Cinema companies, treasure-hunters, speculators—they don't come to us for underwriting. And we don't ever pay in advance. But on delivery—then we pay on the nail, Mr. McLintock, and it smells just as good as gold."

"I believe you—every word. And when Joe gives his word it's his bond. Now this party—he's youngish mm? I wouldn't put him over forty. He's got blue eyes, and fair hair—he's a nice chap. I've run up against him a couple of times, I rather think, but it's a few months back. Likeable guy. Now of course my trust is just as solid as you've been describing it back there, and where we usually ask for the Dun and Bradstreet ratings, our mutual friends are the best of references. Cuts both directions, an introduction like that, to the mutual benefit of all, we may add. You ask me no questions and that is very handsome, yessir, very handsome. And I don't ask any questions but seeing as this is almost a friend and a really likeable guy I forget my conscience and we make it fifteen hundred, right?"

"Waiter . . . bill . . . many thanks. So you're going to the Folies Bergères?—may I wish you a very enjoyable evening? Please do excuse me, I have to make a phone call."

"Well sir, I see you're a business man and so am I and we'll make no more bones about it. Agreed agreed. Before nine tomorrow—no, I thank you, I never wear overcoats. I like the evening and I think I'll treat myself to a little stroll as far as the Saint-Germain crossing. You can rely on Joe, ask anyone who knows. That's settled then. A deal is a deal and a date is a date and if it should take a few hours longer I won't spare the time nor the trouble. Sleep well."

Van der Valk had taken his time about putting on his overcoat and getting his stick organized. The cloak-room attendant called him a taxi and he said, "Continental" in a stiff Swiss voice. A few hundred metres along the quay he saw the big light-grey shoulders moving with a slow easy swagger through a cloud of cigar-smoke down towards the Odéon. The driver crossed the river, tore down the Rue de Rivoli and stopped with a jerk outside the Continental.

"Go round to the Castiglione side, would you?" He took his time hunting in his trouser pocket for change, went into the hotel, straight through and out on the far side, crossed the road, had a little stroll around the Tuileries for his digestion, crossed the Solferino bridge and was back in his hotel surprised to find that it was only nine thirty. A night porter as polite as the day one had been, but fatter and more confidential as befitted a night porter, promised to have Arlette on the telephone by the time he had got upstairs. He had not been followed—not, at least, since leaving the Continental and Mr. McLintock was welcome to that—he might even get to feel at home there.

Van der Valk made affectionate kissing noises at

the telephone, put it down lovingly, rubbed his nose and started to ponder.

Arlette's big news—but it clicked, it fitted, it was alive, right . . .

This man—there was no news, and that was good news. Pointless to feel agrieved about his habits, his accent or his cigars, which were all unimportant. The man was just a little informer like a hundred others who touched a hundred-franc note from DST from time to time. Reliability—complete. Trustworthiness —zero. He plainly did know Laforêt and in exchange for money—assuming anybody gave him money, sniggered Van der Valk, because it wouldn't be him—he would hand over some perfectly genuine information. The only thing was, it might be a little out of date. The fellow was perfectly capable of ringing up Laforêt, touching a few more francs for the news that somebody was asking questions, and keeping an eye on the bird's flight. He would then be most aggrieved at having been diddled, point to the nest still irrefutably warm, congratulate himself on being so close, apologize profusely for the naughty bird, and guarantee to mark its passage for just a bit more money.

Of course, he was too enslaved to DST for any big stuff double-cross. Any police informer knows that the day he sends the cops on a trip with a lump of sugar and a drop of eau-de-Cologne he will be arrested for indecent exposure within thirty minutes.

One would like to know the little something with which DST undoubtedly twisted such people's arms— there always was a little something . . . But the hint had been clear: "Handle him as you see fit." In other words, officialdom considered that it had paid its debts, done him a good turn, and refastened its own shoelaces; it did not intend to bother any further. They had nothing whatever against Laforêt, and at this time of day their interest in him was academic. Borza-the-brown-man had been telling the truth: why not? Laforêt was a dusty and forgotten file, an ancient story about some hanky-panky cooked up in the Algerian time by paratroop commanders. Laforêt had been without active interest since 1960, and that was a long long time.

This McLintock—the way to deal with him might be to move suddenly.

CHAPTER TWENTY-TWO

Even if there were no private planes, there was one place one could always get to in a hurry these days and that was Brussels. One never knew when one might suddenly feel the need to be nasty to the Dutch about margarine or give Italians a rap on the knuckles about secret subsidies. He seized his telephone.

"Is there a night plane to Brussels?"

"Let's see—you've just missed that one—seven in the morning."

"Or a train?" It had struck him that that obnoxious McGuthrie—what was it he called himself?—might have notions about planes. "Oh yes, there's always a night train—you'd catch it easily; you've an hour to get to the Gare du Nord." A pleasure: it was not perhaps among his very favourite railway stations, but it would serve.

Belgium: one never spoke quite the right French for the Belgians, nor quite the right Dutch for the Flemings, so that there was a feeling of being tactless either way and one followed the notice saying Sortie/Uitgang with a mixture of irritation and relief. He got a self-drive from that self-pitying firm which is forever telling everybody that it tries harder. He wished he knew the Russian for "Well, try harder still." And by the time something like daylight appeared through an undecided mixture of fog, snow, and rain he was well into Baluka-Land. This was Arlette's name for the backwoods of Flanders, those gloomy stretches which seem neither properly Holland nor really Belgium, and perhaps the best solution would be to incorporate them into the Grand Duchy of Courland, lying in equally bleak indecision between Lithuania and Estonia.

Poor old Laforêt. Grievances collected in this corner, which thought of itself as being heartily loathed by Holland and Belgium alike—with some justification. Had he any skills, apart from being a soldier? What had his family been like—his home? What had brought him to this hole? An idea of growing mushrooms or some such little business: running perhaps a garage or a small hotel—the kind of job learned from a teach-yourself-bookkeeping paperback in the Home Economics Series?

He had not seen any photograph of Laforêt, but he had two or three descriptions to match together. Ability, charm, good looks, and plenty of brains—how much of that had the years blurred or obliterated? Fair hair, slightly wavy: he might be grey, mudbrown, bald or wear a toupée by this time. Such photos as existed, in files in Paris or elsewhere, were bound to be misleading. In them all he wore a uniform, which he wore well. Square jaw, square shoulders. A fresh healthy face, the kind that never looks tired or yellow. The kind of face that would go unnoticed in any Dutch street. What had he done here in the wilds of Limburg, among villages with names like Opoeteren and Neerglabbeek, in this landscape from an early novel by Georges Simenon? Taken to drink? Van der Valk would have quite understood and been profoundly sympathetic.

Somewhere near Hasselt—a long way. A child's description that was not easy to pin down. Road to Hasselt? Coming out of Western Holland, that could be any of the roads winding southward from half a dozen little Dutch towns—Bergen, Breda, or Tilburg. An airfield—there could not be many. He headed for one of the Customs.

"A little airfield—with a parachute school? Most flying clubs have one. Any amount—let's look at the map. I know them all, more or less. A Frenchman with fair hair? My poor boy, we have no Frenchmen round here! The people who work on these places—yes, I have a nodding acquaintanceship. Ask my opposite number, at Turnhout perhaps. Yes, they most of them have Customs posts—one doesn't know what these little planes might be getting up to, but of course their movements are easily enough controlled. Within the drainage areas, as we call them, of the big towns there are generally a few business men flying private planes, and they hop across to England, Germany, lord knows where. But what are you doing running around the countryside? Surely you could get all this with a few phone calls back in the office."

"It's all very vague and unofficial," said Van der Valk negligently. "Sort of obscure hunch I had last night—and I happened to be in Brussels anyway."

"Well, d'you want me to ring my colleague in Turnhout? He'd be better placed, if it's on the Belgian side."

"I have an obscure feeling that it is on the Belgian side."

"The thing is to distinguish clearly between a commercial airport properly speaking, of which there are only a few, and little private fields—dozens of those, naturally; we don't lack strips of grass round hereabouts that are good for not much else, hm."

"Ring him up—I'd like to talk to him."

". . . Extension seven, please . . . Van Ryseghem?— put him on, would you . . . out on the field? . . . ah, in that case I'll hold on . . . Hallo Johnny, how's tricks, I bet it's slack, there's hardly any visibility here either. So you've got a few minutes? I've a friend here who has a police inquiry. No, no, quite unofficial— shall I put him on?"

"This is extremely tangential," said Van der Valk softly. "A man I think of as having an administrative job, perhaps, on what is probably a private field. French in origin and has perhaps an accent. Around forty, medium build, fair hair, fresh complexion."

"Can't think of anybody like that," said a dubious voice. "Of course there are lots of these little fields— what? Oh yes, a parachute school is a common feature —anything to turn a few extra pennies. Flying lessons for a single-engine license—popular hobby. Gliding, of course. Here we used to have a lot of that, but with the increase in commercial movement involving Antwerp most of that stuff has moved further east. Over towards Hasselt? Yes, two or three—couldn't really say: try Bilsen or Maaseyck." Van der Valk had been saving his high card, but now was the time to show it.

"I've another description, much more precise, which may ring a bell. It is of a big man, heavily built, showy dresser. Thick silver hair, tanned face. Looks about fifty, perhaps because of the hair, and describes himself as to do with aviation. Has an act of being Canadian."

"Sounds like Conny Desmet—except he's not Canadian; Belgian as you could wish: had his passport in my hands a dozen times, he's always in and out."

"Profession?"

"Company director or something like that—I don't recall. Comes from Liège I do believe. But he's a pilot if that's what you mean by aviation—single-engine of course."

"You've helped me a great deal."

"Pleased to hear it," said the voice, surprised.

Snow had fallen. Not enough to mask the lowering country with innocence, but just enough to make the blackened fields look blacker. More would fall, but still not enough. The sky was dour, but had not the yellowish glare of a real snow sky. A day for the electric light to burn even at midday, for cobblestones to be greasy and treacherous, for the depressing bray of the ambulance to sound in all the city streets.

Van der Valk stopped on the Hasselt road at a pull-in café. A failure. The look of the bottle put him off rum, the coffee was greasy and black as the road, and people shook their glum dirty hair at him and couldn't tell him anything—or just wouldn't, more likely. Peasants . . . But he had more luck with a filling-station, where he got a pasty girl with a flat chest but a friendly heart, bless her.

The place was still hard to find. These side roads running crookedly through fields that had been quarrelled over in endless lawsuits, these tiny hamlets all with the same uncouth name. Overcheeserind and Undercheeserind were followed inevitably by Nethercheeserind, and he had already taken the wrong crossroad three times when he came plump on the place—as usual, one didn't notice it till one was grinding one's nose up against it.

"Didn't look much. Could have been any of the obscure little factories, with twenty girls making bicycle repair outfits, that are to be found in this kind of countryside. Same air of a few old farm buildings tarted up cheap and not much money being made. The cheap metal gate was flimsy and rusting, badly hung on wood that had warped; a wooden board said "Aeroclub Polygon." A roughly metalled track led to a group of buildings that looked just the cowshed-and-haybarn they had undoubtedly been. He turned the corner and was surprised. It still had a pathetic aspect when one looked at the wide path of bumpy puddled concrete, the frayed farm-buildings and the three or four workhouse-wagon cars with rusty mudguards, but across this fifty-metre-square patch, unseen from the road he had been following, was a largish, newish, one-storey concrete block with big clean-looking windows, some showing bits of bright-coloured curtain and green climbing plants. Another board, but this one glossy and smartly painted with gold lettering on pale blue. "Polygon Aeroclub and Parachute Training School." At the far side, forming an L, was the end of a biggish hangar. He crossed to where a shiny new Daf was parked next to a Fiat saloon, and pushed the glass swing door. Wide passage with matting. Smell of paint and stuffiness of oil central heating. Ahead, a door saying "Flying" and a door on each side saying "Ladies" and "Gents." To the right it said "Members Only" and to the left "Office," both flanked by notice boards. In the corner was a public telephone both. He pushed the door that said "Flying" and found himself on a concrete apron with rough grass beyond. In front of the hangar were oilstains and one of those planes that reminded him vaguely of his boyhood and Amy Johnson flying to Australia. The hangar was shut. To the left was a glass box with a cluster of radio antennae and a depressed windsock on a pole: flying control, no doubt. There wasn't a soul to be seen but it all seemed less pathetic than at first sight. At the end of the building was what might be a small flat; at the other, where it had said "Members Only," the windows of an obvious clubhouse bar, which at fine weekends would be full, no doubt, of hearty male voices and a smell of whisky mixing with that of sweaty locker-room. He went back and tried "Office." Plastic tiles, steel-tube and imitation-leather chairs, a fluorescent strip light, and a woman sitting behind a typewriter, but doing her nails.

A woman preferring to be thought of as a girl; past thirty but girlish directly the men were about. Tight black ski trousers and excessively brilliant orange sweater, which the nails were going to match when she had finished them. Quite pretty if you like the kind of dark hair that looks just a bit greasy no matter how often you wash it. Well plucked eyebrows, orange lip-

207

stick and a faint moustache. Inquiring, slightly startled look.

"I didn't hear you coming."

"I left the car further back," vaguely.

She was a bit spiteful about being taken by surprise.

"I'm afraid there's no flying today," in a flouncy voice as though it were his fault.

"No," agreed Van der Valk cheerfully. "Lousy weather."

Perhaps he was a customer; better put a foot foremost. "Can I help you?" Standard receptionist brightness.

"Boss about?"

"I'm afraid he's in Antwerp. Was there something?"

"Like to talk to him—or somebody."

Pooh—selling something.

"Are you a traveller?" His clothes were ordinary, and didn't look prosperous: he didn't behave like a traveller somehow, but they had all sorts of approaches.

"You're Dutch—we get plenty of Dutch gentlemen. But you're from Western Holland—I can hear," coquettish. "I don't think we know you, do we?"

"You aren't all alone here, are you?" She was a little scared.

"Certainly not. The chief mechanic's about and Mr. Bos is to and fro all the time—but he had plenty to do —could you tell me what your business is exactly?"

Mr. Bos! Why hadn't he thought of it? *Bos* is a wood in Dutch—or Flemish. At a pinch, a forest, but they don't have forests in Flanders.

"I'm particularly anxious to see Mr. Bos."

She didn't like his look and rose hurriedly, casting a look about to make sure there was nothing pinchable.

Better lock the drawer with the stamps and the petty cash.

"Well, I'll see if he has a minute."

She undulated through the inside door, towards the end of the building which he had guessed from outside was someone's living quarters. He was nervous despite himself. Laforêt, he was quite sure, was not the type to wear a gun. He himself had no gun. But it might not be that easy. He had brought his walking stick; he balanced it between his knees in a nervous fiddle.

Fellow was doubtless reading a magazine with his feet up; he could hear the murmur of voices. The girl came back in.

She had got her confidence back; Mr. Bos must have decided he was harmless. And he didn't look like a policeman, save to a certain kind of eye, like DST —or Mr. McLintock!

"He'll be with you just as soon as he can," pert. He fished a cigarette out.

"Smoke?"

"Oh—those French ones—no thanks. I only smoke Luckies really." To put him in his place! She might be meat for a flyfly boy, but not for a fellow who was just a fellow.

"Oh yes," she was saying, looking negligently for her nailfile, "we have lots of business men from Maastricht, Roermond—even Eindhoven. We've six planes of our own, you know. And several private planes. And Mr.—well, he's from the big pharmaceutical factory—he's bought a Mystère jet and he's going to stable it here. We're turning people away for flying lessons."

"Really." He hoped he sounded impressed.

"We have a plane for sale if you're interested." He

was nervous, and he had a sudden wish to shut her mouth.

"No, but I'm engaging girls to make up a planeload for an oil sheik." She gave him a look designed to be lethal and began a noisy clatter at her typewriter. The door behind her opened and a man came in.

The description didn't help at all, but he knew it was Laforêt at once. He was in sporting flyfly costume; whipcord trousers, ankle boots, rollneck sweater, a sheepskin jacket negligently slung on the shoulders and a Stetson hat. And Laforêt knew him too for what he was—he was sure of it.

"Any calls?" in a crisp bossy voice. But stupid—he could have asked that in the inside room, couldn't he? Giving himself confidence.

The girl pointed her chin at Van der Valk.

"Just this gentleman, who won't tell me his business."

"Oh." The eyes that glanced briefly over were blue, bird-bright. The face was lined around the jaw, reddened and tanned by wind, but not blurred or bloated, and one could still see the young officer.

"Surely Pete's finished the test on that motor."

"He wasn't satisfied with the wiring or something. He's gone for coffee, I suppose."

"OK then, Daisy, just see you catch up on those instruction schedules." Daisy!—she would be called Daisy . . .

"Well, Mister—er?"

"Van der Valk is my name." He would have read the Dutch papers, which announced pompously that Divisional Commissaire Whosit was in charge of the Mystery Slaying. But he held himself steady.

"Shall we go in the bar?"

"Good idea."

There was nobody in Members Only, where a cleaning woman had given ashtrays a wipe with a damp dishcloth and done some desultory dusting. But the lino was polished and the coffee machine gleamed bright and expectant. Laforêt took his hat off; the fair hair was undimmed, thick, still wavy, cut a lot longer than it had once been. He didn't look French in any way, and his accent was not French, though there was something about his Dutch, as though he were a Luxemburger. Perhaps he was. The furrows of the tanned face wrinkled loosely.

"Whisky?"

"A little."

"That all right?"

"So you know."

"More by accident than anything."

"How did you find out? They weren't . . . I should have thought . . . especially anxious to—to . . ."

"Spread it abroad—no, not very. Luck, obstinacy, quite a bit of cheek. And running about. I didn't get as far as Pau, but I wasn't far short, one might say."

"Cheers."

"Cheers."

"Who did you see?"

"Voisin."

"Ah." He remembered Voisin.

"He was extremely nice. And very anxious that there should be no injustice."

"Yes," reflectively. "Yes, he's an honest fellow."

"Things have changed, you know. It's a long way to Hanoi."

Laforêt shrugged. It was a silly remark. Not to him it wasn't.

"They knew where I was? I am surprised that they should take the trouble."

"No. Nobody knew. I asked DST." There was a flash from the eyes.

"No, no—they weren't and aren't after you. Just a file from a long long way back—there was a certain hostility towards the military over Algeria." Laforêt almost smiled. "And you know how it is with files— some tidy-minded bureaucrat discovers it exists and then he wants to put a stamp on the back and send it down to the cellar. It's been in the attic all these years, and I was the—what d'you call it—catalyst?"

He nodded; he was very calm. Possibly too calm. He drank some whisky. And I am much too tense, thought Van der Valk, and drank some too.

"Shall we talk about Esther Marx?"

"You've come—to arrest me?"

"I've no official power to do so. You'd prefer to go with me to the Belgians? Or just come back to Holland in the car."

"You seem very sure."

"I'm not sure of anything. If I'd been sure I would have sent a van with two gendarmes and a piece of paper."

"But I suppose it points very strongly."

"Till we learn something new. Perhaps, for instance, you could tell me where you were, what you were doing, things like that."

"Tell . . ." Laforêt's voice was contemptuous. "You want things proved, with witnesses and things."

"A judge would. I only act on a reasonable presumption. That exists. I want to know more. That would be better in my office, say."

Laforêt was holding his glass, leaning relaxed and

loose against the bar, staring out of the window at the soggy fields and the concrete strip, seeming quite uninterested in what Van der Valk said or did. He probably is quite uninterested, came the thought. Who was it said it?—a type who saw visions.

"I could escape," dreamily.

"You could cause a certain amount of unnecessary trouble," agreed Van der Valk. "I doubt if you'd find it worth the pain."

"You don't seem worried? I'm among friends, here."

"What would be the good of my being worried? And what is the use of our asking one another these questions? I'm obliged to ask you one formal question. You did kill her? In fact I'm even obliged to put it formally, since I am a police officer on duty and under oath. François-Xavier Laforêt, do you admit killing Esther Zomerlust Marx, with or without intending to do so or planning any such action?"

"Zomerlust . . . yes . . . yes . . . I suppose so."

"However stupid these things seem it helps in the long run. What you mean is that it's not as simple as that."

Shrug.

"Just so. You'll find we won't insist on its being simple. We aren't under martial law."

"No? Years of prison—or mental homes—come to the same thing. Why talk about it? Why explain it? What good can that possibly do?"

"The decision is neither mine nor yours," sharp. The eyes looked dopily at him, as though the few drops of whisky had been full of nembutal. "Here."

"I don't smoke, thanks." And we don't commit any fancy suicides either, thought Van der Valk. Let's kick this personage in the pants a bit before he starts this

213

withdrawal lark. If he wants to be schizo let him wait till we're out of the bushes.

"Sit down, here, with me, at this table. I don't want that fool girl listening at the door. Make it look like a business deal."

"She's typing," with a thin smile.

"Look, Sam, there's only one way to handle these occasions and that is to treat them like a hire-purchase agreement. Sit down and I'll sell you accident insurance." He got his notebook out, after looking in two or three pockets, and a pen. It didn't serve any purpose, but it introduced a slight sense of reality—and that did serve a purpose.

"You Dutch," said Laforêt tolerantly.

"Yes. We Dutch. Question number one—why a machine-gun?"

Laforêt sat down, put his elbows on the table, felt leisurely in his pocket, and produced a stick of chewing-gum, which he unwrapped slowly and bit on with firm white teeth. The teeth reminded Van der Valk of Esther Marx. He didn't want to mention Ruth, but if this boy needed a bucket of ninety-degree alcohol over his head he would get it.

"Why a machine-gun?" he said again slowly.

"It's the big fellow's."

"Talk sense."

"He likes guns. He collects them. I haven't any. It was a recent acquisition of his—he was playing with it one day here on the field. It was lying about and I took it. Seemed suitable."

"What did you do with it?"

"Brought it back here of course."

"You mean it's still here?" Narrowly.

"Place is full of guns," in a tranquil tone. "You want it?"

"By and by." Thanks, he didn't want any games with guns. Nice of the fellow, though, to give him the information!

"Just who is the big fellow?"

"He's a bastard," coolly. "If you really want Esther's murderer, and if you don't mind a friendly word of advice, you'd do well to take him. You can take me too, of course," he added, as though that had no importance one way or the other. Play acting, thought Van der Valk.

"Don't feed me fantasies, it leads us nowhere. Let's get back to your trip. Very well, you took the gun. You took your car. That's yours, the Fiat outside?"

"He's real enough. He's no fantasy."

"And you're accusing him? And where is this sinister personage?"

"In Antwerp—or he could be anywhere. He trots about, buying cheap and selling dear."

"And he lives here?"

"He owns the place." Laforêt was staring out of the window again. "And forgive me for telling lies—he's not in Antwerp—here he comes now." But Van der Valk was not taking his eyes off his man.

"He's got a sleigh and reindeer?"

"Listen." From outside, the buzz of a small plane could be heard. The buzz faded as the plane made its circuit, grew again as it came in to touch down, swelled to a vroom which cut off abruptly. Laforêt and Van der Valk watched one another's face: the one was set in sharp hard lines, the other soft, placid and not at all that of a man who had just admitted

215

murdering his one-time mistress. If it were possible he was amused.

"The big fellow," he said softly.

Van der Valk looked. A modern, smart little plane, brightly painted, equipped with gadgets, refinements, and considerable comforts for four persons. A massive figure, relaxed and commanding, got out with a golf-player's agility and came walking over in an easy swagger. The tense hardness left Van der Valk's face and changed to a broad ironic grin. Light soft footsteps passed along the passage, went into the office. Laforêt got up without hurrying and got the whisky bottle off the bar.

"No thanks." He did not take any himself either, but stayed standing with his hands in his pockets and his air of being an interested spectator. The mumble of voices had started with jokes, gone on to the "Any calls?" stage, grown suddenly in intensity, died away to nothing. The soft footsteps sounded harder and then softer on the matting of the passage. The door creaked.

"Good morning, Mr. McLintock," said Van der Valk gently.

CHAPTER TWENTY-THREE

"Mr. McLintock," said Laforêt, entertained. The big man stood still for a moment sizing things up. His thick silver hair looked as benign as ever, but the smooth tanned face was ten years older and twenty years of suspicion nastier. He walked over slowly towards the bar, picked up the whisky bottle and busied himself holding a glass up to the light to make sure that it was clean. Van der Valk struck a match to light a cigarette.

"You certainly made nice time over here. How right I was to wonder what you were after—Mr. Balthasar."

"You know each other?" asked Laforêt, not sounding surprised.

"He's a spy, my boy. Calls himself Balthasar and says he's a Swiss lawyer. He's after you in case you didn't know. The French are interested in you all of a sudden—what you been getting up to, hey? I don't know where he got on to me, though I can guess. I didn't know how much he knew, so I stalled him a bit: thought I'd better get back here and tip you off that DST were offering money to hear your whereabouts." He produced one of his cigars and lit it. "Usual act. You know me—been around enough to know how to handle that. Fed him some cheese but somebody else had flapped his mouth, to judge by what I now see."

"His name's not Balthasar and he isn't Swiss," remarked Laforêt. "He's called Van der Valk. He's a Dutch policeman." Ferocity peeped very quickly out of the watchful grey eyes. He drew carefully on the cigar and said, "Well well well."

"Just a question of getting up a little early, Mr. McLintock. To use your own sensible words, buying a little insurance."

"I'm an interested spectator."

"A little more than that."

The big man grinned, lifted his glass, said "Here's luck" and drank. "Nix. I don't have to tell you. You people always operate on bluff when you don't know where you're going. What you've got on Bos here—Laforêt if you wish—I neither know nor care, but you've nothing on me. No compulsion to tell the truth to somebody nosy that I'm aware of."

"I think you might be a witness. I even think it possible that a judge might want you to tell the truth, which I'm sure would cause pain, though it wouldn't necessarily be lethal, Mr. Desmet—or are you Mr. Desmet?"

"That's my name, Mister Van der Valk. You've been asking—go on asking. Conny Desmet, plain business man and nothing against him. Ask anywhere Brussels, Antwerp—you'll get the same answer. Nothing on him—a plain citizen."

"And in Paris? I already know what answer I get there. A part-time informer, in whose hot little hand DST have slipped a penny from time to time—just as I do occasionally for my own eager little band who telephone me with gossip about their neighbours. Let's not pretend any more."

"Who's denying it?" said Desmet pouring himself some more whisky, "nothing illegal about that. I'm a business man: I keep my ear to the ground. I hear that somebody's looking for a man called Laforêt. Being a friend of his, I think I'd like to know a little more, so I can warn him if necessary."

"And how much is in it to sell him out."

"You know what he offered?" contemptuously, to Laforêt. "A miserable thousand francs to know where you were. Cheapskates."

"How much would you have taken?" asked Laforêt with interest.

"About two," suggested Van der Valk. "He was going to tip you off all right, to get another thousand out of telling me where you'd gone. He was going to nip back to Paris, where I would be sitting on my behind waiting for him. Finding me here is a slight surprise."

He had been hoping to annoy the big man enough to tempt him into imprudence, but insults were small change to him—he had probably got used to much worse.

Laforêt unwrapped a fresh piece of chewing-gum.

"That would be about right," he said. Amazingly relaxed, noticed Van der Valk. Desmet was relaxed in the way a gambler might be who has hedged his bets enough to be sure he will never lose a packet. But Laforêt no longer cared a damn. He had nothing to lose at all. "You've got him pretty well taped," he went on conversationally as though the big man were not there behind the bar an arm's length away from him. "He's a smalltime fixer. Charm boy. Whipped cream to tumble the girls and plenty of cheese for any man who might nibble. Don't underestimate him; he built this business up from nothing. I've never done much more here than earn my keep—he hired me as managerial front man—and parachute instructor of course. He's able, intelligent—he's got a commercial pilot's licence, and he's well in with all the local big-wigs. Right now he's beginning to climb on top and make real money, and he'd be all set to push me off the boat because now he could replace me easily. He's come quite a way. You want to know what DST have on him? He's an ex-Legionnaire—yes, that's where I got to know him; we're ex-comrades." The word "comrades" had a rare sarcasm. Desmet and Van der Valk were both very still.

"He got made a sergeant," went on Laforêt, spitting out his chewing-gum and tossing it in an ashtray. "Always willing, always there, always a smile. But a barrackroom lawyer, knowing all the fiddles. Kept an eye on the main chance. Was very quick to go over to the right way of thinking when the Vietminh told him to, because you see he owed nothing to the French. He was in the Charlemagne crowd when the Germans

220

were looking for sympathizers—joined up as young as he could; really keen."

"I'll remember you, boy, in my will," said Desmet deliberately, "the officer boy—tough para laddie, who crept off into the cave at Dominique."

"That's what he had on me, you see," said Laforêt to Van der Valk smiling.

"I've got a little more than that, and I'm thinking it might be just what this little policeman wants to put you in the bag for—murder."

Laforêt laughed in his face.

"You've missed the bus, big fellow. He's got all he wants."

Desmet smoked his cigar and thought this over slowly, taking his time about it.

"Where's your authority?" he asked Van der Valk suddenly. "You're on my property here, and I can chuck you out any time I feel like it."

"You could indeed," came the mild answer. "It would, though, be a poor tactic. I have a special commission from the Ministry of Justice in The Hague, with which the French, the Belgians and anybody else —I don't know exactly how much petrol you have in those tanks—would make it a special point to cooperate. Suppose I want you taken in by four gendarmes with the wagon—one phone call and a quarter of an hour is what it would take."

"On what charge?"

"Oh, I've the choice of half a dozen," cheerfully. "Obstruction of justice, abetting escape, sheltering a criminal known to be wanted, attempted bribe of a public servant—do I go on?" Desmet was taken aback by the impudence.

"And what proof have you got? Tell me what. What

proof for a second of any of these things? I'd have my lawyer there in five minutes to sue you for wrongful arrest and defamation of character."

"Try it and see," said Van der Valk, "One down another come on. We could hold you for months, sonny, drowning you in bullshit and giving you no end of publicity. Be a setback to all the old pals' circus, all the businessmen in Antwerp and Brussels playing poker dice with Honest Joe McLintock from the Far North—they'd think twice in future about you buying them a whisky."

"You could even do a lot better than that," remarked Laforêt in the pause that followed. "Ask him where he met Esther Marx a month or so ago."

"Do you know?"

"Certainly. What she didn't tell me—she didn't want to cause me pain—he did. Loving every second of it."

Desmet, who was helping himself for the third time to a big whisky, looked slowly from one to the other, his eyes resting on each in turn, coolly weighing it all up, estimating how much harm it could possibly do him. As long as it was only insults . . .

"Sure," he agreed at length affably, "spit it out. Soldier boy has all these years of inferiority complex to get shot of. Spit it out: I'll be real interested. I've got a feeling it's your last few minutes, laddie. You're going to spend the rest of your life behind bars no matter what you do or say. Whereas Conny Desmet is going to walk out a free man, and whatever little scandals you try to go chatting up, people forget. They always forget. Didn't you know? You could do anything, anything—in a few months they'll have forgotten. That's what's so handy about people—they're plastic.

Only little snivellers like you don't forget, who are too goddam stupid to see that everyone else has forgotten." It was getting talkative, thought Van de Valk, but it's drinking quite a lot of whisky there for eleven in the morning. Let it go on by all means—let it drink itself indiscreet and we will see . . .

"Tell me," he said. "Take your time."

CHAPTER TWENTY-FOUR

Esther had been shopping in Rotterdam. About every four months or so she took the car there or to Amsterdam for a day, leaving dinner ready for Ruth and getting back late in the evening. She was always scrupulous on these occasions about bringing back surprise presents, and besides the cotton under-clothes and the pullover marked down, she would make sure that before anything else she got Harry a gaudy sports shirt for weekends, or some new cleaning or mending gadget for the car, or one of the leathery things he liked: a new watch-strap or identity-card folder, a cunning little sheath for his lighter or fountain-pen. Ruth was no problem, since a permanent-wave set for dolls, a miniature dressing-table set—there was always something she had set her heart on within the last month or so and that she would greet with whoops, forgetting the solitary lunch and the lonely wait in the evening while Esther drove back through the rush-hour traffic that always worried Harry, but she was a good driver, with quick reflexes and a cool head.

For herself it was an excuse, really; shopping did not interest her that much. Of course the big stores had more range and a more sophisticated display sense than one found at home, and little expensive boutiques had little expensive frocks—oh yes, one enjoyed looking, and she had a taste for clothes. But apart from the money question she rarely indulged herself—it was too ludicrous. Just every now and then she dressed up for the hell of it, even if it were only to have her hair done or go to the pictures or just lounge about in the flat playing records . . .

She might buy herself a scarf or a pair of gloves. It was much more for the atmosphere that she went. It gave her a tingle still to share pavements with people who moved in a wider world, to have lunch in a proper restaurant and not just a snack bar, to have a pastis and a half-bottle of drinkable Bordeaux and make a waiter skip. Wasn't the Metropole in Hanoi, but there—she didn't want it to be. She knew too well that day-dreams are a more dangerous drug than opium and just as habit-forming. She might be wearing Italian shoes, and perfume, and a coat on her back that had cost money, but she didn't walk about thinking she was the general's wife. Marx has her feet on the ground; she did the same to go to the corner greengrocer. Self-respect. And the old Simca, always spotlessly clean and polished—that was Harry Zomerlust's car and no other.

Nearly six on a fine summer evening—a chilly draught between the buildings but there always was in Rotterdam. She had the car parked down below the Lijnbaan, cleverly, where she could get out into the traffic flow in one smooth turn without any awkward manoeuvring. Damn, some clown had squeezed his fat-bottomed American self in where there was no room, and his front wing so overhung her turning circle that she would certainly not get out without a paint massacre—and she would rather scratch a nearly new Dodge than the silk-smooth home respray on the Ariane, but it was better still to be patient for a few minutes. Belgian registration—they were always like that! Aha, there he came. Company director type with a big black briefcase—lovely soft leather; Harry would like that except what the hell would he do with a briefcase!

"I'm afraid you're jamming me; will you please back out?"

"Sorry mevrouw, sorry. One has to park where one can, you know—why it's Esther."

"I'm very sorry . . . but of course—it's Tuong-ot. You're so damn prosperous I didn't know you for a second. My my, Dodge Dart—I bet you're still flogging penicillin." Great bark of laughter.

"Same old Esther, always insulting everybody. But for God's sake, girl, leave the cars here—perhaps they'll get friendly and have little ones. What's a cross between a Dodge and a Simca?"

Esther laughed. Tuong-ot—a flanneller who would talk his way out of anything.

"A Mickey Mouse designed by General Motors."

"Come and have a drink."

"Well—one—just to let you apologize properly."

"They've pastis at the place across the street—come on."

"Pernod or Ricard?"

"Either—I'm not fussy. I mean it—one. I've an hour's drive."

"Right—I've more than two. Tuong-ot—brings it back. I've almost forgotten—but I hadn't forgotten you." She hadn't forgotten the big Fleming, a Legion sergeant with a notorious creamy tongue and ability to get round any regulation. She hadn't liked him much, but he was harmless. Known as Tuong-ot because of his amazing capacity for the scarlet sauce of pounded hot peppers that went with every Eastern rice dish. The Dutch had it too, brought from Indonesia. Sambal they called it—they spoke Malay over in the Dutch places. But to her it meant Indochina, those little pots of seedy red purée. It had been an affectation of the big Fleming's—smearing it all over everything and shovelling it down as though it were tomato ketchup.

"You still like it?"

"Love it—had it for lunch here—cleaned the pot and sent the boy for more—were his eyes popping!" She laughed, amused. But that was nice about coming to Rotterdam—a harmless silly meeting and a drink at a bar. She picked up her drink and swirled the ice cubes in the old way, as when ice in a drink was the biggest luxury there was and your officers would kiss their fingers in Hanoi with the classic expression "Here's to the terrace outside Fouquet's."

"Here's to old days."

"Here's to the present if you don't mind. To the future if you wish."

"Right," he agreed. "Hell with the old days. Now's the time. Esther—you look great."

"What are you doing?"

"You'll never believe it but I'm in the flyfly industry. Got a little airfield in Limburg, going on great—six planes and they're all mine, and I sit in the driver's seat—every licence you can get on single engines, navigation, the lot. You ought to see us—we get people from Eindhoven, Liège 'swell's Maastricht, Hasselt —you name it."

"Sounds like fun," said Esther mechanically.

"Come on, have another, one for the future and one for the present. What's yours?"

"Dull, feller, dull." She smiled. "Married—yes, army man. What else? I live here—no not here; up the coast. Just quiet. I've had enough excitement."

"Go on, what do you do? Any flying?"

"Not unless I fit the Simca with wings."

"You should come and look us up—no, I mean it— no distance in a car. Fly all you like—teach you to drive—do it myself. Charge? What's that? What, for the girls who flew for us? Nix, nix. And jump—you should come and teach a few of our fat business men to jump. See them shaking like a jelly before they're pushed . . . yes of course we got a parachute school— we got everything except you." He made her laugh with a dramatic funny description of business men who wanted to be heroes, and one massive tycoon from Eindhoven who brought his secretary . . .

"Made her jump ahead of him he did—so that in case his chute didn't open she could catch him on the way down!" Crafty twister he had been in the old days, but people changed. Confidence in themselves, a new career for which they were better suited—this one, he'd never been a real soldier, not what she called a soldier.

She was tempted to take him up on it. Not now, not in a hurry; Esther knew better than to do things in a hurry. But she would turn it around, see how the idea looked.

"Shouldn't be calling you Esther now you're grown up and married and everything."

"That's right, Madame Zomerlust to you, and what's more I only sleep with my husband. But I don't mind —call me Esther if you like—it's the last sentimental corner I have left." The two pastis had made her a bit too relaxed, but she would watch it.

"No, no more."

"Esther—who'd have thought it, gone Dutch! Why you speak Dutch as well as me."

"Better, I hope—le gros Flamand!"

"There's the girl—I haven't been called 'le gros Flamand' in years!"

But he didn't make any passes, treated her with politeness, opened the door for her, gave a little bow when he left her at the car . . .

Ach what—harmless! A tiny touch of nostalgia— like a touch of Tuong-ot on the plain rice of Rotterdam. And she'd been careful to tell him nothing.

It hadn't occurred to her that he had her married name and the number of the Simca—plenty of information for someone with a taste and a talent for working things out.

Ruth had a school holiday—trades union conference of teachers; they never had such things in holiday

times! Agitation about their pay or their pensions—
the army couldn't do such things! One could not speak
of a decision, and anyway she was tired of deciding
things. She had had to decide so many things, from
sometimes speaking French to Ruth to accepting the
fact that she was not going to have another child: she
could not blame Harry, poor devil—it was just one of
those things, and had forced her to yet another decision, that was—almost—as hard, which was that she
was condemned to the Van Lennepweg, or somewhere
very like it, for many many years.

She had had dreams—so much the worse for the
dreams—of a house of her own. Of planting roses and
watching them grow. If she had had two children or
more . . . Regulations!

A bright sunny day. Really she did not care whether
she was making up her mind or whether she was just
drawing a straw to see who got the shortest. She would
take Ruth. It would be exciting for her, to go up in an
aeroplane. And what did it matter—what importance
had someone like the big Fleming? He knew nothing
about her anyway—he had not come back to France
after the summer of fifty-four.

There was another thing; if she went alone he might
consider it as an invitation of sorts. Taking Ruth at
least made it clear that she was not looking for any
"adventures" today, thank you.

It was not the first time she had been out of Holland, even since living in the Van Lennepweg. They
had spent the meagre fortnight of a Dutch holiday in
Denmark, and on a Rhine cruise—and Norway this
year. She had not wanted to go to England, and Harry
—she neither, come to that—had not wanted to go to

France, and small blame to him. Hell, there were plenty of other places. She had sometimes suggested working, tentatively, to make a bit more money for these holidays—just a part-time job. For a few weeks. But no, he wouldn't have it and she didn't press it. He had the right to be awkward about things. He wasn't awkward, anyway. Did he not show absolute trust in her? Did he not give her complete freedom, as far as the Van Lennepweg could give anyone complete freedom? Did he ever ask where she had been, ever ask what she did with money, ever knit his brows at whisky bottles or ciagertte packets? No, he did not.

The border already; the road went easily. Ruth was not a chatterer, and neither is Esther, she thought, smiling slightly. I am a pretty bad mother. I am not exactly a prize packet as a wife either. I try. Marx, quite a good report for effort; I suppose that's something. Takes pains with her appearance, keeps that stinking little apartment in reasonable shape, doesn't get drunk, doesn't whore about.

The big lummox of a Fleming—should she after all turn back? No—Ruth would be horribly disappointed. She was looking forward to it, and had even begged to make a parachute jump. Esther had to promise to make one herself. Didn't have to feel defiant about it, either. It wasn't nostalgia, and it certainly wasn't self-indulgence. Esther didn't know what it was: didn't have much imagination, thank God. Maybe just a bit of snobbery. Nobody in the Van Lennepweg thought much one way or another of little Mevrouw Zomerlust: she wasn't particularly liked, nor was she disliked, she hoped. But she was damn sure of one thing —none of them knew how to make a jump.

Was there disloyalty to one's husband in putting on

overalls again and a jump helmet? Honestly she couldn't see it. She would tell him if it worked. Almost certainly he would laugh in his unmalicious generous way, and tell her to go ahead and enjoy herself because what gave her pleasure pleased him too.

This must be the place. A dozen cars—all a lot grander than the Ariane but she was not going to be ashamed of the Ariane any more than of herself. Fat business men. Give them lessons—all right she would. Remember Gilles—le père Gilles with his glass eye which he took out when he jumped. Been over forty when he made his first jump.

Office place—Ruth was exclaiming with excitement. Now she had to go through with it.

"Just wait outside a moment—I have to go in here. Why don't you go through there, and you can look at the planes?"

She had to be patient for several minutes while a big sporting golfing character went on about putting the papers through and how many hours he had. Her turn at last—soppy girl with stupid clothes and a ghastly shade of lipstick, who looked at her as though she wasn't rich enough for this league.

She had to straighten the cow out a bit. Conny Desmet was giving a lesson and would be down in twenty minutes, but . . .

"No, I'm an old friend." *Le gros Flamand* was not exactly a friend but that was no business of office girls. "I came to do a jump."

"Oh, but that's Mr. Bos—he's in charge of that— oh yes, he's around." Who the hell was Mr. Bos? But Ruth would be fidgeting. The girl got up and looked through the window.

"Oh yes, there he is on the apron. Is that your little girl? Well, that's him talking to her."

Esther walked out into a smell of creosoted wood baked by a bright September sun, of dried grass and motor oil, her heart lifting and contracting at remembered smells, remembered excitements. It was Pau again, Pau where she had made her first jump ever. Yes, she wanted to buckle a harness on again, tighten the heavy straps around her thighs, feel that sharp empty air as she jumped into it and the exquisite second after one punched the release on one's stomach and felt the snatch of the chute. There was a glare that blinded her a second and then she saw him. The muscles in her calves and thighs jumped and twitched furiously; the blood roared in her throat and head.

Him. Talking to his daughter. She walked slowly, shakily, as though the dusty concrete on which the air danced and shimmered were the thigh-deep black mud of a delta ricefield. She stood there a metre behind Ruth, waiting for him to see her. She said nothing because there was nothing to say. What could one say?

"Drop dead?"

"I love you?"

"Good afternoon?"

"Hallo Mevrouw—seems I've a pupil here, or have I two . . ."

His turn to stand rooted. Esther made a monstrous effort not to be a fly stuck on the flypaper.

"Come, sweetie." Ruth looked properly astonished, never having been called sweetie in her life.

"She's told me her name," said Laforêt slowly.

God it was cowardly. Look at him. Speak to him. Say something. Jump you fool. And she couldn't jump . . . Esther Marx . . . couldn't jump . . .

233

"Come, Ruth."

"Why?" She was flabbergasted, naturally. She was getting along fine!

"I don't know—it's the wrong place or something. I must have got something wrong but they've no place —no room or something. They're booked up. Come; I'm going to buy you an ice."

She had gone to a great deal of trouble, working out all sorts of elaborate details to forget her cowardice. Buying a picnic lunch, taking Ruth swimming and hiring two bathing costumes from a Belgian who plainly thought her an imbecile, driving all the way over beyond Liege into the Ardennes, getting stranded with no petrol—lord, behaviour of a startled virgin—going back through Spa and up to Maastricht, letting Ruth drink beer mixed with lemonade and spending an awful lot of money . . .

She had managed to raise her eyes after bending down stupidly, dizzily, to fix Ruth's sandal strap, with which there was nothing whatever the matter. Just for a moment she had managed to meet his eyes before dragging the protesting child back to the car. She didn't know what her expression had been, but she hoped it had somehow managed to convey "I'm sorry" and that he would have understood what she meant.

For weeks she had waited for the consequences, knowing there would somehow be consequences, uneasy and frightened, cursing herself for a fool, trying to be less surprised at her agitation. After all, seeing somebody for the first time since the night in the bar you shot him—bound to be a *bit* of a shock however you looked at it. Even after twelve years. It made her furious that she could not even tell Harry, even hint —caught in her own trap: had it not been herself that had laid it down so adamantly that whatever happened the past would never never never come up between them?

Had he seen in that one second that whatever she did or said she would go back to him at the drop of his hat—if something did not stop her?—and one minute she found herself praying desperately that something would not stop her, and the next second that it would.

Would he find out where she was? Perhaps through Desmet? Would Desmet? She knew—she knew—that sooner or later she would find one or other of them waiting for her.

Esther did not tell anyone what she went through in the fortnight which followed. Laforêt—who was cursed with too much imagination—later thought that he had some idea.

It was Desmet who came. She was quite glad when at last it happened. And glad that he was so easy, so unembarrassed, so casually ready to admit he had spied her out. He had enough brass for a whole military band, that one. And the easy accustomed swank of a drum-major marching at its head.

Esther lost hers. Her head, she meant. Right bang there in the Van Lennepweg he walked in at the door as unconcerned and confident as the man come to tell you you've won ten thousand on the football pool. "*Good* morning, Mevrouw. We've a simply great piece of news for you."

Of course the great piece of news that people like Desmet brought was their own marvellous self. There he was, in his beautifully cut suit and shirt, with that lovely soft black leather briefcase exactly as though selling insurance, and his broad sunny smile. Walked

235

in before it entered her head that she could have shut the door again.

"Hallo, Esther." Cheerleader.

"I'm sorry, the place is a mess. My girl's at school. I wasn't expecting anyone. I'm sorry, sit down. Can I offer you something?—I've some whisky," desperately.

"I'd love that. Trust Esther to have something good." In her nervousness and haste she poured herself an enormous one, far bigger than she intended, slopping some on her fingers. It was a brand new bottle of Johnny Walker, bought just that morning, the tissue paper still wound round the bright red and gold label. When he went it was empty, and she stayed sitting there looking at it, tipping it up to her mouth to get the last drops out, throwing it in the bin and crawling after it to get it back out, with an absurd notion of sticking it up on a bracket with a ribbon round it and a little gold-edged card saying "Esther Marx is a whore—everybody knows that." Esther Marx is a whore, Esther Marx is a whore, beating in her head, beating with drums, in march time. The drums swelled and banged inside her head, and the boots of a column of soldiers following, cracking down in rapid rhythm. Boots, boots, boots, boots . . . Go on, boots, kick me to death.

A slogan. Chant it, *sur l'air des lampions*. Esther Marx—*is* a whore.

"I thought now Conny, you have to pass by to apologize. Without knowing or even guessing—and that was damn stupid of you, boy, you've caused her one hell of an embarrassment, and now how could you be so damn dim?

"Sure I knew where you lived. Went to some trouble to find out. Couldn't leave you thinking that old Conny would be such a bastard as just not to do anything at all, just laugh and say too bad, let's forget it. Wouldn't do that to any girl. And Esther! No no no no no.

"Honest, you won't believe a man could be such a total clot, but I never thought. Why sure, I knew you used to go about with him in Hanoi, but then we all used to do some queer things in those days. I never knew, of course, there was anything big in it. And those days—well, jesus, we used to do some things then, didn't we? I reckon there's a lot of us did things we'd be a bit ashamed of now. But it's all such old stuff, isn't it? I mean to say, these people that go about holding reunions and remembering where they were back at good old El Alamein or wherever, they're simply not for real. Stuff like that one keeps for kids who've never grown up. Mean to say—I'll admit it; couldn't be less than honest with a girl like you —I had heard something years after from some guy I knocked up against who used to be in the old mob, good old Third Thirteenth, and he told me some garbled story of a row back there in France. But I mean, I never gave it a thought. Long forgotten. You too— why it's obvious, you've got your own life, went off and got married and all, didn't just hang about brooding.

"No, I'll explain. I was setting up the airfield deal and I was just wishing I knew somebody who was a parachute instructor because that's great stuff and who do I run up against in a bar in Brussels but Lieutenant Laforêt and who else do I remember as one hell of a crackerjack jumper and who else is better-looking for a job like that—and what's more he's thinking of changing jobs. Well I mean there's no question of his being an employee or something, but he makes the ideal partner, and if he's got no money to put into the business that's all right, he works and takes responsibility. Managing director you'd say, and Conny's president or something, belting round the countryside to whip the businessmen into garaging their planes at Conny's place . . ."

How it had gone on. And she had drunk more and more in her fever and uncertainty and fear, and had got drunk, for the first time since the night in the bar when she had taken the pistol out, the one she had taken from his suitcase. Drunk. Drunk as a stinking slut. And of course it had ended the way such scenes always ended, with her getting up to empty ashtrays, and being pushed up against the wall in the kitchen, pushed back through into the living-room, pushed over on the living-room sofa. Didn't it always end that way? What else was Esther Marx good for, in heaven's name?

She had gone into the lavatory and vomited and vomited and then got under the shower, sitting huddled on the tiled floor and letting water wash over her until it was time for Ruth to come home and she had drunk cup after cup of strong coffee and forced herself to be a suburban mum.

Suburban mum tumbled by the milkman.

She hadn't wanted to live any more. And then one day he had come, ten days after the other.

CHAPTER TWENTY-FIVE

He hadn't come barging into the house. He had waited lord knew how many hours outside being unobtrusive. Days for all she knew.

"Esther." It had been hardly over a whisper. But at least the Desmet episode had broken her out of the rigid shell. She didn't have to play the blushing house-wife. She could look at him naturally, speak to him unselfconsciously, have a normal human contact without freezing, or opening and shutting her mouth like a gaffed fish.

"You shouldn't have come here, you know."

"I know. But I had to. You know?"

"Yes. But not here. I'll meet you. Wait—in an hour.

239

No—tonight. Nine tonight." Harry had a duty, a guard or a fire picket or something.

"I was very amenable," remarked Laforêt with his tissue-paper smile. "A well-brought-up little boy, and a malleable, suggestible man."

He went on speaking in the same slow careful voice; he seeemed to have forgotten Desmet standing just the other side of the little bar, immobile and menacing, sipping whisky with an ugly detachment.

"Where did you meet her?" interjected Van der Valk, colourless.

"The railway station buffet—there's nothing more classic than that, is there? An emotional scene would not be noticed." But there had been no emotional scene. Esther had flinched, once, but she would not flinch again.

She spoke bleakly; when she spoke of herself she spoke harshly. But her voice was gentle.

"I have tried to make something. I wanted to make a human being happy. I suppose it will fail, but I will have tried. It must seem very laughable and somehow pathetic, what I tried. You haven't seen my home, and you're not going to. Well, it's just a rotten little council flat. You haven't seen my husband, and you're not going to, because if anybody tries to involve him in my dirty stories I'd kill him. I mean kill him, as I would a cockroach, with no more feelings about it. He's just a quiet working man. Nobody thinks much of him. He doesn't think much of himself. But he's worth the lot of us put together. I don't love him, but I'd go to prison for him, and if need be I'd die for him. You don't understand that, because once I went to prison for you, and would have died for you, and you thought that quite all right, because I loved you.

"It won't even surprise you to hear I still love you. You'll take that as quite evident and normal. That's how it should be. Faithful Esther, through all these years, I'm her man.

"So I'm going to ask you to go away. Just for once to consider yourself something unimportant. Are you able to do that? I'm not going to see you again, and won't run away with you, or sleep with you in secret, or anything, much as I'd like to. I've looked after your daughter, and I'm trying to let her grow up in a way you'd be proud of, but I'm not letting you see her either. Even though with you I could have been very happy.

"You see, you go around with this certainty that everyone looks at you. That you are under a curse, just because of a moment when your nerve failed. It's just egoism, can you see? One isn't important enough. You keep on creeping around thinking you are being humble, and you're just exalting yourself. You've blamed yourself all these years for not being like Hervouet. You remember Hervouet?"

Of course he did. Nobody had forgotten the young tank captain, with the pale, fragile-seeming student's face, who had fought the battle with both arms in plaster casts, who had come through to the last day, only to die on the march to the Viet camps.

"Romantic," and the word in Esther's mouth was a distillation of derisory bitterness. "You are asked to be like Guérin, who lost both legs and shot himself rather than risk the lives of the men he knew would come for him. Understand that of all things the last I ask you to do is to shoot yourself. That would be just one more crowning egoism. Just remember instead what Langlais said—yes, I know, you don't care to be reminded of him. Somebody complained of being tired.

" 'Tired?' he said. 'And us? You weren't asked for your advice, but to come and have your face broken with us.'

"Remember all the boys who got up from their hospital beds. The boy with one eye and his face in pieces. Fox, Le Page, Guy de la Malène. You think that because you once broke the solidarity and they threw you out you are forever in exile, forever in darkness—and you've loved it. Now rejoin."

He had stared at her stupidly, mechanically stirring the spoon in half a cup of cold railway station coffee, thick and syrupy in the thick white railway station china.

"I want to ask you another thing," went on Esther, inexorable. "You've got a pretty good job there, haven't you?"

"Not bad—not that good," hastily.

"No, but comfortable," and there was irony in the word "comfortable." "A soft easy job, undemanding. And you can show off to people. And you don't have to rub yourself against the ruck of common stupid folk. A select, classy lot."

"Not a bit of it," but she brushed his words aside.

"Jammy. Those little planes, and that windswept airfield stuff. You've learned to pilot and all, and you teach them to jump."

"I had to take what I could. I'd no training, no skills—I knew nothing else." Esther picked up her handbag and stood up.

"Leave it," she said softly. "Go far away. Not for me or because of me. That man is a bad man. A vicious man. I do not know why. But I know that he is only waiting for an opportunity to blackmail you. Just as he is only waiting for a chance to blackmail me. But he knows that I will not yield to that. Though I yield to everything else. Goodbye." She had walked straight away from him.

"Esther," he had called, jumping up from the bewilderment of her finality. But she was already gone, and he dared not make a scandal. He had reason to know that Esther was not to be trifled with.

His peace was gone and he fidgeted about unhappily, trying to think it out. It was too bad, really. Say what she liked, he had a job in which he could respect himself. And in the three years he had had it he was a new man. What had he ever done before? A pack of rubbishy salesman jobs in Brussels, till he had had the luck to meet Conny one day, and over a drink Conny had said, "By God this is a stroke of luck" with a conviction not only fervent but genuine.

Conny had found the wilderness of fields and tumbledown farm buildings. He had his first plane, and a tiny bit of money. He was giving all he had to persuade the bank to back him up, and a few business men to give him a loan. And he had worked; how he had worked. But he had to be constantly away, nourishing and watering the "tap roots" as he called them, and he knew no one whom he could trust or who would work at the day-to-day unglamorous task of turning the depressing mudheap down in Limburg into an aeroclub. Laforêt was his man.

A bad man? He had known Conny's reputation as a barrackroom lawyer. A fiddler, shifty, dishonest; servile and insolent in turn. But a good sergeant, whom his men liked, and who could get the best out of them. A driver. And that had been in the army, and Conny was not a soldier, it was plain to see. He was a businessman, and he didn't want to become sergeant major—he wanted to become rich, to be respected, to carry weight. To forget all the little mean tricks and extortions to which he had been forced to resort in his frenzy to climb out of the ruck of anonymity.

Laforêt himself got on with Conny. They both knew that in the past of the other were some not very brilliant episodes. And they disregarded it. It was as though each was determined to show the other the best that was in him. And together they had worked. It had grown to be a genuine powerful bond between them, the work that they did together. They had built the aeroclub literally brick by brick, themselves, just the two of them. Laforêt had spent weeks on end isolated in that dump, day and night, guarding the little heaps of pathetic equipment as though it were Fort Knox. And Desmet had been away nearly every day, but nearly every evening he had returned, bearing loot. A few bags of cement in the old Mercedes (they still used it to tow gliders), a mysterious wheezing junk-heap lorry he had picked up for two sous and which had been cajoled and bullied into carrying sand. For concrete was what they needed before anything, since for nine months in the year the place was a bog, and neither car nor plane could manoeuvre in the clinging mud.

Desmet used to bring supplies of anything he could pick up—a bag of potatoes or a box of oatmeal had sometimes been the only food they had. Sometimes sausage, crates of beer, great lumps of smoked meat. No matter how hard his day had been Conny would carefully wash a shirt, press a suit, polish his shoes—

ready for next day. And then get his overalls on and lumber about like a bull. He was tremendously strong and it was good to see him sweating and bawling, thundering across wobbly planks with the wheelbarrow full of liquid concrete.

He remembered the triumph with which Conny had brought home the puttering one-horse cement mixer, the friendly architect who had drawn plans for them (he was now one of their best customers), the plumber who had advised about drainage, old Pete the mechanic who was fed up with his bankrupt Antwerp garage—he was no businessman. Old Pete wouldn't shovel sand, but he could and did make the plane and the precious auto go, and he ate what they did, slept where they did—he was one of the team. But he, Laforêt, he had built this place, he and Conny.

And Conny was never discouraged, never failed in his confidence, his tough gaiety, his songs and laughter, even when things had gone badly, those long evenings of the first summer when the bank withdrew support and it all seemed doomed. On Sundays he would put on his good suit and walk around like the big businessman come to see how his investment is getting on, to impress the Sunday drivers, the tourists who stopped out of curiosity and asked what was going on. He would take the plane up, just simple circuits over the field. "To believe that this will be a real aeroclub they've got to see a plane flying," he used to say. "Otherwise to them it's just another cattleshed." He had taught Laforêt to fly, those summer Sundays, had brought back parachutes and harnesses fiddled heaven knew where, and they had made whitewashed circles for a jump target out by the road to give a free exhibition the moment more than half a dozen cars had parked there of a Sunday afternoon.

He couldn't let Conny down.

For they had won, in the end. Conny had bought the Chevrolet (it too now towed planes and gliders) before he had got the Dodge. And before he had the Dodge he had come back with the Fiat, which was a demonstration model from a big agency, as good as new. Italian racing red, the twin carburettor high-performance model, throwing the keys to Laforêt and saying, "This one's yours, cocker. You've been stuck here damn near two winters, as good as never going out. Now's the moment to take off for a week. Go to Brussels and live it up a bit."

From that day they hadn't looked back. There had been money in the bank. People had started coming, for lessons, flips. Conny had gone on, never looking back, never sitting still, never contented with himself. Charters, gliders, the gymnasium where the enterprising could learn jumps on the static line.

The flat too had been Conny's idea. He still slept in a cupboard affair behind the bar, along with the fuse-boxes and the fire extinguisher, but he had insisted that Laforêt should have proper living quarters.

"And this is not just to impress customers. This is needed for you. Hell, for every night I'm here there's one I can sleep in hotels, have a proper bath, go into the restaurant and pick up a menu. You have to have something to give you self-respect." And the flat had been built, with its kitchen and bathroom, and the cleaning woman had been found. Laforêt drove most mornings into Hasselt to pick her up; by then she would have done the marketing, and would bring food, fresh vegetables and fruit. A wine merchant from Liège came out and stocked the bar. Conny knew how to get licences and permissions—never once were they held up with administrative paperwork. And now there was even a girl receptionist to keep accounts and plan schedules. Daisy thought she ran the whole place singlehanded . . . Conny's doing again. He knew how to manage women!

One could not let Conny down. He was puzzled, worried, and bit his nails more than he had in ten years.

CHAPTER TWENTY-SIX

He mentioned it himself, finally. And as soon as he had he saw from Conny's expression that he himself was just a simpleton. What had he ever been but the pick and the shovel? Conny Desmet was the brains. He had known how to flannel round regulations and how to wheedle ten thousand francs. He knew how to swing hardheaded business men off their feet, as well as how to put the girls floating horizontal. And above all, he knew how to be patient, never to hurry a deal, never to show himself anxious or nervous, never to appear pinched or crowded. A good business man, who will hold on to the slightest little thing that may turn out one day to have value. Stow it away and let it accumulate interest, and when you have a market for it you can hold out for a good bargain. Laforêt could never do that. He wouldn't know how.

When he did finally mention Esther's name he understood that Desmet had been waiting quietly for this moment, sure it would come, sooner or later. Had been playing with him the way a cat would with a mouse.

Has Conny then been playing with me all these years? Suddenly he did not know, and there was no solid ground any more at all.

They were drinking coffee together; a still morning of early autumn when the thin bony easterly has turned the dew to frost and sends long pale spears of sunshine through the white mist. Laforêt was grilling the day-before's bread on an electric toaster. Desmet, hairy across the shoulders, smears of talcum powder on his thick upper arms, was hunting clean things out of the laundry suitcase.

"It amuses me occasionally—" Laforêt in a drawl, stirring his coffee—"the possibility—I mean it's remote but it can always happen—seeing someone from old times. Kind of funny sensation. You know how much you've changed yourself, and how everybody else must have changed, and suddenly you see a face that was once familiar. Like when every now and then you hear someone talking French in Flanders and you wonder who the hell that can be—somebody out of a different world."

"You talking about Esther Marx?" asked Desmet nonchalantly, his thick fingers picking a sleevelink deftly from between his teeth and working it into the cuff. "Yeh, I ran across her up in Rotterdam a few days ago—she lives there along the coast some place.

I was chinning with her a while on the parking lot, and 'having a drink in memory of the good old days' —these old days you're always brooding about and which have about as much importance as a potato you chuck out because it's frozen."

"What's she doing now?"

"There you are—all flustered and lamentable straight off."

"Chuck it, Conny."

"She's married to some bum in the Dutch army—I ask you."

"So what?" allowing irritation to creep into his voice —Conny's trick of always knowing everything about everybody invariably rasped, which was illogical—he wanted very badly to know . . .

"Why, in that time—and no offence to you, old son, because I remember you escorting her about everywhere in Hanoi—nothing ever did for those girlies below the rank of officer. Things find their level like I'm always telling you—married to some technical sergeant—how dim can you get?"

"You know she turned up here a week ago. Backed out when she saw me—that's natural enough. You're never embarrassed, but other people are."

"What about it? Yeh, Daisy told me. You mean you were embarrassed?"

"A bit. After all—awkward situation. I suppose she was curious after seeing you. She was what d'you call it—disconcerted. You've got a brass gut; it beats me how you can be so insensitive."

Desmet was drinking coffee placidly.

"I've got weak spots, same as anyone else—but when I think them just damn stupid I try and get rid of them. A soldier second class or a general—all equal now, no? Look for the other fellow's weak spot is my motto—don't go about parading your own. Give me some more coffee, would you?

"Yeh, I got a laugh out of seeing little Marx— amusing girl. I was kidding about a bit over a drink, saying why don't you come down and show a few of our fat chemists here how to jump without getting their foot in their mouth. I didn't know she'd take it so seriously though. Must have a hankering for those good old days all right, when she was a sort of heroine."

"Now hell, Conny," exasperated. "What did you do that for, knowing perfectly well I wouldn't be exactly delighted."

"Now Frankie," mimicking head in the dust, mock apologetic, "I never meant to upset you. But snap out of it, brother. That old shindy . . . this little mare dropped you in the shit once—you've told me and I'd heard rumours once—but who cares now? Bit of ass's skin. You can't go round the world scared of meeting people. Look at you—climbing up steady, same as me. Are we respected by all? Sure. Despite having come from nothing? Not a bit; because of it, more like. Do we boast of the time we had nothing to eat but potatoes? Not specially, but we aren't bloody well ashamed of it either. What's this girl now? All these years gone by, and just the same tarted-up little fancypants with dreams about the good old days when you could tell who was the big guy by the number of his shoulder-straps. You wonder why she comes here? Just an attempt to pretend she isn't pushing forty by now. Recapture her youth. Going about begging for diversions. Gave me her address—here, you want it?" hunting in his pockets and producing an old envelope, "no good to me—I got other fish to fry. You could have her back tomorrow if it amused you. Fall off in your hand like a ripe plum. Ought to try it really—you never have enough confidence in yourself. Jumpy little trout still too—be a good joke to put horns on the Dutch army." Desmet laughed at this gay thought, and finished tying his tie. "Ey, I got to get up on my toes. Did I tell you about that Piper Navajo?—fellow's hesitating still. I got him in my little eye. Going to appear a bit casual over in Aachen, and if the price is right—and I'll make damn sure it is right . . . Ey?"

The envelope had the result of Conny Desmet's detective work scribbled on it.

"PX 7799-25. Zomerlust." Under was scribbled "Tech sarg. Juliana Caserne Alphen." Lower down was 'Van Lennep 432." Laforêt brooded about this for some days. Later, he would ask himself how on earth he could have been so astonishingly naïve. It simply never occurred to him that if Esther had really given Conny her address she would hardly have bothered to dictate her car number.

"George," shouted Desmet. "Hey, George!" It was one of his tricks when in an especially good mood to call people by imaginary names. "Come on out here 'n' I'll show you my new gun. Boyboyboy, what a sweet job. Fellow I met in Antwerp in a bar, one of these United Nations clowns, was a bit short on drinking money and offered to sell me a souvenir of Sinai. Israeli—Uzzi it's called. These Yids, they know how to handle Arabs—say that for them. Look, the trigger and the grip are synchronized, kind of a safety device. Have a good day? Say, at that, you were up in Amsterdam, did you think of giving Marx a bang on the way?"

"No," lied Laforêt stoutly. "No—you were quite right—the past has no importance. Good gun, this. You want to try and get one of these Chinese ones they're talking about—AK something. No: no, it doesn't matter to me; I've forgotten about it."

"I thought of it," chuckled Desmet, handling the gun lovingly, taking it down and putting it together with a grunt of appreciation at the simplicity and cleverness of the mechanism. "Wish I'd had this—to poke her with, ha ha. Boom boom. Yeh, I flannelled her with 'Aw, Esther, never meant to embarrass you.' Got her a bit pissed—likes her whisky. There never was anything easier—it's just not possible how easy she fell over. Don't need to point a gun at that one, I can tell you. Mmm—baby! Now look—see the old notice board—that's an Arab." He fired an expert half-second pattern. "Dead Arab. What a little beauty. Christ—better clear that up all the same, or the Customs men will think I'm training to go out to Angola to fight for liberty, haw."

The café was the model of all Dutch cafés, with its polished nickel, Oriental-pattern woolly tablecloths, Heinekin beermats in a regimented square. The place was nearly empty in mid afternoon, and the neat grey-haired cafékeeper quite ready for gossip.

"Gimme a beer, would you? . . . Get a lot of soldiers I dare say, with the barracks opposite?"

"Not really—I don't encourage that noisy crowd. Get the permanent staff—they're quiet. Come in for a beer at knocking-off time—they all live out, you follow me." He polished the spotless coffee machine carefully.

"I've an idea I know one of the sergeants—Zomerlust." Nod, indifferent.

"Quiet chap—nice fellow. Belgian, aren't you? Never rains but it pours, as they say. Was a Belgian chap in the other day who knew Zomerlust—been in Korea together I do believe: they were having a beer together."

"I was in Korea myself."

"Old soldiers talking over the campaigns, what. I was in the Resistance myself. Another beer?"

"No thanks. Got to be moving."

"On the way through to Utrecht? See quite a few Belgian cars on the road—one of these big American sleighs this other chap had. One guilder—I thank you kindly. Good road to you."

He hadn't needed the confirmation of the car—Desmet beyond doubt. Trust him, to check up on the husband before going on to the wife! He stood for a moment looking at the barracks. It seemed to him that he lost all sense of time, and that past and present and future were all there mingled in one thread. Desmet . . . taking his little pleasures in Holland . . . Esther . . . "That is a bad man" . . . Zomerlust, who had been in Korea. Been in France—another to enjoy Esther's favours. Who hadn't, after all? Probably a well-known bicycle for half the camp. Odd—the soldiers there in fatigue uniforms, cleaning up the half-track . . . their berets were wrong. Not French soldiers.

He shook his head out of its daze. Idiot—for a moment he had thought this was France. Or was it

Hanoi? He looked around the big cool café as though expecting to see Esther in uniform sitting waiting over a whisky. Waiting for him . . . And a couple of Indochina captains in the corner, laughing across the Ricards. Silly . . .

Trust Desmet. The little bastard.

CHAPTER TWENTY-SEVEN

Desmet was helping himself to more whisky. Was it the fifth, or only the fourth? Van der Valk had lost count. It didn't matter much, with the size they were!

"Biggest load of bullshit I ever heard," said Desmet contemptuously.

"I quite agree," said Van der Valk with great politeness. "You would reply, I gather, that he has mixed all this up together in his mind. Brooding over it has blurred the outlines between fact and imagination. Now he's telling a pack of lies but he doesn't realize that himself. He believes in it all. That about it?"

He had been studying Desmet quietly for some time, while the recital of grief and bewilderment went on in Laforêt's dulled monotone. He had talent, the fellow! Would make a good policeman—of the kind that takes bribes . . . He could see the crafty sod though, spreading persuasive warmth through a café, finding, with that odd instinct of his, the right words, the right tone to palm a man like Zomerlust, who had exactly the innocence, the peculiar military purity, that made him vulnerable to a man like that. Desmet could have sold him insurance, a secondhand auto—anything . . .

"The interesting thing about all this," he began gently, almost pedantically, "is that of course either of you could have killed Esther Marx." His turn to get a contemptuous look from the lounging Desmet. "We have no material proof."

"Don't be a fool, man—he admits it!"

"Dramatics," said Van der Valk coldly. "It's commonplace. He feels guilt, as he always felt guilt. Now that he has found something to confess to—something he finds fitting and properly tragic—he's only too pleased."

"You mean you don't believe him?" incredulous.

"Mr. Desmet, you are a man of some intelligence, and experience."

"I'm that all right."

"But if you had heard the number of false confessions I have you would be less confident."

"Christ, man, he was there."

"So were you. Both of you knew where to find her, knew enough of Zomerlust's movements, could plan a little assassination without any real technical snags. Both of you knew about the gun, could handle it, had access to it. There is no strong material probability either way."

"But," the deep throaty voice rose suddenly, ready to crack, "what about his motive? He had every motive. What possible motive could I have, in God's name? The woman didn't matter a burnt match to me one way or another."

"Oh, as to that," said Van der Valk almost shyly, "I could construct motives for you very easily. If only your enormous vanity. I begin to understand Esther. She realized, at a given point—quite possibly the moment after you had filled her with whisky and pushed her over—that you were a far more contemptible person than the man she had once shot—and would have killed. She could—and to my thinking did—find the words to bring that home to you in pungent terms. I am speculating and it has no importance. You know this yourself, you live with the constant, uninterrupted knowledge of your own character—it is possibly what makes you at once an aggressive salesman and an accomplished actor. None of my business, fortunately."

"I'll say it's none of your business," grunted Desmet. The immense quantities of whisky were making his eyes tiny. Reddened and malevolent they squinted at Van der Valk as though trying to figure whether this lunatic really meant what he said.

Laforêt seemed lost in some obscure vision of his own, the head tilted forward so that the bright blond hair obscured the youthful healthy face. Psychologically immature and oh, etcetera etcetera, thought Van der Valk impatiently. So oddly likeable. He hated those jargon terms, so glib and plummy, so pitifully inexact and inadequate. Laforêt, for the last hour, had put a more concrete image into his mind, that of Wozzeck. The soldier who saw visions, who was bullied by the Doctor and jeered at by the Drum Major, who killed his Marie without understanding, virtually without knowing . . .

"There are other hypotheses," he went on, his voice beginning to take on the rough joviality, almost vulgarity, with which he conducted business. "It would be quite permissible to suppose that Desmet killed this woman with considerable calculation, knowing as he did that he possessed the perfect patsy. Laforêt was a useful tool, no doubt, but had outlived much of his value, besides being a continual reminder of Esther Marx alive or dead. The man kept his ear to the ground, as he says with pride. One of his little insurance policies, as well as an occasional small supplement to income, was to act as an informer for DST. Very prettily thought out. The big Fleming, very patriotic—he hated the French. He always hated Laforêt just as he always hated Esther Marx. He had collaborated with the Viets, and finished with what amounted to a bad conduct discharge from the Legion. His endless loud protest that the past meant nothing to him shows in itself that it rankled more than he cared to think. The French were repsonsible for many past humiliations. But it would be wise to keep a foot in their camp—just as at Dien Bien Phu. When he heard that DST, for obscure reasons of their own, were taking an interest in Laforêt, the time had certainly come to rid himself of an embarrassing accomplice."

Desmet's big head hunched between his massive shoulders, and his whisky breath came hoarse across the bar counter.

"Very nice, very ingenious, very fancy." His hand flapped heavily on the shiny plastic. "All froth. Prove it, that's all I ask, prove it."

"You mistake the function of an officer of police,
Van der Valk told him pleasantly. "Proof is a juridical
fiction. All I do is present a person to a judge. The
judge then decides whether there is a case to answer."

The big man changed at once to his purring, whee-
dling manner.

"Look, fellow, what you're after is too complicated
and involved for a simple chap like me. I say that
what you've been telling us here is all moonshine, and
I'll stick to that—that's my right, isn't it? If this guy
here chooses to admit to a lot of killings that's strictly
his business. No judge could hold me on what you're
building up. He killed her. You got a prejudice against
me—all right, I admit I'm no saint, and then what?
You're trying to fix this on me. Nix friend, nix."

Van der Valk stood up, straightened his shoulders
and looked the man in the eyes, his face and voice
heavy and serious.

"You're right again, Desmet. But there's a point the
judge won't miss. A thing that's been worrying me
since the day I started on this, the day I was called to
look at Esther Marx's dead body. She was killed completely, unemotionally—and smoothly. The assassin
thought of waiting until the television was broadcast-
ing a loud gangster serial, full of bangs and gunshots,
which could—and to a certain extent did—cover
whatever noise he made. That was not spontaneous—
that was planned. The noise was heard by one person,
a housewife across the hall. She thought that Mevrouw
Zomerlust had fallen off a ladder or some such accident, and being a helpful soul she came to see. She
knocked on the door. With striking presence of mind
the assassin opened it, hid in the bathroom just behind

it, waited till she had gone forward nervously, hesitating, into the living-room, waited for her to be hit by the shock—and slipped quietly out, in as steady and unflustered a way as could be thought of.

"I don't like Laforêt for that bit of business, and neither will the judge. But I do like you for it. Whether the judge will remains to be seen. He just might find a witness who remembered seeing you. So eat it, and like it—I'm taking the two of you in." He walked to the door and opened it. "Don't make the mistake of running. There's nowhere to run to. That plane of yours—a general alarm, and the radar screen picks you up inside three minutes. On the end of that telephone line," he pointed to the phone box across the passageway, "is the machine. Be a big boy, and let me handle this quietly."

He walked across the hallway to the office, and flashed his badge at the astonished young woman.

"Commissaire van der Valk, criminal brigade of the Dutch police. Ring the local station, ask for the duty officer, and give me the instrument." The girl stared at him frightened, hesitated, and stretched a limp hand towards her phone.

"Put it down, Daisy." Desmet stood in the doorway, rumpled, sweaty, drunk. Must be drunk. It seemed the only explanation for a foolish move. He had a gun in his hand, an American police positive. Van der Valk did not care for the look of this in the hands of a drunk. He half turned, centred his stick on the ground between his feet, and rested both hands upon it.

"A gangster serial," he said cuttingly. "You propose to shoot me, shoot this girl who is a witness, shoot Laforêt who is another, and burn the whole place down in flames, ringed around by all the cops in Limburg. A James Cagney movie, nineteen thirty-six. Put it down, clot. Ring the number," he added to the girl.

Desmet started to back towards the door to the field, holding the gun pointed towards Van der Valk, who stood watching, unamused.

"You're a bloody paratrooper, Laforêt—take the thing away from him."

"No."

Laforêt stood in the other doorway, his hands in his pockets, chewing a matchstick.

"No, Mister van der Valk. Let him go, if he wants. You've got what you want—you've got me. But by myself. I don't want him. This business is between Esther and me. Just the two of us. Not him. He hasn't anything to do with this."

"Ring that number," snapped Van der Valk over his shoulder—this halfwit was going to muck everything up. But the girl was too paralysed by the melodrama to do anything.

"Come on, Frankie," shouted Desmet suddenly. "Don't let youself be bluffed, boy. I'll hold the gun on him—cut the bloody phone wires. Take them half an hour before they know what they're doing, and I'll have you out of this. Stand on me—I don't care for him and his Interpol. I know how to fox the radar."

"Whisky talking," remarked Van der Valk to the floor.

Laforêt appeared to make up his mind. He stepped forward quietly, softly, moving on the balls of his feet, looking very like a paratrooper. He took a knife out of his pocket, grinned at Van der Valk with a broad boyish charm—it was very like the photo he had had

262

taken after he got his parachutist's wings, aged nineteen, thought the policeman. He cut the telephone wire, backed so that the gun stayed pointing at Van der Valk, did the same with the instrument in the hall.

"Retreat through the jungle," he said with a tone that sounded boyishly gleeful. "Leave it to me, Conny. Anything you want? Clothes—money?"

"Just my briefcase—there on the chair. Don't worry boy—I've got friends. Dutch people!" He spat, like a street urchin.

"Have it your way," said Van der Valk coolly. "Perhaps it's just as well."

"You tanked well up?" asked Laforêt.

"Plenty, Frankie, plenty. Conny's thinking of these things. Conny's mind has nothing wrong with it. Never hesitate. Pity about all this, you're thinking. Have no fear. Leave it to Conny." He flattened himself against the wall to let Laforêt pass, and wiggled the police positive nastily. Van der Valk moved his stick a little forward to lean on it more comfortably. The gun went off with a sudden blast that made the girl scream, and the bullet sent the stick across the hallway.

"You think I'm drunk," said Desmet quietly. "Don't think I won't plug you if I have to. Walk forward—this way. Out on to the strip." He backed down the wooden steps on to the concrete. The plane motor ground, throbbed, caught, turned over smoothly. He walked leisurely over to it, the pistol nudging Van der Valk out on to the steps. He climbed in, motioned to Laforêt to move over, said something to him, wound himself into a comfortable driving position. The little plane turned, started to taxi. Van der Valk watched calmly, and as it reached the runway and gathered speed he grinned a little. The girl spoke behind him in a nervous gabble.

"I've got my Daf—shall I go for the police? I only hope I don't crash into anyone—but the shop in the village has a phone."

"Don't bother," said Van der Valk quietly. Into his mind had come a phrase—who had quoted it? Had it been Arlette? Or Colonel Voisin? Or the general? The plane was racing; its tail came up and ground showed under the wheels.

"The 'parachutist's prayer' . . . Give me, God, what nobody else asks for. And give it to me quickly, because I may not have the courage to ask a second time . . .

The plane, taking off into the wind, banked in a low circuit to make its course; he went on watching. Behind him, the girl stood stupefied. It came flying over at a hundred feet, no more than three hundred yards distant. In mid-air it rocked; had a violent gust of cross wind caught it? The motor seemed to lose power, exactly as though a petrol filter had suddenly blocked.

"Oh," screamed the girl with her hand in her mouth.

The door slammed open suddenly and a figure appeared, climbing over some obstacle. It braced against the wind with its hands, gripped the door-frame, got its feet together, tensed both knees. The plane lost speed, put its nose up, seemed to meet an unseen barrier, went into a classic flying stall, wavered, dropped with startling swiftness. It crashed over on the edge of the field, above a moribund fence and a drainage ditch, and was no more seen, but an instant wuff of pale flame sprang up, and the dull thud of the exploding tanks reached both pairs of ears at the same moment. The girl screamed and Van der Valk paid no attention. Dramatics to the last drop, he thought, suddenly tired. The figure in the doorway had had time to spring clear. A paratrooper had jumped.

CHAPTER TWENTY-EIGHT

"Dramatics," he repeated sourly to a disturbed officer of police. He had fire brigades to deal with, Police Secours, the local criminal brigade, and a protesting magistrate. Irritable telephone calls were bombarding ministries all over the shop. DST, thought Van der Valk crossly, were probably convulsed in gales of merriment. That goddam stupid fool hardhead of a Laforêt and his infernal dramas, messing everybody up to the last second just for the sake of messing himself up. He had felt pity for Laforêt, but he was feeling precious little now. These infernal egomaniacs who had acted the goat during their entire life and still could not learn, but had to make a gesture.

Ach, he couldn't complain too much. The gesture had not been so much for him. It had been for him too, of course, a final gesture of rage and bravado addressed to the DST, to the Colonial Parachute Regiments, to the Legal Department—to the hills around Dien Bien Phu. But most of all, it had been addressed to Esther.

"All this administrative mess," grumbled the Belgian. They were both being scolded by agitated superiors. "I'm damned if I understand anyway. I know about this Marx murder, of course; it's been on the teletype and everything. Who's that outside?—oh God, the Press . . . I suppose one has to be grateful that the maniac with the machine-gun is finished with—yes, we found it there, Ballistics have it. Easy to match it with the bullets your people have—they'll have photos before this evening for comparison but it's the Marx gun all right. But in heaven's name who was it killed her? I'm all muddled."

"Truly I don't know," said Van der Valk apologetically. "It'll stay open unless somebody round the flats recognizes a photo. Could have been either."

"But this Laforêt surely . . ."

"Killed her learning she'd slept with Desmet? I'm not too sure. He'd have killed her and been caught, or given himself up. Can't see him sitting on that airfield, alone most of the time, sweating it out. I think he didn't understand what had happened, couldn't work it out, till I appeared, and then he threw himself into a confession—for him that seemed a sort of atonement for letting Esther die. Basically immature."

"But the other? Why would he shoot her?"

Van der Valk shrugged.

"Why be so silly as to hold a gun on me? Because

he genuinely thought he'd get away with it. Put a certain pressure on a certain kind of psychopath and he goes violent—I ought to have seen it coming. But when I went there I was still ninety per cent sure it must be Laforêt. And what was the way to handle him? Fill him up with loads of argy-bargy. Isn't that what they like? They want to be important, to be made much of, given the feeling that they're the centre of everyone's loving care. Give him that and I was certain he'd come back across the border with me like a good child—and I wouldn't have had to bother with any mandates for arrest—notifying you on the way, naturally."

The Belgian policeman sniggered.

"Notifying us on the way naturally, the hypocrite. Well, you got caught," with a relish that was not spiteful really; a little gleeful, possibly, at the spectacle of an esteemed colleague getting bellowed at by higher authority.

"Well," said Van der Valk defensively. "I wasn't to know there was any material evidence. Those two chuckleheads didn't even throw the gun in the river."

The higher authorities were, it was true, displeased with Mr. van der Valk. No news state of affairs. They were, however, mollified by the thought that it was all going to save the state a great deal of money. They did not keep him hanging about more than three hours, and he promised to submit a fully detailed written report, together with an exact note of expenses incurred and petty cash disbursed, a confidential memo about DST, a brief historical précis about the battle of Dien Bien Phu together with remarks about the mentality of paratroops between the years 1953–8, and a footnote on Flemish-French antagonism. The

Belgians were mollified at the thought of confiscating all the late Mr. Desmet's various properties both mobile and immobile pending an inquiry into various suspected income-tax irregularities, and were read a little lecture about the type of person who made a very pleasant living from collaborating with absolutely anyone, coming up like a cork to the top of whichever wave happened to be boss wave.

He still had his self-drive car; damn it, he knew that the Comptroller would notice that, and only allow his expenses as far as the Dutch frontier. Had he not the right to travel on the Dutch railway system free of charge? A lot of good it would do him to tell them that on this particular evening he didn't feel like travelling on the Netherlands Railways. He left the coast, passing through Alphen on the way to The Hague. He looked at his watch in Alphen. Yes, the thing was possible, especially now that the man was not in a hurry to get home to his wife. He parked outside a large café opposite the barracks, and surveyed several tables occupied by groups of quiet men talking shop.

"A small gin for the morale, an apple juice for thirst—got any French cigarettes?"

"You Belgian?"

"No, but is Zomerlust here?"

"Everybody's always asking for Zomerlust. Ja, he's over there in the corner."

"His wife got killed, remember?"

"Oh that. I read about it in the paper. He won't talk about it. You a journalist?"

"That's right."

"They get the chap who did it?"

"They did, yes."

269

"That's something, anyhow."

Sergeant Zomerlust was not a drinking man.

"No thanks, Mr. van der Valk, two beers is my limit. Ruth behaving herself?"

"No misgivings?"

"No."

"I was going to suggest you drop into my office. It's finished. Two men were concerned. They tried to make a getaway in a plane, but crashed it. They both got killed. There'll be a spread in the papers—hopelessly garbled, of course. If you want to know more you know where to come—it's your right."

The mild blue gaze settled on him thoughtfully. The bumpy shiny forehead, still reddened and flushed from that year's suntan, wrinkled.

"I won't read the paper. And I won't come to see you, unless I'm ordered to, that is. I've—" he searched for a phrase "—put it behind me. All right. Two men. You're not going to tell me any nonsense about lovers and jealousy and such because it's bullshit, and you know it."

"Nothing of the sort," placidly. "Just a question of the past, as I always thought—and you knew, naturally."

"Esther's past was her affair—and still is." Not for the first time, Van der Valk felt admiration for this plain man, who with his simplicity and dignity had made Esther such a good husband.

"There is nothing that you—or she—would feel ashamed of. Two men whom she once knew. Soldiers. Both had an episode in their past which they feared would come to light. They met her, quite coincidentally, and were alarmed at the realization that she recognized them and knew them. One was a man himself in the habit of any petty blackmail that came his way. The other was a hysterical fellow with no particular harm in him. They were afraid that the past would come to light."

Zomerlust gave a short, perfectly mirthless laugh.

"They were safe with Esther."

"Their tragedy was that they did not understand that."

"She was absolutely faithful. To herself, to her husband, to what she believed in. She's' gone. You will never know what she was like."

"I'll be getting along then," said Van der Valk.

"You get a lawyer—about Ruth. I've given you my word. I won't go back on it. When I say a thing I mean it."

"I know."

He had not had the time to phone, and nobody at home was expecting him.

"Lightly boiled egg all round," decided Arlette, much too pleased he was back to be cross having no warning.

Ruth was doing her homework dutifully at the writing table. Her face lit up when she saw him, and he was touched. All that was left of Esther—he would try and give some of that fidelity.

In the kitchen, changing his shoes, he told Arlette, briefly. She began to cry quietly in front of the stove, keeping her back obstinately to him. Tears fell in the boiled-egg water. He gave her an affectionate gentle smack.

"Now you needn't put any salt in." He put his slippers on painfully, conscious of enormous fatigue, and limped back to the living-room—she needed to be left alone a few minutes.

"I've got a recitation," said Ruth. "It's for tomorrow."

"Do you know it?"

"Nearly all, I think."

"Give it me here and I'll hear you."

"Hear me here," said Ruth giggling. The poem was nicely written, and the page decorated in coloured pencil with apple-trees. Four spelling mistakes had been corrected in red ink, and the mark was six-and-a-half out of ten.

"*Automne malade* by Guillaume Apollinaire," she announced importantly. "It's a nice poem."

"It's a good poem."

> "*Automne malade et adoré*
> *Tu mourras quand l'ouragan soufflera*
> *Dans les roseraies.*
> *Quand il aura neigé*
> *Dans les vergers.*"

"Very good so far. Second strophe, please."

> "*Pauvre automne.*
> *Meurs en blancheur et en richesse*
> *De neige et de fruits mûrs . . .*"

"*Aufond. . .*"

"Oh yes.

> *Aufond du ciel*
> *Des éperviers planent.*"

"*Au fond du ciel des éperviers planent . . .*" He had forgotten for a moment when he was . . . "Sorry. Last strophe."

"Aus lisières lointaines
Les cerfs ont bramé
Et que j'aime ô saison que j'aime tes rumeurs,
Les fruits tombant sans qu'on les cueille,
Le vent et la forêt qui pleurent
Toutes leurs larmes en automne feuille à feuille.

I like this poem."

"I think," said Van der Valk judiciously, "that you have certainly earned sixpence."

"Did you forget my smoked goose?" asked Arlette, bursting in violently.

ABOUT THE AUTHOR

NICOLAS FREELING was born in London and raised in France and England. After his military service in World War II, he traveled extensively throughout Europe, working as a professional cook in a number of hotels and restaurants. His first book, *Love in Amsterdam,* was published in 1961. Since then, he has written a number of novels and two non-fiction works. Mr. Freeling was awarded a golden dagger by the Crime Writers in 1963, the Grand Prix de Roman Policier in 1965, and the Edgar Allan Poe Award of the Mystery Writers Association in 1966.

Mr. Freeling lives in France with his wife and their five children.